THE BITTER SWEET LIFE OF ANNIE JENKINS

ANN BROUGH

Thicket Books

*To my son, Matthew,
and my daughters, Tracey and Kirsten,
for their love and support.*

A NOTE ON POTTERY DIALECT

I chose to depict the conversations between people who would have spoken in the Pottery Dialect, by only dropping the 'h' at the beginning of a word. This makes it obvious they are speaking in a dialect, yet makes it easy to read and understand. A few words may not be familiar, but I hope that the context may carry the meaning for you.

It may be interesting to see some of the dialect written down, to help you understand why I only dropped the 'h'.

Here goes:

O things come ter those oo weet
All things come to those who wait

Yer conna git blood ite o stoon
You can't get blood out of stone

Eh cudna fate eeze wee ite o peeper bag
He couldn't fight his way out of a paper bag

> **Eets better ter bey an owd mons darlin thun a yung mons sleev**
>
> *It's better to be an old man's darling than a young man's slave*

> **Thees now plees lark wom**
> *There's no place like home*

* The above quotes are from a publication called *Arfur Tow Crate in Staffy Cher: A Humorous Guide to Potteries Dialect* by Alan Povey (Novel Productions, 1986).

Translation: "How to Talk Properly (right) in Staffordshire."

A few readers of my previous books commented that there were "many spelling errors," which turned out to be dialect words. I hope this will help clear up the confusion - I do indeed have an excellent editor, and several "first readers," who I trust implicitly to catch most of the errors.

Thanks for Reading,

Ann

MAY & ANN

1948

CHAPTER 1
AUNTY ROSEMARY

My gran had promised me a trip to The Pear Drop, the sweet shop owned by her sister, Annie. I had walked past the window a few times when I went to the downtown market with my mum, but we were always in a hurry to get the shopping done and I never had a chance to stop and look inside. Gran had lots of stories to tell about The Pear Drop, going back to her own mother, who had worked there as a girl.

I was looking forward to our trip, but then everything changed.

Great Aunty Annie died!

When I went next door to stay with my gran for the morning while my mum worked, she told me to keep my boots and coat on.

"Put your 'at and mitts on as well. It's a cold morning. We're going to visit the old aunties this morning," she informed me. "First Rosemary, then Lizzie, then Daisy. You'll 'ave to be a good girl, Ann."

I gazed up at my gran and nodded my head. I could tell

she had been crying by her red-rimmed eyes. I felt sorry that her sister, Annie, had died. Even though she was old.

Memory is always linked to smell. It's the sense of smell that lasts. Even now, as I struggle to remember the early years, I smell the musty, dank aroma of Aunty Rosemary's house. With the smell comes the claustrophobic sensation of entering a dark parlour, with high ceilings, cluttered with austere walnut furniture, and only the dim light from a heavily-draped window casting shadows on the patterned walls.

At just four years old, I was very small and the step from the outside pavement into the house was more than I could climb. My gran took my hand and hoisted me up, reminding me to only speak if I was spoken to.

"Your great Aunty Rosemary likes polite little girls," Gran whispered. "So you sit still and be a good girl."

My skin felt itchy. I wanted to leave before we had even begun the visit.

Great Aunty Rosemary was Gran's sister-in-law. She had married Gran's older brother, John, back in 1907, but he had been killed by a motorbus, leaving Rosemary with two little girls, Enid and Nancy.

"Come in, May," Aunty Rosemary greeted Gran, as we walked into the kitchen. "Oh, I see you have your granddaughter with you. Well, child, sit on the sofa quietly while your gran and I have a cup of tea."

The kettle whistled on the old black stove fuelled by a coal fire. The black fireplace shone like ebony it was so polished—as were the sideboard, the straight-backed ornate chairs, and the bookcase in the corner. The table legs were just visible below the rich maroon chenille tablecloth.

China cups sprinkled with a pattern of rosebuds and edged with gold sat in saucers to match. Aunty Rosemary brewed the tea and offered me an arrowroot biscuit, placed in the center of a small plate, and a small glass of milk. I remained on the sofa, while my drink and biscuit were placed on a small round polished table with three legs, covered with a lace cloth. I was content to nibble on my biscuit, listening and watching the two old ladies over their tea.

Aunty Rosemary was very tiny, even smaller than my gran. They were about the same height, maybe five feet, but Rosemary was so thin and fragile. Her fingers fascinated me as she lifted her teacup to her lips: so delicate, so beautiful, even though age had defined the blue veins crisscrossing the backs of her hands. She wore a black ankle-length skirt and a long-sleeved dark green blouse, fastened at the neck with a mother-of-pearl brooch. Her hair was streaked with silver and gathered into a bun at the nape of her neck. Gran was dressed almost the same, but her skirt was a bit shorter, her mauve blouse was not buttoned quite so high, and her wavy hair still had the radiant flashes of red running through it.

"'Ow is poor Kathy?" asked Rosemary. "'Ave you been to see 'er today?"

"She is taking it very badly," answered Gran. "She won't even answer the door."

Gran wiped a tear from her cheek.

"What are we going to do? I would imagine nothing could be said to give 'er comfort," Rosemary continued. "Annie was a good mother to 'er. More than good. Maybe that was the problem."

"Yes," was all Gran could say for the moment.

I watched the two old ladies closely, and listened carefully. What could be wrong with Kathy, I wondered. She was grieving the loss of her mother—but not answering the door? Was there something I didn't know?

"I'll go again this evening," Gran said between sips of tea. "She 'as the door bolted from the inside, so I can't open it with the spare key. I didn't 'ave any luck this morning."

"I should go with you," offered Rosemary.

"I think I should try on my own again," said Gran. "More people may upset 'er even more."

Finally, the visit was over and Gran took my hand to lead me back out into the sunlight where I could breathe and see the sky. I carried two of my buttons in my hand that I had managed to pick off my dress. Mum would understand when I told her about sitting with nothing to do for so long.

We left Aunt Rosemary to wash the china cups and begin preparing tea for "the girls."

"The girls" weren't girls at all. Enid was forty years old, and Nancy was thirty-eight. Aunty Rosemary thought they were still her little girls and treated them as such.

Enid had a good job as office supervisor in a large pottery factory. She had been trained in Pitman shorthand and could use a typewriter. She ran the office with a rod of iron, giving orders to the junior staffers like a regimental sergeant major. They made fun of her behind her back, but to her face they wouldn't dare. She dressed the part, always wearing a smart suit or dress, short-heeled sensible shoes and immaculate stockings. She had very black hair, curled at each side of her head and rimmed glasses, and she always wore bright red lipstick.

Enid hardly ever smiled—what was there to smile about? Twenty years ago, when Enid was a young woman, Sam Williams, a carpenter attending the Chapel, had talked to her after the morning service and even sat beside her at the Sunday night hymn sing. He was the only man to ever pay her any attention, but it came to nothing and she was left looking a fool, vowing she would never go into the Chapel again and be the cause of everybody's gossip. There was nothing to smile about in Enid's life.

Nancy "lived" at the Chapel, a small brick building in the middle of the row houses of Normacot, when she wasn't working at her day job as a free-hand paintress at the Aynsley Pottery factory. She supervised Sunday School twice every Sunday, and helped run the Boys Brigade every Wednesday. She never wore makeup and her hair was always pinned back severely from her face. I was in the preschool class at Chapel and couldn't call her "Aunty Nancy," only "Miss Jenkins." I was quite scared of her because she always looked so strict, but my Gran said she had a heart of gold, so every Sunday I smiled my best smile.

As we left Aunty Rosemary's house and faced the biting wind, I braced myself for the long walk to visit the next Aunty. I hoped Aunty Lizzie would have a roaring fire going and the kettle on the hob for tea.

CHAPTER 2
AUNTY LIZZIE

My fingertips and toes were frozen when we reached Aunty Lizzie's house, but there was a roaring fire to welcome us, just as I'd hoped. Gran and I warmed ourselves while Aunty Lizzie busied herself brewing the tea in a big brown pot, pouring the hot liquid into two plain cups and adding a generous amount of milk and two spoonfuls of sugar for both her and my gran.

I think I was a weird kid. I was actually quite fascinated by Gran's sisters. She had a big family, so we never ran out of places to visit.

Aunty Lizzie lived very close to Gran. Just around the corner, in fact. Aunty Lizzie was wider than Gran. She wore a tweed skirt, just above her ankles, and always a white blouse with a v-neck. She said she couldn't breathe if she wore a button-up blouse. Winter and summer she always topped the blouse with one of her beautiful hand-made knitted cardigans. Her hair was thick and streaked grey and white. She wore big waves down each side of her face, covering both her ears, then gathered the back into a roll at the nape of her neck. Gran said she slept with big curl clips in her hair every night to make those waves. It didn't do much to improve her looks, because she had such a big nose and wore round spectacles with thick lenses, which slipped down her nose when she talked. Her breath came in short gasps much of the time, and there was a peculiar raspy sound going in and out. Gran said she'd always been "delicate" and had to take a tot of brandy every night before bed to help with her breathing. Even though she'd signed the temperance pledge at Chapel, she had special permission from the elders to take it for medicinal purposes.

Aunty Lizzie's house was one of six tiny row houses at the bottom of Lower Spring Road, which ran along the bottom of our avenue. A small square window faced the road and a narrow wooden door beside it heralded Aunty Lizzie's home. Gran and I stepped into the kitchen over the low step. The smell was different than at Aunty Rosemary's house. It was earthy and sweet, with a hint of damp wool. I felt cramped and closed-in. The room was so tiny that the small table, three wooden chairs and small cupboard on the opposite wall to the door, filled the space. There was the usual black grate, but it was dusty and very ancient, with patches of rust showing through. There was only one other room down-stairs, called a back-kitchen, housing a big stone sink and a single cold-water tap. A variety of pots, pans and a wash tub were kept in the cold, dark back-kitchen, along with a broom, mop and bucket. I never asked to use the toilet at Aunty Lizzie's. They shared with the people next door. There was a tiny brick shed out back at the top of three steep steps, which held a rough wooden platform with a hole in it. There was no flush chain like at my house, so the smell was unfor-gettable. I only used it once—never again!

Aunty Lizzie had one son, named Lenny. I had never heard him speak. He was the same age as my dad, but hadn't been in the army because he had something wrong with his chest. He was very small and frail, not like my dad who was tall and broad shouldered. The last time I saw Lenny was at his wedding just a month ago, when he had married his very tall and large girlfriend, Sally.

"It's a quick wedding," Gran announced in a whisper to my dad the night before the big event. "There's a bun in the oven! Lizzie will never get over it. She says she won't be able to lift 'er 'ead up in Chapel ever again, she's so ashamed. Who would have thought it? Lenny of all blokes. It's the quiet ones who are always the worst. Still waters run deep, that's what they say."

My dad laughed and laughed. He was still laughing as we walked to the Chapel on our way to watch the wedding. I heard him tell my mum that Lenny was a bit of a queer kind of a bloke and dad never thought he would meet a girl, let alone… More laughing.

I wondered what was so funny about "a bun in the oven." Had Lenny let them burn? Why would that make Aunty Lizzie be ashamed? I couldn't figure it out.

Lenny stood at the front of the Chapel looking paler and thinner than ever. He was a few inches taller than Aunty Lizzie, which must have made him all of five feet, three inches. He had no lips, at least I couldn't see any, and his thin jet-black hair was plastered to his head with Brylcream. I thought he looked nice in his new suit, even though his trouser-bottoms were so wide and long I couldn't see his shoes. I felt my dad shaking beside me and knew he was trying not to laugh. They were the most unlikely couple, but I thought it was nice they were getting married because they probably wouldn't have found anybody else.

With the tea poured, Aunty Lizzie turned her attention to me.

"Look at this big girl," Aunty Lizzie said, pinching my cheeks with her fat fingers, which I absolutely hated. I was allowed to sit up at the table with the old ladies, where the usual biscuit and milk appeared in front of me. I was also given a small basket full of tangled wool.

"There's a job for you," said Aunty Lizzie. "You work on untangling that lot for me, there's a good girl."

Aunty Lizzie was a great knitter. She always had knitting in her hands. She knitted very slowly, but the result was outstanding. People from the Chapel and all over the neighbourhood ordered knitted items from her, because they were so beautiful. I never saw her without her needles in her hand.

She showed me how to wind the wool around my hand to make a ball, and I was quite happy winding the tangle of different coloured wool into little balls, and placing them back into the basket—they looked like colourful eggs in a nest.

Before the tea was even brewed, the question came up:

"What about Kathy?" whispered Aunty Lizzie, although I could hear her quite clearly. "Is she all right?"

"No, she's not," answered Gran in a low voice, with a quick glance my way. "She's locked 'erself in the 'ouse and won't open the door. I don't know what to think."

"It's been such an upset, losing Annie so suddenly. I'm not sure I would be of much use to 'er grief-stricken daughter," Lizzie said.

"We all 'ave to find our own way through these trials in life, Lizzie. Kathy was our Annie's pride and joy, but now she's gone, that girl 'as to carry on with 'er own life, but I'm not at all sure she can. She should 'ave come back sooner. She never even saw our Annie for almost two years."

"Kathy's wedding announcement finished 'er off, that's what 'appened," Lizzie mouthed the words, hardly making a sound, but I could still hear. "We all knew our Annie's mind was fragile. She lived every day 'oping for Kathy to come

'ome. The thought of 'er beloved daughter being married in another part of the country was just too much for 'er."

Aunty Lizzie sniffed as she refilled the china cups. Both sisters dabbed at their eyes and noses with their handkerchiefs, and sipped the hot tea.

"I'll go to the 'ouse again later today, Lizzie. Maybe I can persuade Kathy to open the door."

While we were having our tea, Uncle Albert came in from work. I had to give up my chair for him, and squatted on the floor in front of the grate with the basket of wool.

Like their son, Lenny, Albert never spoke. I inspected him carefully from my vantage point on the floor. He was a mystery! He had a very white face and very white hands, but there was a definite line around his neck and wrists where his skin turned black. Was his body black? Even his fingernails were black, but his hands were white. He always wore a cap, but I could see his ears were encrusted with the same black hue. His clothing was all black and he never took off his big boots, which were very dirty. I could see the mud caked onto the bottom and sides of his boots from where I was sitting on an eye-level with his feet.

As we walked up the slippery street towards Aunty Daisy's house, Gran explained that Albert was a gravedigger at the Anglican Church. That's why he was covered in dirt.

"Why doesn't 'e have a bath?" I wanted to know.

"'E doesn't like water. Not many men do," explained Gran. "'E 'as a bath once a year on the day before the Chapel anniversary. That's the only time 'e changes all 'is clothes and gets 'imself clean. Lizzie insists 'e be clean for the anniversary, although I don't know why, 'cause 'e's rarely set foot in the Chapel, except when 'e was married and to 'ave Lenny christened. I was surprised 'e showed up for young Lenny's wedding last month."

"Why doesn't the gravedigger talk?" I continued to ask.

"Some men don't like to talk," answered Gran as we walked up the narrow street. Young Lenny's the same. Never speaks! Mind you, there's worse things than not talking. 'E 'ands over 'is money every week and doesn't spend it at the pub. Because 'e doesn't talk, 'e never complains. That's a bonus in a 'usband. Must be a quiet 'ouse though'"

I thought of my own dad, who was a quiet man. Our house wasn't quiet though because my mum was a talker, always chattering away about something. She made my dad laugh a lot, and he never seemed tired of listening to her tell about her day. He would take me onto his knee every night after our meal and listen intently while I shared all my secrets with him. He knew all my dolls' names and even knew about my imaginary husband, Bill, who worked at the coal mine and came home covered in coal dust. My dad loved to sing and whistle. I was very impressed that he could sing the Welsh National Anthem in the Welsh language. He sang songs from the war years and sometimes he would grab my mum and they would dance together around our tiny living room, which usually ended with my dad crying and my mum laughing.

Our last visit was to Aunty Daisy's house. I loved my gran for saving the best until the last.

The end house in our avenue had twelve steps leading to the front door. I counted them every time we visited Aunty Daisy. She was Gran's younger sister and I loved visiting her.

Because we lived so close, Gran and I went there just about every day. Aunty Daisy never visited Gran. I wondered why.

Daisy was always happy and welcoming. She folded me in her arms every time she saw me and snuggled me into her fat chest. She was very soft and warm and smelled of toast and wet dog.

"'Ere she is," she greeted me. "Little princess. Come on up onto the sofa, duckie, and give your Aunty a kiss."

There were always at least two biscuits for me and Aunty Daisy made her own sweet lemonade to go with them. She had three children, but no grandchildren yet. She told my gran she couldn't wait for the babies to start coming, and I could see why—she would love them like she loved me.

Tea was made in the kitchen, as Daisy didn't have a black grate like the other two old aunties. The main room was called the living room, like at our house, and the kitchen had hot and cold water, a gas stove, a table and even a pantry for all the food. Gran and Daisy both agreed tea never tasted the same when the water wasn't boiled on a black grate stove. Why would it make a difference?

Aunty Daisy didn't have a husband. He was dead. He'd been dead for a long time. A framed picture of him stood on the mantle. He looked like a kind man and I thought Aunty Daisy must have been a very happy wife, because she was even happy now she was alone.

Aunty Daisy had a big dog named Sheba, who let me pet her and lie on her and cuddle her. She let me pick up each of her paws and check her toenails, which I thought were very impressive. She licked me with her long pink tongue, and tickled my cheeks with her breath.

Aunty Daisy didn't go to the Chapel. Gran said that's why she sometimes said swear words. My mum said swear words as well, so I didn't mind. It was made perfectly clear to me that I should not say those words out loud, but I did like the sound of them. I even practiced saying them under my breath when I was playing in my favourite spot at the bottom of the stairs in my house.

"'As anybody been to see Kathy today?" Daisy asked in a lowered voice. "I 'eard she won't leave the house. Our Annie spoiled 'er from the beginning. Always favoured 'er over the eldest girl. Look where it got her. Kathy hasn't been near 'er for years."

"I'll go this evening," said Gran, taking off her little round glasses and dabbing her eyes with her handkerchief. "It's up to me, being the eldest sister. I'm still so upset about Annie though, I don't think I'll be any comfort to Kathy."

"Somebody 'as to go, and you're the best person," continued Daisy, sipping on her strong tea. "Kathy was never an easy girl to get along with. Always wanted 'er own way. I can get along with most folk, but I 'ave to admit she rubbed me up the wrong way every time I saw 'er. Always thought she was a cut above the rest of us."

"That was Annie's fault, and you know it," Gran chimed in. "She worshiped the ground that girl walked on. Gave 'er everything she wanted and more. Now Kathy's left with more money than she could ever spend, and probably a guilty conscience that won't be easy to live with."

Both old ladies sat staring through the window, sipping on their tea, absorbed in their own thoughts of their sister, Annie, and the legacy she had left.

I lay on Sheba watching them. Like the other aunties, Daisy wanted to talk about Annie. I suppose it was because she was dead. Old people liked to talk about dead people! Others in Gran's family had died. I had all their names memorized. Gran had lost a brother and two sisters before Annie had died. We regularly visited their spouses, so I knew where all the dead people fitted into the family and who was married to whom.

I prayed my gran and grandad wouldn't die. God didn't seem to have a plan where age was concerned. Some folk died young, even kids, and some, like old Miss Barlow in the next street, lived to be ancient. Gran's siblings were all now younger than her, so I worried about that. It was probably something to do with going to Chapel. If that was the factor, then Gran and Aunty Lizzie would live to be very old indeed.

Aunty Daisy struggled to her feet to reboil the kettle and make more tea. I noticed, from where I lay on the rug, that her ankles were very swollen and spilled over the sides of the soft slippers she always wore in the house. She was always short of breath, like Aunty Lizzie, but she didn't go to Chapel. Maybe she would be the next to die!

We walked across the avenue to Gran's house, and I ran next door to tell my mum all about the visits we had made. I was so full of milk and biscuits, that I didn't eat my meal. I watched through the front window for my grandad to come home from work. I would often go next door to share his meal, which was usually bacon or sausage with cheese and tomatoes. He always gave me a big wad of bread dipped in the bacon fat and spread it with melted cheese. I saw his cap bobbing above the hedge as he walked up the avenue, and shouted a goodbye to my mum as I scampered through the back door and into Gran's house to meet my grandad.

Once Grandad had his plate of bacon and cheese at the table, with me standing beside him ready for my share of his meal, Gran put on her hat and coat and headed for the door.

"I'm going over to Annie's house," she announced. "One more try to see if Kathy will let me in."

I heard the familiar knock on the wall between our house and Gran's, summoning me home. I didn't want to leave. I wanted to wait for Gran's return to find out if Kathy had opened the door, but if I waited for a second knock I was running the risk of my mum coming to get me, and she wouldn't be happy.

I put on my nightie and sat at the kitchen table drinking a cup of warm milk. I listened intently for the sound of next door's front door opening and closing, to let me know Gran was back, but I heard nothing except the low murmur of Grandad's radio through the adjoining wall.

My bedroom was at the back of the house, so there was no chance of hearing when Gran returned. When my dad had read me a story and tucked me in with a kiss goodnight, and I was sure he was downstairs talking to my mum, I crept out of bed and into their front bedroom and peeked through the window. Gran was long overdue according to my reckoning. Annie's house was only a ten-minute walk away. Surely Gran should be back by now. I became pretty cold waiting there by the icy window, with bare feet and no blanket around me, but before long Gran came around the corner, her head bowed against the wind, as she trudged towards her house.

I wondered if Kathy had opened the door. I would find out in the morning.

CHAPTER 4
KATHY

Gran was taking a break from doing the laundry. The house smelled of soap and steam. Gran usually let me stand on a stool at the sink and wash her thick lyle stockings in special mild soap flakes. The soap flakes made wonderful bubbles and I would usually plunge my hands up and down in the sink, washing and washing those stockings until my fingers looked like prunes. Today, I was too late to wash the stockings and Gran had already filled the washtub with clean water for the rinse cycle. She must have been up very early to be this far along at such an early hour.

I couldn't wait to hear if Gran had seen Kathy the night before.

"Gran," I began. "Are you going to visit Kathy today?"

"Don't you start," Gran said. "'Aven't I 'eard enough from my sisters about Kathy?"

"Well, I was just going to ask to come with you. If you go."

"If I go, I'll probably go on my own."

I was undeterred.

"Gran," I tried again. "I think I should go with you. People like children around when they're sad, I've noticed. Children are a definite distraction in a stressful situation."

"I don't know where you get those words from," Gran said, looking at me closely over the top of her glasses as though she could see into my mind to discover my secret. She sighed before adding, "You may be right. Out of the mouths of babes…"

"Can I then? Go with you?"

"All right, you little clever-clogs. You'll be bored though, because there'll be nothing for you to do at Kathy's."

"I'll take my book bag with me then," I suggested. "I have a new baby animal book to look at."

That was settled. I would go with Gran on the epic visit to Kathy's. I didn't dare ask when we would go. I had pushed my luck far enough already.

When the washing was rinsed, put through the mangle and hung out to dry on the clothesline, with me passing the pegs, my gran told me to put on my red wellies. She took off her aprons, pinned her hat on her head, and, picking up her handbag along with her cavernous shopping bag, told me we were going to Kathy's. I grabbed my coat and my book bag, ready for the big visit.

Gran looked around the house before we left. She always checked that everything was in perfect order before she could leave. There was never anything out of place in her house.

Gran liked to clean. Her house shone from all the polishing. There was a big carpet square in the middle of the living room, leaving a border of linoleum showing on the edges. Gran then had rugs on top of the carpet to keep the carpet clean: one in front of the fire, one beside Grandad's chair and one in front of her bible-reading chair. She then put down newspaper to keep the rugs clean. When she was at home a big apron covered up most of Gran's clothes. It had a bib front and long skirt and tied in the back with a big bow. On top of the apron, Gran put on another smaller one, without the bib, to keep the first apron clean. It seemed very complicated to me.

There were special rags for cleaning, which were kept in a green box under the kitchen sink. Some were for putting on polish and some for buffing up the wood once the polish had been applied. I had my own buffing rag and took great pride in polishing the bottom two drawers of the chest of drawers, which held all Gran's special linen.

Gran always wore a dust cap over her hair when she was cleaning. I thought she looked like Little Bo Peep. I wished I had a dust cap.

We walked down the avenue and along Lower Spring Road, with me finding every puddle on the way to wade through, testing my new wellies. Gran didn't mind. She walked slowly anyway.

I had been to the big house on the corner, opposite the post office, before. I remembered the sweet smell of caramel and chocolate. I remembered the dish on the table full of sweeties. I remembered Annie wrapping some of the sweeties in a small white bag, tying it with a blue ribbon and giving it to me to take home.

Gran knocked on the door and waited. She had her "stiff" face on. Her lips were in a line, which indicated that she was worried or annoyed about something. She knocked again. We just stood there, the two of us, side by side, staring at the closed door. Once more Gran knocked, this time harder and longer. She was not about to give up.

"Go away," said a raspy voice from inside. "Go away."

"Kathy, it's me, Aunty May," Gran said quietly through the letter box in the door. "Please let me in. Just for a few minutes."

The door opened a crack. I could see the dim shape of a

woman inside the dark house. She put her face close to the crack to peer out at Gran.

"I don't want you here," Kathy said in the same raspy voice. "I want to be left alone. Go away."

"I won't stay long, duck," Gran cooed. "I've brought you some things to eat. Soup and a few scones."

The crack in the door grew wider.

"The house is a mess."

"Don't worry about it," Gran replied. "I've seen messes before."

Gran pushed gently on the door as she talked and Kathy didn't resist, allowing us to step into the hallway.

The house smelled of moldy cheese, or was the smell coming from Kathy? Wherever it was coming from, it was very unpleasant and I swallowed hard to quell the gag reflex in my throat.

Kathy closed the door quietly behind us. It was like entering a jail, where the door had slammed shut and we were trapped. It was so gloomy and damp inside the house, even though the hall was spacious with a wide curved stair-case ascending to the floor above. Kathy didn't speak, but glided noiselessly past us along the hallway and into a room to the left of the stairway. As we followed her I began to regret asking Gran if I could accompany her on the visit. The house was creepy and Kathy was weird. I wished we were on our way to visit the Pear Drop, like Gran had promised, instead of visiting Kathy.

The room we entered was large with high ceilings. A stone fireplace dominated the wall facing the door and I could see, even in the dim light, the dust clinging to book-cases, chairs and tables in the beautifully furnished living room. There was a large pile of debris in the corner, with an axe beside it. Kathy stood with her back to us gazing into the unlit fire grate. I stood beside Gran in the doorway, waiting.

I didn't know why we were waiting, but we stood there for a long time. I tugged on Gran's skirt but she shook her finger at me and gave me a frown, indicating that I should stay still and wait. Wait for what?

"Kathy," Gran finally said in a low voice. "I don't want to intrude but we're all worried about you. I've brought you some soup and a few scones. Why don't we go through to the kitchen so I can warm up the soup and we'll 'ave a bit of lunch, the three of us."

Kathy didn't move or speak. We waited again.

"Come on now," urged Gran. "You look like you could use something to eat. We'll be cozier in the kitchen."

Gran took my hand and marched down the hallway to the door at the end. We stepped into the big square kitchen with a red tiled floor. Sun was streaming through the window over the sink, catching all the dust mites in its rays. There were cupboards all around the kitchen. A stove, twice the size of my mum's, stood beneath a copper range hood, and saucepans and pots of every size hung from a rack over a butcher-block table in the center of the room. Gran rinsed one of the pots in the grimy sink and dried it with a cloth she took from her own bag. She poured the soup into the pot and lit the gas on the stove, carefully placing it over the heat to warm. She put her lovely clean cloth on the soiled table and laid out scones, butter and even a slice or two of cheese.

"What about Kathy, Gran?" I asked in a whisper. "She didn't follow us. She's probably still standing in the other room."

"Don't you worry about 'er," Gran answered. "I'll go and get 'er when the soup's warmed through. She can't ignore us forever."

Gran found three bowls in one of the cupboards and three spoons in a kitchen drawer. She rinsed them all carefully and polished them until they shone with a second cloth from her bag of treasures. My Gran was the cleanest person I ever knew.

The soup was steaming and the wonderful smell of ham and pea soup filled the air. It was my very favourite soup, especially the way Gran made it. My mum made it with the same recipe—it was rich and thick and salty. I could eat a whole bowl of it without hardly pausing for breath.

My mouth watered at the thought of the soup. Despite the delicious aroma Kathy still didn't appear.

Gran left the kitchen on her mission to persuade her niece to come and eat with us.

I wondered if I should try to stir the soup. Maybe it would burn if I didn't stir it. I would be breaking a rule about going near the gas stove. If I burnt myself Gran would blame herself and mum would be very angry. I stood looking at the pot steaming away and decided I should turn the knob until the flame went out. I was very careful and particularly brave as I twisted the knob and watched the flame die. Now the soup wouldn't burn.

I listened for any sound of Gran coming back along the hallway, but heard nothing.

I opened the kitchen door and peered into the hallway. It was dark and dank and quiet. I crept towards the living room door, which was standing open, to see what was happening.

Gran was sitting on the big dusty couch and Kathy was kneeling in front of her with her head on Gran's lap. She was sobbing quietly and Gran was stroking her hair. I backed away from the door and tiptoed back to the kitchen to wait. This was a very boring visit so far. Adults took a long time to actually do something. It seemed all we had done was wait.

I climbed up onto a high wooden chair and set my book

bag on the table. At least I had something to do, other than wait.

I heard footsteps in the hall. Gran pushed open the kitchen door, and led Kathy by her hand to an empty chair at the table.

I stared at the woman who sat across from me: wild red hair in a tangled curly mass like a halo around her face. Her unblinking eyes stared at the wall behind my head. Her face was as white as a sheet, there were dark circles around her eyes and her lips were cracked and dry. It was how I imagined dead people would look.

Gran lit the stove under the soup to reheat it and bustled around the kitchen, filling an oversized black crusted kettle to boil water for tea. Was there no ending to the assemblage of items in Gran's bag: two white face cloths, a small tin filled with black tea leaves, a tea strainer, a bottle of milk, sugar lumps in a small tin, even three of her everyday china cups. Her bag must have been heavy to carry and I wished I had offered to help her.

I watched as she found a heavy earthenware bowl in the pantry, rinsed it under the tap, then filled it with water, adding some of the hot water from the kettle. She wet one of the facecloths in the warm water and gently began to wipe Kathy's face and hands. I could see the white cloth changing colour as the dirt and grime was washed away. I wondered why this grown lady was acting like a baby. Even though I was still small, I was expected to wash my hands and face by myself every morning.

Kathy didn't move. I wondered if she was crazy!

Soup was poured into the bowls, the scones were buttered and the tea made. Gran blew on my soup to cool it before placing it in front of me. She smiled and winked at me, trying to reassure me that all would be well.

"Right then," Gran said cheerfully. "This looks like a good

lunch to me. Let's bow our heads and ask a blessing before we dig in."

Gran always prayed before she ate. I thought that was a nice thing to do. I knew how busy Harold must have been looking after the whole world. Gran said it was good to say "Thank you" to him. I knew his name was Harold because I was learning The Lord's Prayer in preschool Sunday school and we always began with "Our Father, who art in heaven. Harold be thy name." Martha James, who sat next to me, said I was wrong and God's name was Art because we said "Art" before we said "Harold." Maybe he had two names: Arthur Harold!

I dipped the buttered scone into the middle of my soup and sucked the rich, thick green soup into my mouth. Delicious! I smacked my lips and made "yum, yum" sounds, hoping it would encourage Kathy to eat something.

I couldn't believe my eyes when Gran began to feed Kathy.

"Now then, duck," Gran murmured. "You get this down. You just need a bit of food inside you and you'll feel better. Open your mouth. That's it. Good girl."

Gran broke a scone into small pieces to feed to her niece. Kathy didn't refuse the food and Gran seemed pleased with what she had accomplished.

"You're doing very well," cooed Gran. "Look at that. You've eaten 'alf your scone already."

I slurped down my soup, engrossed in watching the scene before me. So this was why all the aunties had asked about Kathy. She had turned into a baby and needed somebody to take care of her.

Spoon after spoon of soup went into Kathy's mouth. Her fixed stare shifted slightly and she blinked rapidly, as though she was making up for all the blinks she had missed. Finally her gaze moved down the wall and onto me. I paused with the soup spoon half way to my mouth. We held each other's eyes. Me, not daring to break the contact and the wild looking lady, once more, unblinking. The stillness and silence was eerie. Gran sensed the uneasy atmosphere and rubbed Kathy's back, while she smiled and nodded at me with reassurance.

"You remember my granddaughter don't you?" Gran asked. "She begged me to let 'er come and visit you today. She wouldn't take no for an answer."

I smiled my best smile. Kathy didn't respond, but she did break the eye-lock, and looked down at her soup bowl for the first time. She frowned as if she was trying to remember something. Gran took the interest in the soup as a good sign and she put the spoon into Kathy's hand. Puzzled at first, she sat just looking at the spoon and Gran and I held our breath. Then, slowly, the spoon dipped into the soup and she began to eat by herself. Gran let out a sigh of relief and pushed the half-eaten scone closer to the soup bowl. Soon the soup and the scone were gone and I felt like Gran and I had just won an important soccer game. Elated by such a small thing as eating lunch!

I carried the bowls and spoons to the sink and Gran rinsed them carefully before drying and putting them away. She packed all of her belongings into her bag, then sat down at the table to finish her tea. I loved the weak tea that Gran made especially for me, with lots of milk and a spoonful of sugar. Kathy drank her tea slowly, her eyes buried by the rim.

How could Gran and I ever leave her alone again? Who would take care of her when we were gone?

I think my Gran was worried too because she dawdled over washing the tea cups, frowning and glancing at Kathy as she did so. I put my book into my book bag and climbed down from the chair.

"Are we going now, Gran?" I asked.

"We are in a bit," Gran answered. "Be patient, there's a good girl. We want to make sure everything is all right 'ere before we go."

It seemed to me that things would not be "all right" no matter how long we delayed. The house and the person living in it were both a mess.

"Now, my duck," Gran cooed. "Why don't you come and stay with me for tonight. You can 'ave a nice bath and we'll find you some clean clothes. You'll feel like new."

"That's all right, Aunty May," Kathy answered slowly. "I can have a bath here. I'm feeling better now. Thank you for taking care of me. I should have come to see my mam sooner. Now it's too late."

Kathy began to cry softly and my gran held her close, patting her back and shushing her.

"The rest of your family will be 'ere tomorrow—Nora, Norman and the boys. Me and the other aunties will come first thing in the morning and clean up a bit and open up the bedrooms. Don't you worry about a thing."

On the walk home, I looked up at my Gran and realized what a strong little lady she was. She accepted Kathy and the state she was in, and helped her be better.

"Gran," I asked. "What was your sister, Annie like?"

MARGARET

1880

CHAPTER 6

A HOUSE FULL OF LAUGHTER

Jacob and Margaret Jenkins counted themselves lucky to have procured number thirty-one Newhall Road. They were newly married so the expectation was that they would live with family until they "got on their feet."

Jacob Jenkins was already "on his feet."

He had worked since he was fourteen for a printing company in Stoke, beginning as a skivvy doing errands and odd jobs: cleaning the press, the floors, the privy. Every day he set off on his bike from Normacot to ride the mostly uphill, two and a half mile journey to Stoke. He prided himself that he had never had a day off in all those years, except for Christmas Day. He was promoted to press-hand, helping mix ink and keep paper, card and canvas in good order. Now, at twenty-one years of age, he was a type-setter, responsible for setting out the complicated system of letters, words, sentences and even some illustrations to be printed in the weekly magazine, "Gentleman's Business Weekly." Indeed, Jacob Jenkins had his feet firmly planted.

A small slender girl with chestnut hair worked at the

sweet shop on the corner of Webberly Lane in Longton. Every morning as Jacob rode by on his way to work, he glanced through the window hoping for a glimpse of her. He eventually plucked up enough courage to push open the door and step inside, where he entirely lost his nerve and couldn't even talk. He had never been shy, and he struggled to understand why all of a sudden he had been struck dumb.

"Can I 'elp you?" the girl with the chestnut hair asked.

"Eeeer. Mmmm," mumbled Jacob miserably.

"Perhaps you could point to what you want," the girl said, trying to help the young man who was obviously distressed.

Jacob pointed to a jar of pear drops.

"Pear drops. What a good choice," the girl continued, mouthing the words slowly for Jacob.

"Thank you," he said, finally finding his voice. "I'll take a quarter pound please."

The girl blushed, turned her head away and reached for the jar of pear drops. She had noticed Jacob riding past on his bike, how he always looked into the shop and sometimes caught her eye. He was taller than she was, which wasn't saying much, and very handsome; he had lovely eyes and curly dark hair. The heavy glass jar almost slipped from her hands as she carried it to the counter.

"What's your name?" asked Jacob, becoming bolder.

"Margaret," she said, giving him a smile.

"I'm Jacob," he said, returning the smile.

That was two years ago and they had loved each other from that moment. Two pear drops sat on top of their wedding cake and Jacob was never without a small bag containing the delicious sweets in his pocket.

Jacob's well-paying job and frugality gave the young couple an uncommon start to their marriage—a rented home of their own. A home in Newhall Road, where the houses were newer and where they could see trees in the distance. In fact it was only a short fifteen minute walk to Weston Woods where the grime of the town felt a hundred miles away.

The tiny row houses all looked the same in Newhall Road. Built in the mid nineteenth century, two up, two down was the standard of the day for the working class. Two up meant two bedrooms up a steep flight of stairs off the kitchen. Two down meant a kitchen and a living room, called a parlour, on the main floor. The parlour was used only for special events: a visit from the vicar, the birth of a baby or laying out the dead. It was sparsely furnished with a sofa, and a sideboard containing linens and family possessions. A large black leaded fireplace took pride of place in the kitchen. The coal fire in the centre of the fireplace provided warmth and heat for cooking the family meals. A hob over the fire boiled kettles for tea and heated soup and porridge, and warming ovens on either side of the fire baked bread, scones and cakes. The kitchen usually had a table and several wooden chairs, a cupboard for dishes, and sometimes additional seating like a narrow horse-hair sofa. In addition to the two rooms there was a back-kitchen, which was not counted as an actual room. It was often open to the outdoors, and contained a large stone sink with a cold water tap, which was the only source of water in the house. Many tenants built makeshift shelves for pots and pans, and the washing tub and brush, mop and bucket were all kept in the back kitchen.

There was no bathroom, but each house in Newhall Road had its own outside privy in the backyard, with a wooden plank seat. Every house had a net curtain covering the downstairs window in the parlour, next to a dark wooden door with a brass knob, and at the foot of the door, the pride of the house - a red step, polished to perfection every day by the woman of the house. Nobody could see what was behind the door, but everybody could see the red step, and judgement was harsh for the women whose step wasn't up to standard.

The row houses looked the same and the families living behind the closed doors had many things in common. Most men worked in the pottery industry or a coal mine, earning a pittance for their long days of hard labour. As a result, many of the homes housed more than one wage earner. Often multi-generational groups including dads, brothers and sons lived together, bringing in a wage to help pay the rent and buy food. Women stayed at home trying to hold things together, taking care of too many children who arrived with startling regularity. Life was hard in most homes. Not much to smile about.

The exception was number thirty-one. Laughter spilled through the door and through the open windows in the summertime, causing the neighbours to stop and smile to themselves, despite their lot in life. The squeals and giggles coming from the upstairs window on warm evenings, when the neighbours sat on their steps smoking pipes and drinking ale, produced embarrassed glances between the women folk and winks and chuckles from the men.

Jacob and Margaret smiled their way through life, not allowing the gloom of their surroundings to abate their happiness.

"They'll not be laughing so 'ard once the first babbie comes," Mrs Trainor scowled. "Life 'its you with a slap in the face once you're on your own with a babbie."

"Aye, you're right there Gladys," agreed Mrs Thomas. "They'll be takin' in a lodger to 'elp with the bills then. Once she's not working. Watch them laugh their way out o' that."

They poked each other in the ribs and rolled their eyes when they saw Margaret's obvious baby belly begin to show.

Margaret was ecstatic about the baby. Jacob would be the best father in the world and their baby would want for nothing. Jacob treated his wife with such tenderness, making her cups of tea and rubbing her tired feet. How he adored her.

How he was in awe of her and the life she was carrying inside her. His baby. He lay with his head on her belly listening to the sounds inside her and imagining the tiny life in there turning and twisting, although Margaret assured him it was probably gas he could hear. No matter! To him he was convinced the baby knew he was there, so he spoke gentle words or sang softly knowing his baby was listening.

"You must get Mrs Browning from Uttoxeter Road," advised Jacob's mother. "She's the most experienced midwife around these parts. She's delivered 'undreds of babbies in 'er time. She'll look after you very well, my ducks."

Margaret's mother had been gone for five years. Swept away, at the age of forty-two, in a tide of people who succumbed to the dreaded diphtheria outbreak of 1875. Margaret missed her mam every day, even more now she was to become a mother herself. How her mam would have loved all the preparations for the baby. How she would have loved being at the birth and helping the midwife. How she would have loved holding her first grandchild.

"Thank you, Ma," Jacob said. "I'll go round to 'er 'ouse this week and book Mrs Browning for the birth."

Borrowing and scrimping to gather together all the things they would need for the baby was not for Jacob and Margaret. A baby cradle was ordered from Barnabas McAlister, renowned creator of wondrous wooden furniture. A requisition for a matching wooden trunk and three-drawer chest quickly followed. When the horse-drawn delivery wagon turned into Newhall Road, all the doors flew open as neighbours spilled out of their houses to witness the phenomenon. They watched with mouths agape as the two delivery men proceeded to lift first the three-drawer chest, then the trunk and lastly the beautifully crafted baby cradle, off the wagon and into number thirty-one. Jacob strutted up and down, holding the door as wide as he could and helping guide the precious furnishings through the small doorway without a scratch or a scrape.

People "oohed and aahed" as they craned their necks to get a better view. The children elbowed each other as they jostled to get to the front of the crowd.

"Well I never," gasped Mrs Trainor. "No drawer from an old chest for their young 'un to sleep in. Did you see the fancy carving on that cradle? Fit for royalty I'd say."

The chest and trunk were placed in the small bedroom, which had been decorated with wallpaper covered in yellow rosebuds. A new carpet square filled almost the entire room and Margaret had hung three framed pictures of nursery rhymes—"Twinkle, Twinkle, Little Star," "Baa Baa Black Sheep" and "Hey Diddle Diddle," on the wall. A wooden rocking chair, a gift from Jacob's grandmother, rested in the corner by the window. The cradle was set beside the double bed in the big bedroom for the time being, so that the new baby would be close to Margaret and Jacob.

The chest was filled with nappies, soft undershirts, white nighties, swaddling blankets and knitted sets of bonnets, matinee coats and booties, made by Margaret. The wooden trunk held an array of knitted blankets in pastel shades, along with a warm woolen shawl with long tassels to cover Margaret's shoulders while she was nursing the baby.

The whole of Newhall Road seemed to be holding its collective breath awaiting the arrival of Jacob and Margaret's baby.

CHAPTER 7
HELEN

Warm water flowed over Jacob's legs as he entered the pristine, turquoise blue ocean. He loved the way it felt on his skin and couldn't wait to submerge his entire body but somehow his legs wouldn't move any further into the water. What was stopping him?

His eyes shot open taking in the dawn-lit bedroom, with Margaret asleep beside him, the rhythm of her breathing like the waves washing onto the shore in his dream. It had seemed so real. His legs still felt warm and wet. Reality came upon him with a jolt. His legs were wet! The bed was wet! Not just wet, but soaked.

"Margie," Jacob whispered in his sleeping wife's ear. "Wake up. Something's 'appened."

Both wide awake now, they surveyed the mess they were in. They stripped off their wet nightwear and towelled down before pulling on dry clothes. Similarly they stripped off the wet bedsheets and put thick towels over the mattress to soak up the water still remaining.

"What 'appened?" Jacob asked, wide eyed.

"The baby must be coming," Margaret answered. "Mrs Browning said this might 'appen. I wish she would 'ave explained just 'ow much water we could expect. There's an ocean of it 'ere."

Jacob started to laugh at the mention of "ocean", remembering his dream.

"Let's get you downstairs and wrapped in a warm blanket, my girl," Jacob said, taking charge of the situation. "Are you in pain?"

"No, not at all," answered his smiling wife. "In fact, I feel so good I may want a bacon sandwich for my breakfast."

Margaret kissed Jacob goodbye as he left for work.

"No point 'anging around 'ere all day," she said. "Your mam is coming over this morning, she'll keep me company, and the single bed is all made up and ready in the front room."

Margaret boiled pots of water to fill up the small bath kept in the back kitchen and washed herself from top to toe in the new lavender soap she had kept for this special day. Jacob's mam helped her wash her hair. Margaret towel dried it and brushed it out, then pinned it up into a soft chignon at the nape of her neck. She felt wonderful.

At the printing shop, Jacob wasn't doing so well. He couldn't eat. He couldn't concentrate on his work. He looked at his pocket watch hundreds of times during the day, which didn't make the time go any faster. He envisioned Margaret screaming in agony, sweating and writhing as she struggled through the pangs of labour. He couldn't bear that he wasn't with her at such a pivotal point of their lives.

"Jacob," Mr Matthews, his boss, said quietly. "Go 'ome lad. You're no good 'ere. Go 'ome and be with Margaret."

"But Mr Matthews, it's only four o'clock," was Jacob's reply. "I've never gone 'ome before my time."

"Never mind, now. Go on. Off with you. It's Saturday tomorrow and you'll 'ave a couple of days to settle in with your new baby. See you on Monday."

With that, Jacob jumped on his bike, completing the down-hill journey to home in record time.

"You're 'ome early," Margaret greeted him, moving across the room to greet him with a kiss. She looked and smelled wonderful.

"What is it Jacob?" his wife asked, noticing his pale face. "Do you feel sick?"

"I thought I'd find you thrashing about in agony by now," Jacob said, shaking his head at the worry he had been through all day.

"Ah, well, things 'aven't moved along very quickly," explained Margaret.

Waiting causes time to slow. It turns minutes into hours. Energy is sapped from doing nothing. Hearing becomes acute, making the slightest sound loud enough to startle the senses. Too much tea is brewed yet it never quenches thirst.

News soon spread down Newhall Road. Margaret was in labour. Her "time of grief" had come. She was in her "time of trouble." Many of the women in the adjoining houses could relate to confinement and the dangers and joys it produced. Women gathered in each other's houses to brew and drink pots of tea while they waited for news. The children kept watch outside to report any activity.

As the sun was setting over the chimney tops, Jacob rode his bike to Uttoxeter Road to fetch the midwife.

"Jacob's gone off on 'is bike," yelled Sally Trainer through the front door.

"Keep watching," yelled her mother. "Tell us when he gets back with the midwife."

Twenty minutes later, Mrs Trainer and her three neighbours were alerted that Jacob was back, along with the midwife.

"I'll put another pot on," Mrs Trainer announced. "Looks like we'll get some news before the night's out."

Mrs Browning bustled into the front room of number thirty-one, big black bag in hand.

"Lovely day for a baby to be born," she said. "Let me get settled and then we'll take a look at you, my lovely."

Laying out the contents of the black bag on the sideboard under the window, the midwife took one look at Jacob and gave him quick instructions.

"Off you go, young man," she ordered. "Put the kettle on and make a good strong cup of tea for yourself with lots of sugar. I don't want you fainting on me anytime soon. The father can be more trouble than the mother sometimes. You look like something the cat's dragged in."

Tea was the backbone of the working class. It was brewed and drunk on every occasion—good or bad. Whether a death or a birth, an anniversary or a funeral, a fight or a reconciliation, tea was the great calmer of frayed nerves and the pick-me-up in times of grief, tragedy or joy.

The midwife was a kind middle-aged woman, who had birthed hundreds of babies in the past twenty years. She had helped her mother do the same job, learning from her the skills needed to help mothers who were afraid and in pain. She was calm and cheerful, giving Margaret the confidence she needed to face the next stage of her labour.

"There, there, my girl," Mrs Browning cooed as she slid her fingers inside Margaret to check what was happening. "You've just about done it all by yourself. Almost no need for me at all. You're a brave girl."

Margaret thought she would tear apart. Even the calm, quiet words from Mrs Browning didn't help the panic that rose in her throat as the torturous pressure relentlessly increased. She tried to squeeze her legs together to stop the pressure, but that was worse. She gained some comfort from the soft warm cloth Mrs Browning placed over her perineum. Then she gently massaged the area with lard to help the stretching.

"You're doing real well, ducky," encouraged the midwife. "I can see the top of your baby's head. Lots of hair. The next few pains will be the worst and the best—once the head is out the rest will just slide through."

Mrs Browning slowly eased the taut skin around the baby's head as Margaret pushed her firstborn into the world. As the midwife predicted: the worst and then the best. The baby girl slid out of her mother and screamed her arrival to the world. A plump healthy baby, angry at being thrust from her warm bed. Mrs Browning laughed at the commotion she was making. No need for a tap on the bum for this one. There was certainly nothing wrong with her lungs. She expertly tied and cut the umbilical cord and wiped the furious baby's face and head.

"Come on in, Dad," shouted Mrs Browning as she wrapped the precious baby in a cotton blanket and placed her on Margaret's chest. "Come and see your baby girl."

Before the midwife had finished her invitation Jacob was in the room and at his wife's side, gazing with teary eyes at the wonder she was holding. He stroked his daughter's tiny hand which had escaped from the blanket, in awe of the minute fingers, each with a fingernail, and the delicate lines etched into the palm of her hand. The skin was so soft that Jacob could barely feel he was touching anything. He closed his eyes tightly, letting the tears spill down his cheeks as he thanked God for the safe delivery of his firstborn.

Margaret ran her fingers through Jacob's thick dark hair. She was tired now. Tired and completely euphoric.

The baby looked like her father. She had stopped screaming and lay quietly sleeping on Margaret's chest.

"What will we call 'er?" she whispered. "She looks so much like you with 'er curly dark 'air. We'd talked about naming 'er after your grandmother and I think the name suits 'er very well."

"'Elen it is then," smiled Jacob. "My mam will be so 'appy."

The women in Newhall Road waited for the young family to crash under the stress of a new baby and one wage earner, but they were disappointed. The printing company Jacob worked for became more and more successful, enabling the workers to profit from wage increases and bonuses paid by the generous owner, George Fellows. He was unique among company owners in North Staffordshire, who were renowned for paying low wages, making high profits, and becoming rich on the backs of a downtrodden work force.

Babies arrived at regular intervals in most families. Breastfeeding prevented pregnancy until the baby was old enough to be weaned, with few exceptions, so another baby usually arrived about every two years.

True to form, Margaret's second daughter was born almost two years to the day after Helen. They called her Sarah. She looked almost identical to her sister, although a much quieter version.

Regular as clockwork, Mrs Browning was called to number thirty-one Newhall Road a third time. Childbirth was much faster after two babies, so the midwife was summoned as soon as Margaret knew she was in labour. Helen and Sarah were picked up by Grandma Jenkins and the neighbour's lad cycled to the print shop in Stoke to let them know Jacob wouldn't be at work that day.

"All set then?" Jacob asked, as Mrs Browning went through her ritual of unpacking the black bag and checking to make sure she had all she needed. The borrowed single bed had stayed propped up in the back kitchen, as it was put to regular use every couple of years.

"Yes, ready to go," replied Mrs Browning. "You know the ropes, Jacob. Do you still need that cup of tea before things get exciting?"

Jacob laughed, thinking about the day Helen was born. Now he was an old hand at becoming a father. Would they have another girl, or did he dare hope it would be a boy this time?

"I'll make a cuppa anyway," Jacob said. "Would you like one, Missus?"

"Not until I'm all done 'ere, thanks," said the midwife. "Then I'll be 'appy to take you up on the offer."

"Tea for me as well, once it's over," grinned Margaret. "Away you go now, Jake. Let me get my work done."

John-Bernard was born just as the sun was setting on a fine spring evening in April. There was no means of weighing a baby, so the midwife announced a baby to be small, medium or large. John Bernard was definitely a "large." Like his sisters before him, he also looked like his father. He had fat little arms and legs and his cheeks were so plump he could barely open his eyes. He looked like he was already two months old compared to most newborns.

"Isn't 'e wonderful?" cooed Margaret, holding him to her chest and gazing down adoringly at her first boy.

"Wonderful is the word," answered Jacob, whose tears

spilled down his cheeks at the first sight of all his babies. "You too, Margie. You're the most wonderful. A baby boy. 'Ow blessed are we?"

Margaret's breast milk couldn't keep up with the demands of her growing son and she had to give him extra food at a very early age, mixing her milk with bread and a bit of butter to make "pobs" which helped keep him content.

The unfortunate side effect of weaning her boy so early was another pregnancy for Margaret. By the time John was six months old, she was pregnant again. This baby would be born only fifteen months after the last one. Even contented, positive spirited Margaret balked at the thought of having four babies under the age of five.

"I should 'ave slept downstairs on the sofa," Jacob sighed, when his wife told him there was another baby on the way. "I blame myself. I really do. But when I'm lying next to you in the same bed, you are so 'ard to resist. I 'ave no will power at all when it comes to loving you."

He wrapped his arms around his irresistible wife and held her close, stroking her long auburn hair.

"Don't worry, Margie," he said. "One more baby won't be too hard for us. We can ask that nice girl, Naomi, from number nineteen to come and 'elp out after school. We can easily pay 'er a few pennies for 'er time and she loves the girls already—always wants to play with them."

The following summer, on a hot July morning, Margaret delivered another baby girl. May was an easy birth compared with her brother, for which her mother was grateful. She looked the same as the other girls in every way, and was instantly adored by her parents, as the others had been.

Now, surely, thought Jacob, their family was complete. Four children seemed like the perfect number to him.

"She was born beautiful," everybody agreed.

The first four children born to Margaret and Jacob looked like their father. The first three had Jacob's dark curly hair and even May, born with her mother's auburn hair and blue eyes, followed the family trait of noticeably large nose and ears. Four children under the age of five, born in quick succession, challenged the young parents to the limit. The house seemed suddenly smaller, the hours in the day shorter, and sleep non-existent, as they struggled to give each precious child enough attention and provide the basic needs every new day demanded.

With Jacob's cooperation, their fifth baby didn't arrive until May was four years old. With the three eldest children in school, Margaret was excited to have another baby in the house. Everything was prepared weeks ahead, and the tiny house buzzed in anticipation.

Mrs Browning gasped in surprise when she caught sight of the fifth Jenkins' baby, holding it carefully in her experienced hands and gazing down at the tiny face.

"Oh, Mrs Jenkins," she exclaimed. "It's a beautiful baby girl."

Margaret was sure the midwife said the same thing about every baby, but as the baby was laid on her chest, she believed what she had heard. She was beautiful. The first of their five children to look like her mother, with delicate features in a perfect face surrounded by a soft auburn fuzz. No big nose. No big ears. She looked as different as she could from her siblings.

Jacob came from the kitchen leading a line of children, who watched as he kissed their mother and gently touched the baby's hands, tears wetting his cheeks.

"Come and see this wonder," he said, bringing his children close to the bed to see their new sister. "We're calling 'er Annie. Do you like that name?"

"It's lovely, Dad," said Helen, the eldest who had just turned nine years old the week before. "She's lovely too. Look at 'er fuzzy 'air and 'er tiny lips—just like a rosebud."

While the midwife attended to their mother, each of the children took a turn holding Annie. Jacob had to time each "hold" with his pocket watch, so that they were sure they each had a fair turn. Four girls and one boy. Jacob was a very happy man. He thought his family was even more complete. It was a perfect family and there would be just about enough room in their two-bedroomed house to fit them all in quite nicely.

The family at number thirty-one was considered lucky by many of the other residents of Newhall Road. Other families never had enough to eat. Their children were dressed in cast-offs and hand-me-downs, or jumble sale clothing. Men worked hard for little pay, coming home drained of energy to a houseful of children and little nourishing food. Some men drank too much, causing grief beyond endurance for their wives and children.

Several of the men on the street, however, didn't drink—Jacob included. The Working Men's Temperance Movement held weekly meetings and every man who joined signed a pledge saying he would never consume alcohol. Another reason for the other women to envy Margaret.

"She thinks she's somethin' special, she does," observed Mrs Hill from number forty-one. She hung the grey sheets over the line stretched down the backyard, while she gossiped over the brick wall separating her yard from Mrs Lovatt next door. "Five young 'uns now and look at 'er. Still spry and slender. Still getting into clothes she wore before 'er first was born. Who does that?"

"I know what you mean, Elsie," replied Mrs Lovatt. "I've been behind 'er at the corner shop and seen 'er buy bacon on more than one occasion. She regularly orders rabbit and one day she bought a piece of pork big enough to feed ten people."

"We should be so lucky," continued Mrs Hill. "An 'usband who doesn't spend all 'is money at the pub. My old man swills 'is wages down 'is throat. I get the dregs of what's left to make ends meet for me and the little 'uns. Bread and lard's no substitute for bacon and rabbit."

The two women went back to hanging their laundry to dry, knowing they would be collecting it in a couple of hours covered in black soot from the factory kilns. They looked down at their old, thread-bare clothes, stretched over their distended bellies and envied Margaret Jenkins until they were green. Their dreams had long departed in the bleakness of their existence. Gone were the hopes of a happy home where food was plentiful and children were content. Beer took all that away, along with the handsome young men they had married.

To top it all, Margaret had given birth to another girl

who, unlike the other Jenkins children, had the look of an angel. The women on Newhall Road agreed: Annie was the most beautiful baby they had ever seen.

Cause for more envy.

CHAPTER 10
A PLACE OF THEIR OWN

With Jacob's house bursting at the seams, he suggested to his two best mates, Joe and Bill, that they should have a meeting at Joe's house.

Three steaming mugs of tea sat on the table in Joe Baker's kitchen. He had lived at number seven Newhall Road for more than thirty years, taking the tenancy over from his parents when they died. His family was now grown, with only his youngest son still living at home. For the three friends, Joe's kitchen was the quietest place to meet.

"Well, lads," began Joe, looking intently at his two friends. "We're all agreed, right?"

"Aye, Joe. We're agreed," Jacob answered. "You're in, right Bill?"

"Aye, I'm in," Bill said. "It's worth a try. The land's just sitting there empty. I believe we 'ave as good a chance as anybody of getting it."

"What about the cost?" Joe asked, his forehead wrinkled with questions. "None of us 'ave that kind of money."

"We'll 'ave to be prepared to do some collecting," Bill suggested. "You know. Go door to door, like."

Jacob looked at his two friends and shook his head at their naivety. It would take more than coppers collected door to door to realize their dream.

"We'll probably need some big donors, I'd think," observed Jacob. "Like the boss at work, or old Mr Snape who owns the tobacco shop. We should make a list of rich folk who may help us."

Joe wrote a very short list of rich people they knew in his notebook. One of the biggest questions, though, was: Were they religious? Were they Methodists?"

"I've yet to meet a rich fella who was Methodist," Bill said. "They're mostly Church of England, those lot. Or Catholic."

Topping up the mugs of tea, Joe paused and held the teapot over Jacob's mug. His face lit up. His eyes opened wide and a big smile spread across his face.

"We're going about this all wrong, lads," Joe finally said. "We don't need to ask for money. I propose we ask the Duke of Sutherland to give us the land."

Jacob and Bill stared at their friend in disbelief. Who would give away land? Particularly a duke.

"You're batty, Joe," laughed Bill. "The Duke of Sutherland owns just about every piece of land in Normacot. 'E's not going to give any of it away. Land's worth money. A lot of money. You're not thinking, mate."

"Wait a minute, Bill," Jacob interjected. "Why don't we give it a try? 'E'll probably laugh at us and say "no", but we don't know until we've tried."

"I'm laughing now," Bill said. "Give it a try? Please, Mr Duke, can you give us this piece of your land on Newhall Road to build a chapel? 'E'll flip his lid."

They decided Jacob should write the letter. He had the best handwriting and he could get the best paper from his company. They all had input into the wording, working on it until they were happy with the end result. Jacob's boss helped him find The Duke of Sutherland's address in London.

"Well, Jacob," Mr Fellows, owner of the printing company, said. "Good luck to you, lad. There's enough pubs in your end of town to keep every man drunk for as long as he lives. Asking for land to build a temperance chapel in the middle of all that is a brave step, I must say. Mind you, I've heard The Duke of Sutherland's a fair man—he'll consider it. He's done no end of good for the folks around Normacot. The rental houses he's built are in high demand. Lovely wide streets and well-built terraced homes with more space and light. Yes, he's one of the good ones. You may just be onto something."

Several weeks later an official-looking envelope arrived at number thirty-one, addressed to Jacob. It was an invitation to meet with a Mr George Colclough, representing the Duke of Sutherland, at an address in Trentham, a village a few miles west.

❧

"God bless The Duke of Sutherland," sang out Bill, raising his mug of tea in a toast. Jacob's long interview, six weeks before, resulted in an official donation of the proposed Chapel site in Newhall Road. Now it was all systems go to raise money for the building.

The members of the Working Men's Temperance Society threw themselves into the project with great enthusiasm. Using the old dance hall, they organized dances, picnics, talent shows, and band concerts, with all proceeds going to the building fund. Mr Fellows started them off with a generous donation of £50, a small fortune. Shops put donation boxes on their counters, and even the pubs collected money, which was irony at its best.

Newhall Road was a buzz of excitement as the fund increased to a sizeable downpayment and the building society agreed to lend the trustees the money for the construction of the chapel.

"I never imagined our dream would come true," Jacob said as he sat in his chair by the fire, gazing into the flames. "What do you think, Margaret? A chapel across the road!"

"Your faith never wavered, Jacob," Margaret responded, putting down her sewing and reaching for her husband's hand. "God is good. The chapel will become the center of all our lives, you mark my words. It's a heaven-sent blessing."

"As are you, my love," Jacob said, raising Margaret's hand to his lips.

Watching the erection of the chapel was the favourite pastime for Jacob's oldest four children. Helen, who was ten years old, held May's hand as they stood beside their brother John and sister Sarah and gazed out over the mud-covered ground.

In fact, the building site was the favourite place to be for all the children on Newhall Road, who dashed home from school to join their friends and watch the bricklayers at work. As the walls rose the excitement grew, and Margaret walked over to join the children, carrying one-year-old Annie on her hip, to watch as the roof trusses were placed. There were mums and dads, grandmas and granddads, aunties and uncles, all watching as the workers built the roof. A cheer rippled through the small crowd as the roof structure was finished. It was only a matter of weeks before the roof was tiled, the windows and doors installed and the simple interior completed.

The three friends, now trustees, who had begun it all stood and watched as the doors swung open to welcome the first meeting of worshipers.

The stone above the door read "Workingmen's Temperance and Christian Society 1890."

It was finished and it belonged to them—they had a place of their own.

As it turned out Annie was the middle child. Five more children arrived at regular two-year intervals over the following ten years—three girls and two boys.

Over the years the house on Newhall Road was changed many times to accommodate the growing family. The parlour was put into use as the boys' bedroom. A double bed for the three of them took up half the room. During the day it was piled with cushions along the wall and used as extra seating. The long sideboard under the window had three rows of sturdy drawers, one row for each of the boy's clothing, and Jacob had installed a long row of hooks across the wall leading into the kitchen, which served as hangers for everybody's outdoor coats. Margaret and Jacob slept in the smallest bedroom, where a double bed, small dresser and wardrobe made it difficult to move around, sometimes causing a riot of laughter as the forever-happy couple tried to get dressed and undressed without falling onto the bed.

The largest bedroom was furnished with two double

beds, with only six inches between them. Two eight-drawer tallboys faced the beds—two drawers for each girl's clothing. The girls slept four in one bed and three in the other, the smaller ones sleeping in the middle so that they didn't fall out of bed. Each girl had her own small pillow, made by their mother, so that it afforded some measure of comfort.

Annie was the only one in the family who looked like Margaret. May had lovely wavy auburn hair too, but that is where the resemblance stopped. Annie had pale delicate skin, large blue eyes surrounded by lush auburn lashes, a perfectly shaped small nose, full pink lips, and level white teeth. Her cascade of glorious auburn hair curled and caught the light making it shimmer with different shades of red. She turned heads wherever she went.

Margaret never lost the joy of living her life with Jacob. The house in Newhall Road was kept as clean as a new pin, even with the babies coming so frequently. Margaret was grateful to have birthed ten healthy babies, with not one lost. Quite an achievement in an era when miscarriage and still-born babies were common. The family thrived on the love and affection they received on a daily basis from both mother and father, whose love for each other never wavered.

They were not without their hardships over the years. In the winter of 1895 it snowed for three whole days, until the drifts had reached the top of the window sills and the wind was enough to cut them in two. Margaret and the children huddled together around the fire in the kitchen with blankets wrapped around them, sipping hot lobby—a meaty soup —from the pot over the fire and prayed Father would be able to get home from work safely. Jacob had walked to work for those three days, the journey taking him more than two hours through the worst winter storm in living memory. On the third day he made it home, but his feet were so frozen he never regained the feeling in some of his toes. Margaret used every morsel of food in the house during that time, down to the last crust of bread and last drop of milk. As the storm abated, John-Bernard, at eleven years old, braved the still-biting wind and walked to the market in the hopes there would be food available. He returned with two rabbits and enough potatoes and carrots to make a fine stew. A stew that had never tasted so good.

Later the same year all the children caught the measles at the same time. The bedrooms were kept dark because the light hurt their eyes, and Margaret had little sleep as she bathed them with cool water to keep down the fever, and sang them lullabies, holding them close when their eyes glazed over in delirium. The young couple worried they would lose one or more of their precious babies, but the children slowly recovered and Jacob thanked God over and over again. Other families were less fortunate and funeral services were held for several weeks as other people's children succumbed to the disease.

The little chapel was kept busy with grieving families—the men forgoing the pub to be at home during the epidemic. Terrified of spreading the terrible disease, families stayed in their homes, not daring to visit or send their healthy children to school. The men had to work, but hurried home at night to barricade themselves indoors with their loved ones.

The primary school finally closed its doors, staying dormant until two weeks after the last reported case of measles. Cautiously, mothers allowed their precious young ones to attend again, scrutinizing each child every night for signs of a rash.

Skinny and bedraggled, the children gradually regained strength. Benger's Food, a powdered wheat product with added pancreatic enzymes to help digestion, was the diet of every household. The magic gruel-like tasteless grey substance transformed sickly children, fleshing out their thin bodies and restoring their appetites. Death and disease behind them, the working people of Normacot had picked themselves up and carried on, as they always did.

CHAPTER 12
OLD ENOUGH

At the turn of the twentieth century, pottery factories filled the landscape of the five towns known as Stoke-on-Trent in Staffordshire. They provided the world with the finest china, and jobs for a vast percentage of the working class. Sixty-eight factories were located in Longton (one of the five towns) alone. Each factory belched out black smoke from the coal-fired kilns, filling the air with soot, rendering the middle of the day dark as dusk.

Life expectancy for pottery workers was short: mid-forties for men who had worked constantly since eight or ten years of age. Some jobs were more dangerous than others—scouring or smoothing china was a job for young girls; the china glaze contained lead that often caused an early death for these girls. Clay dust filled the air and the workers came home with the white clay powder covering their skin, hair and clothing. Bronchitis and pneumonia were a constant threat and it turned young girls into old women in short shrift.

School ended for Helen at eleven years of age. She remained at home, helping with the younger children, as did

Sarah two years later. When it was May's turn to leave school, Margaret realized she couldn't keep them all at home. The older two girls had to find work somewhere. But where? A caring and loving mother, Margaret didn't want her girls working ten hours a day at a menial job in the clay end of a pottery factory, where the work was back-breaking and the conditions deplorable.

Mrs Millington, at number three Newhall Road told Margaret about a new getting-up shop that had just opened in the high street. A getting-up shop brought in produced china ready for decoration, and they were looking for girls to learn the trade.

"Your two girls would do well there, Margie," Mrs Millington said. "It's walking distance from 'ome as well. Our Alice started there two weeks ago. She's learning 'ow to paint flowers. Loves it, she does."

Needing no more encouragement, Helen and Sarah put on their Sunday best clothes and walked to the high street to find the new getting-up shop.

The sign read "Winston Field China." The double doors were freshly painted and opened onto a small vestibule where a stout middle-aged lady sat behind a desk. She greeted them with a smile and asked them to fill in an application form. She asked them questions about their schooling and their home life and if they enjoyed drawing. The age of the girls was an advantage. At thirteen and fifteen they were regarded as good candidates to learn the skills of decorating. They were both offered jobs learning to gild gold onto cups, saucers, plates and dishes.

The small factory grew quickly, employing more and more people. The quality china was in high demand, and the exceptional working conditions made it the most desirable place of work in the entire city. The building was expanded to accommodate more workers, but the standard never dropped. Under the watchful eye of Mr Masters, the production manager, every room in the factory was clean and well-organized. Long benches were installed under the windows for the best possible light. Each worker had a comfortable stool. Regular breaks were incorporated into the day, with an opportunity to take a short stretch or walk, have a snack or a drink. Best of all there were two huge tea urns in the centre of the maze of rooms, where the workers could fill up their mugs and take their "cuppa" back to their work bench to enjoy while they worked.

Each of the girls from the Jenkins' family began their working life at Winston Field China. May followed after her sisters. Annie couldn't wait for her stint of helping her mother at home to be over.

"Please, Mam," Annie begged. "You know 'ow good I am at drawing. I'm ready for work. You've only got our Charlie at 'ome now—the others are all in school. Our 'elen and Sarah are both married."

"Annie, you will never listen, will you?" replied her patient mother. "Don't be in such a 'urry to go to work my dear girl. Your dad and me 'ave talked about it and decided you will stay at 'ome for a year, at least. Even now the government's raised the age to twelve for leaving school, it's still too young to be gone all day. I need you 'ere Annie. With your two sister's married, we still have eight, plus me and your dad, to see to every day. You need the experience of running a 'ouse and cooking for a big family. It might come in 'andy one day."

"But Mam," Annie pleaded.

"No, Annie. That's my final word."

Annie sulked her way through the next several weeks, making it conspicuously clear to the entire family that she was staying home under duress. A year was a very long time for a twelve-year-old to wait.

Time dragged by for Annie, while the rest of the family seemed to be quite contented. Her two oldest sisters and their husbands came to eat Sunday dinner with them every week, when stories of work in the decorating shops would entertain the family for hours, only sending Annie into more of a sulk. She was missing out on so much of the fun.

Her life revolved around cleaning, cooking, and watching the younger children. Washing the never-ending pile of clothes then trying to dry them in rainy weather was Annie's least favourite chore. The damp clothes were hung from the rack in the kitchen, then hoisted up to the ceiling on pulleys. Condensation beaded and streamed down the walls and windows. Everything in the house felt damp—it sometimes took days to dry.

When she turned thirteen, she finally had permission from her parents to apply for a job at the decorating factory. Annie was thrilled.

ANNIE

1905

CHAPTER 13

EYE OF THE SON

"Number one flower painter," announced Annie as she handed her pay packet over to her mother. "Mrs Newbury says she's never seen a girl take to it so quickly. Only sixteen and I'm earning as much as some of the girls in their twenties."

It had taken Annie three years to perfect the art of flower painting.

"Now, now, Annie," Margaret said, trying to hide a smile behind her hand. "No bragging. Remember what we learn in chapel about God's gifts. 'E's gifted you with an eye for painting flowers. All 'is doing."

Annie took her sixpence pocket money and skipped up the stairs to put it away in her tin full of other silver sixpences stashed away. She was saving for a bicycle, so that she could ride across the recreation ground, over the brook by the Cinderhill pub and into the countryside. She loved feeling the fresh air on her face and wind in her hair. Sometimes she borrowed her brother's bicycle, but it was too big for her and she couldn't sit on the seat and reach the pedals.

Many changes had occurred at the factory where she

worked. A Royal Commission had been procured, which had enhanced the profile of the factory. The owner, James Benton Esquire, had taken a personal interest after that, visiting the decorating shops on regular occasions to gain a firsthand knowledge of how the china was decorated. His wife had ordered a full dinner service in a green lily of the valley pattern, edged in liquid gold. Annie had been part of the decorating team who had expertly painted each individual lily. The gold edges and bands were done by Annie's two older sisters. The owner himself came to thank all the girls who had worked on the project.

"Who's the nice looking young man with the manager?" asked Annie, as she glanced up from her work bench into the adjacent room.

"Don't you know?" Annie's friend Hilda said. "The owner's son, that's who. 'E went to a posh school down South. Supposed to be real clever. Eddie Jones says 'e's coming into the business in a big way. Working on the selling side of things."

Daniel Benton was tall and lithe, with thick brown hair and deep blue eyes. Every girl on the factory floor stole a glance at him as he walked past them, taking everything in as he asked questions of the manager. Annie felt her heart skip a beat as he passed behind her. She caught a slight fragrance of sandalwood mixed with fine leather, and suddenly felt a radiation of warmth spreading into her neck and face.

The factory workers never saw much of Mr Daniel Benton. He worked in the manager's office, only venturing into the factory work-spaces to gain knowledge about a particular new design or a commissioned dinner service. A photographer had been hired to take some promotional pictures and Daniel was talking to him now, as they wandered through the factory.

The purple crocus Annie was painting blurred before her

eyes as she steadied her hand to finish the petal. It was a warm June day and the windows had been opened earlier to let any kind of a breeze float into the painting shop. Her cheeks burned as she felt the blush flooding her face. The two men had stopped behind her and were intently watching her paint the crocus.

"It's the light on her hair, of course," said the photographer. "See how it catches the tones of red and amber —beautiful!"

"You're the expert," replied the young Mr Benton. "Make your choice and we'll arrange for the sitting."

"I don't think I need to look further," was the statement. "Would you arrange for this girl to be photographed in the room we chose earlier? It will be an eye-catching piece for your sales convention in London next month. I think we have enough photographs of the china. Something more personal always makes an impact."

They walked away, leaving Annie in a state of disbelief.

"What do you think of that?" her friend whispered. "They're going to take your picture. Your picture's going to be seen by people in London. Well I never."

"Come with me, Annie," ordered Mrs Newbury, the shop supervisor. "Bring your paints, girl. And run a brush through that hair of yours. Why they'd choose you I just don't know, with that mass of red hair in disarray."

Annie scurried after the older woman. Nobody had bothered to ask her if she agreed to having her picture taken. She was regarded as the factory owner's property and, as such, she did what she was told to do.

"Put this clean apron on," Mrs Newbury said. "And don't smile, or do anything unless the photographer tells you. It's a big 'onour to be picked out of all the girls working 'ere. You mind your manners."

Through the tea urn room they went. Through rooms

where men sat at tilted desks drawing flowers, leaves, land-scapes and patterns of all kinds. Annie could have stayed in that room all day, watching the talented artists work their magic, bringing their drawings to life with coloured pencils.

A small room filled with light was their destination. A table and chair were placed near the window and the photographer was busy placing panels of white board around the back of the table and chair.

"Come, come," he said as he saw Annie enter. "Come and sit here. I will tell you how to sit, how to hold your head, your hands, your shoulders. But for the moment just sit."

He walked to a tripod supporting a giant contraption, which Annie assumed was a camera, and peered through a black funnel, where he fiddled with knobs and adjusted the position of the tripod until he was satisfied.

Explicit instructions were given to Annie. The photographer posed her expertly and with great precision for each picture he took.

"Look up, dear. Now look down at your hands. Hold the paintbrush higher. Brush your hair away from your face. Smile—not that much! Good, good, that's it. Turn your face more to the light."

Through the sitting, Daniel stood in the corner of the small room watching the process. Aware of his eyes on her face, Annie felt suddenly shy. She never looked at him, but his very presence in such close proximity caused her breath to catch and her throat to tighten. It was only because it was such a strange experience, she told herself. She had never had her photograph taken before and had been completely unprepared.

Daniel was riveted to the spot as he watched Annie pose for the photographs, her red hair curling around her perfectly oval, flawless face. Her plump, pink lips parted in a half smile exposing a row of even white teeth. She was small in stature yet carried herself with an air of confidence rarely seen in one so young. She somehow exuded joy—something in her eyes and the curl of her lips gave the impression that laughter was close to the surface. She was beautiful and Daniel was captivated.

CHAPTER 14

HEADING FOR TROUBLE

"Are you setting the table for tea, or just staring into space?" Margaret asked. "I can't imagine what's going on in your 'ead these days, our Annie. Stop daydreaming and get the table set. Your dad'll be 'ome any minute."

Annie snapped out of her musing and quickly put the finishing touches to the table, piling the plates in the middle, along with the forks, salt and pepper. Her mam had made a giant meat pie for tea. A favourite of Jacob's as well as most of the children. The meat had been cooking slowly for a good part of the day, along with onions and carrots, until the broth was thick and full of flavour. The fluffy pastry crust was more than an inch thick, and golden brown when it came out of the oven beside the coal fire grate.

"Something smells delicious," called Jacob as he hung his coat on a hook in the front room and hurried to the kitchen to give his wife a kiss. "Must be meat pie."

Soon the kitchen was full of hungry children, all with their eyes on the meat pie in the middle of the table. Margaret scooped out the pie, giving a heaping portion to each of her family. Jacob said a blessing and, finding a place to sit, the family tucked into their tea.

"You're the best cook in the whole world, my Margaret," said Jacob, his mouth full of meat and pastry. "And we're the luckiest family, for certain."

Annie picked at her meat pie, her thoughts still elsewhere. She found it hard to think of anything but the photograph session and Daniel Benton's eyes. She was expected to grow up and marry a local lad like her sisters before her. A lad who worked hard and didn't drink. Preferable somebody from Chapel who had signed the pledge of sobriety. Any other scenario could not be considered. Annie was a working class girl, from a working class family, and the working class didn't mix with the middle or upper classes, ever.

Daniel Benton sat at the table in the dining room of his family's home on Trentham Road, waiting for the footman to serve him soup. His father sat in his rightful place at the head of the table, with his mother sitting at his right. Daniel's younger sister, Felicity, made the fourth diner at the evening meal. The rest of the table, which accommodated twelve people, was empty, which made the large room feel echoey and cold.

"You are very dull tonight, Daniel," Mr Benton Senior observed. "Why don't you tell us about the photographer and your plans for the exhibition next week in London?"

With the cream of asparagus soup before him, Daniel told his family about his day.

"Nothing much to tell really," he began. "The photographer was a nice enough chap and spent a great deal of time displaying the china. I think the results will be very good."

Daniel paused, wrestling with his thoughts about the red-headed girl.

"He also chose one of the working girls to photograph. A flower painter," he continued, hoping his voice didn't crack and that the fluttering in his stomach wasn't visible on his face. "The photographer thought a more personal photograph would do wonders for the promotion of our product."

"Which girl did he choose?" questioned his father. "I can't imagine any of them making much of a model, particularly not for the clientele we are hoping to reach."

"Her name is Annie Jenkins," replied Daniel. "I think you'll be surprised with the results, Father. She was quite stunning."

Daniel wished he hadn't said "stunning" the minute it was out of his mouth. His father and mother just about dropped their spoons in their soup and Felicity gave a small squeak.

Flustered, Daniel tried to explain, only digging himself a deeper hole.

"Well, I mean, she had red hair. In that way, she was different. Yes, I definitely should have said different instead of stunning. I mean how could she be stunning? She's a factory worker."

"Quite so," mumbled Mrs Benton, continuing to eat her soup. "Your father will be the judge of whether or not you use photographs of a flower painter in your presentation, Daniel."

The footman cleared the soup plates and served the grilled halibut as an awkward silence fell on the diners.

Daniel forced himself to eat the fish. How stupid to have talked about Annie as "stunning." It was a word too inadequate to describe her. The image of her had never left his head. She was far more than "stunning." She was beautiful, wonderful, delicate, lovely! At nineteen years of age he had seen a few lovely girls at house parties and summer barbecues. All from well-to-do families, mostly daughters of factory owners or even junior peerage. He was encouraged to acquaint himself with the daughters of these wealthy families, seeking out a future wife from his own class. He had to put all thoughts of Annie out of his head.

The photograph of the flower painter was the talk of the London Exhibition. People flocked around the Winston Field China booth to gaze at Annie's picture. Orders flooded into the factory, many of them requesting that their china be painted by the girl in the photograph. Mr Benton Senior was delighted that his son had talked him into displaying the artwork as part of the exhibit. In fact, he had gone into the factory and sought out Annie just to see what she looked like in real life, and pronounced her to be a very attractive working girl.

When Daniel returned to Normacot, he was greeted with elation from the manager and staff at the factory. Orders continued to stream in and they had enough work for more than a year already. A celebration dinner was held at the Benton mansion, where other pottery owners congratulated Daniel on a job well done. The publicity from the much acclaimed picture of Annie had influenced buyers from all over the world to order china from the pottery factories based in Stoke-on-Trent, benefitting many of the competing factories. It was a victory for them all.

Annie heard Daniel had returned from London and that the exhibition had been a great success. She was happy for him. He was so young and always under the critical eye of his father. She had no idea, however, that the source of all the excitement and resulting sales were in a great part due to her.

Daniel, for his part, stayed off the factory floor and remained in the offices, supervising the orders as they came over his desk. At some point he would have to go into the factory and check on the progress of some of the more lucrative orders, but he trembled at the thought of seeing Annie again. He vowed to avoid the room she worked in, so that the image he had of her, which was his constant companion, wasn't embellished even more.

Annie was taking a message to the design room from Mrs Newbury when she turned the corner and almost collided with Daniel Benton.

Stunned into silence, Daniel and Annie stood inches apart, rooted to the spot. Time stopped. The peripheral world became cloudy and dim. The air between them seemed thick as syrup. Slowly, Annie raised her eyes to meet Daniel Benton's eyes. It was like looking into another person's soul.

Reality hit with a force so powerful they both stepped back at the same time, as though the air between them had suddenly evaporated. Annie fled up the stairs into the design room and handed the note to Mr McKenzie before running down the stairs again, praying Daniel would be gone. She hurried back to her workbench, still flustered from the unexpected collision. She swore to herself that she would never leave the factory floor again. Never run the risk of intercepting young Mr Benton again.

Daniel poured himself a glass of whiskey, which was totally out of character for him, particularly in the middle of the day. Anything to stop his hands from shaking and his heart from pounding. How had this young flower painter infiltrated his mind? Why was he so affected by just being near her? Why couldn't he stop thinking about her and find a girl from his own class to fixate on? But he didn't have any answers to his own questions. He only knew that Annie seemed part of him. He couldn't separate himself from her. He wanted her more than he'd wanted anything in his life. He loved her—he had loved her from the first moment he saw her.

For weeks Daniel avoided the working area of the factory and immersed himself in his important role as head of sales and promotion. Singing floated through an open doorway as he walked along the passageway towards his office. He turned back to stand in the doorway and listen.

"Happy Birthday to You," sang the girls from the flower painting shop. "Happy Birthday, dear Annie, Happy Birthday to You."

Annie blew out the seventeen candles on the chocolate cake her friend Hilda had made. Through the smoke from the candles she saw him standing in the doorway.

"Do you want a piece of cake, Mr Daniel?" called Hilda as she handed out slices to the girls in the shop. "Come and wish Annie a happy birthday."

Daniel accepted the cake graciously.

"Happy Birthday, Annie," he said.

With everybody watching, Daniel took Annie's hand in his and kissed it gently. An audible gasp reverberated around the room. Then he was gone, back to the security of the top floor offices.

"Annie, what just 'appened?" gasped Hilda. "He kissed your 'and. We all saw it. What could 'e be thinking? Annie, 'e's the boss's son."

Dazed and confused, Annie sat at her workbench, her piece of cake discarded. He had kissed her hand and she could still feel the imprint of his warm lips. She put her other hand over the spot he had kissed, trying to keep the kiss on her skin for as long as possible.

She couldn't love anybody else. She loved Daniel Benton, despite the taboo of loving a man from a different class. She knew there would never be a future for them. She knew the Benton family would never accept her, just as her family would never accept Daniel. They could never be together. The beautiful kiss on her hand would be the only kiss.

"Annie, what will you do?" asked Hilda.

"I don't know what you mean," retorted Annie. "He was just being a gentleman that's all. He probably didn't think anything of it. I'm not giving it another thought."

The girls went back to their benches to paint flowers. All of them thinking the same thing: *Mr Benton Junior is in love with Annie.*

As Annie arrived at work the following Monday, the first thing she saw was an envelope sitting on her bench. It had nothing written on it, but was sealed tightly. She used the end of her paintbrush to slit it open.

Dear Annie,

Would you please consider meeting me outside work? Somewhere private. Maybe I could suggest the flower clock at Longton Park on Sunday. If it's a dry day, would you meet me there at 2.00pm? I'll be there.

If you decide not to come, I will understand.
Don't try to reply. It's too complicated.

Please come,
Daniel Benton

So the kiss on the hand wasn't the end of it, thought Annie.

Sunday afternoon couldn't come soon enough for Daniel and he was at the flower clock at 1:30, waiting. He wondered if she would come, guessing she probably wouldn't. Why would she? She would know that meeting him was the precursor to a whole lot of trouble. He walked away from the clock and back towards it, pacing up and down in his anxiety.

Annie almost ran to the park. The last half-mile was all uphill and she was out of breath as she reached the top of the steep avenue. She slowed her pace as she went through the park gate and took the long walk around to the flower clock. The path was well-trodden and she couldn't see the clock until she turned the corner. He had his back turned towards her and she stopped, her heart thumping, to watch him. As though he could feel her eyes on him, he slowly turned to look directly at her.

Annie didn't move as her employer's young son strode towards her, his eyes never leaving her face. The space between them decreased until they stood only inches apart. They had never spoken directly to each other, and even now they were alone, words seemed somehow unnecessary. To be together at last, away from the prying eyes of the factory floor, was enough. Eventually Daniel broke the silence.

"I'm happy you could meet me, Annie," he said quietly. "I've dreamed about being alone with you since the first day I saw you, almost a year ago."

Annie blushed and fell into step beside him.

"It's nice to be away from everybody," she said, smiling. "The park's lovely in the summer. Flowers everywhere. So much to see and admire."

Conversation was easy between them as they walked under the trees towards the pond. Annie had worn her Sunday best—a dark blue skirt and white blouse. She had wrestled her voluminous hair into a soft bun at the nape of her neck, although curly strands had escaped and danced around her face in the breeze. She was very aware that, despite her carefully chosen outfit, she was no match for Daniel Benton, who was attired like the gentleman he was. Dressed in the finest cloth and latest fashion, he was a dashing figure, somehow out of place in the middle of Longton Park, where the working people came on Sunday afternoons. He attracted curious stares as he sauntered along beside the petite red-headed working girl.

"Will you meet me again next Sunday, Annie?" asked Daniel.

"I would like that," Annie answered. "Rain or shine?"

"Yes," laughed Daniel. "Rain or shine."

Sunday afternoons became their regular meeting time. They both kept their meetings a secret. They both worked during the week with their minds set on Sunday at the flower clock, when they could be together.

The secret was hard to keep, especially when they desperately wanted to tell everybody they knew how much they loved each other. They were both aware that their secret would shatter the worlds they lived in, particularly Daniel's privileged world. Daniel's parents would never understand. There would be a family commotion like none before, and the young man dreaded the conflict it would cause.

When Elizabeth Walker, one of the flower painters who worked with Annie, saw them in the park together their secret was out. By the time Annie arrived at work on Monday morning, the entire factory knew about it, including her sisters and Mr Benton Senior.

"What do you think you are doing?" yelled Daniel's father. "Damn and blast you. Are you out of your mind? You stupid, stupid boy! Walking out with one of the factory workers!"

"Father, please," began Daniel, walking over to his father's desk.

"Stop," James demanded, holding up his hand. "I came into the office this morning to be informed by my manager that there was a 'situation' involving my son. A 'situation' damn it! You had been seen out in public with this girl, by one of the other flower painters. I could barely believe what I was hearing."

"Father," interrupted Daniel again, "let me explain."

"Explain? Explain what?" said his father, jumping up from his chair and charging around his desk to confront his son. "That you fancy her? You have obviously forgotten who you are and the family you belong to. It will kill your mother, I swear. A factory girl. You could have gone to Manchester and bought any high class trollop."

"You evil old man," yelled Daniel, seizing the lapels of his father's jacket and glaring into his face. "How dare you even suggest any such motive in my relationship with Annie. I adore her. I love her more than life itself. There, now I've said it and you can go to hell for all I care!"

Daniel struggled to quell the urge to hit his father squarely in the jaw and dropped his hands to his sides. Having professed his love for Annie, there was nothing more to be said.

James Benton's visage changed. His face was a pallid grey. He looked suddenly old and his hands shook as he tried to control his emotions.

"Get out," he finally muttered between his teeth. "When you have come to your senses and told the flower painter you've made a mistake and the liaison cannot continue, we will talk again. Until then, stay away from me. I have nothing more to say to you."

Every word of the confrontation had been heard in the outer offices and design room. The silence was tangible as Daniel walked briskly through the adjoining rooms and out of the building.

"Get on with your work," yelled Mr Benton Senior from the door of his office. "Keep your noses out of my business."

He slammed the door and retreated behind his desk, where he put his head in his hands, still shaken from the argument with his son. He poured himself a large glass of whiskey and sat sipping the fiery liquid until his hands had stopped shaking and he felt the colour return to his face. He had such big plans for his only son. He was a talented boy. Intelligent and artistic. The success he had achieved at the London Exhibition showed his propensity for sales and promotion, and his father dreamed of Winston Field China becoming renowned internationally. America was where the new money was. He would send Daniel to New York on a promotion trip. That would get this nonsense out of his head in a hurry.

Meanwhile, there was another positive step he could take. He sent for the production manager immediately.

In the decorating shop, the last half hour had been filled with a barrage of questions and innuendoes.

"Well, well, Annie," Elizabeth Walker had greeted her. "In the park with the boss's son were you? I saw you both with my own eyes."

"Annie, what's this we've heard?" her older sister whispered, coming into the flower painters shop from the gilding shop to find out what was going on. "You must be crazy. You shouldn't have agreed to meet 'im, Annie. You know it will only mean trouble for you."

"I want to know what 'e's after," sniggered Joan Turner from the back of the room. "Or 'as 'e already got what 'e was looking for?"

"That's right, Joan," goaded another flower painter. "There's only one reason the boss's son shows interest in the likes of us."

"Stop it!" shouted Annie. "None of you know anything about it. Daniel's not like that. 'E's been a perfect gentleman. 'E would never take advantage of me. It's none of your business anyway."

Annie jumped up from her workbench and ran to the privy to wash her face and calm herself.

When she returned, they began again, berating her and asking crude, hurtful questions.

Mrs Newbury marched into the decorating shop, her mouth set in a line and her arms folded in front of her chest. Gossip was a constant companion of the factory workers' lives. This particular piece of gossip had all but stopped production throughout the factory and Mrs Newbury was having none of it.

"Back to work, girls," she ordered. "Enough talking and gossiping for today. You're getting paid to paint flowers, not to natter about stuff that doesn't concern you. Any more of it and I'll dock your pay packets. Annie, you're to come with me."

Annie followed her supervisor up the stairs and into the production manager's office.

"Your wages are in the pay packet," he said, handing her the brown envelope and speaking in a quiet voice. "I'm sorry, Annie. It's not my decision. You're dismissed immediately. Pick up your personal belongings and leave the building right away."

"What?" asked Annie, unable to comprehend what was being said. "You can't sack me. What for? What's the reason? I haven't done anything wrong. I'm a good worker, you know I am."

"Please, Annie," said Mr Masters. "You are a good worker. If it was up to me you wouldn't be sacked, but it's not my decision. It's come from higher up."

"I want to see 'im. I want to see Mr Benton Senior."

"He won't see you, Annie. It's the last thing he'll agree to under the circumstances."

"Where's Mr Benton Junior?" asked Annie.

"He's left the building. There was a bit of a row earlier and he walked out," explained Mr Masters. "Be a good girl now. Take your pay and don't make a fuss. Nothing's going to change the old man's mind, I can tell you that."

Daniel had fled from the factory in a daze of emotion. For the first time since he was twelve years old, and his dog had died, tears welled into Daniel's eyes. Not because of the fight with his father, but because of what his father had said about Annie. His innocent, lovely Annie, who he hadn't even kissed. He rushed down the high street and turned into Newhall Road, knowing Annie lived at number thirty-one.

He paused as he reached her house. It was the middle of the day and the street was quiet except for two women sweeping off their front steps and staring at him. He continued his walk across the recreation ground and into the Cinderhill pub.

"Your best scotch, Landlord," Daniel ordered.

"Yes sir. Glenfiddich's the best we 'ave," said the landlord, pouring the golden liquor.

Daniel sipped his drink, his thoughts flying in every direction. The cat was out of the bag now. Everybody knew, which meant Annie's family too. He was consumed with how Annie must be feeling. The teasing from the other girls she worked with, her sisters asking her all kind of questions, her parents—how would they react? He had to speak to her. He had to find a way to comfort her and tell her everything was going to be all right. Yet how would it be all right? He had no intention of ending his relationship with Annie. It was unthinkable. He had to find a way through this.

He drank another scotch and left the pub still puzzling over his dilemma. A long walk through the countryside helped to clear his head and settle his emotions. He focused on what he knew as fact: he would never leave Annie, he was a talented and successful businessman, he enjoyed his work, and he had some money of his own.

What if he called his father's bluff?

CHAPTER 17
RESOLVE

It was quiet in the Jenkins' house. Jacob, Margaret and their five eldest children sat in the kitchen sipping their tea. The five youngest were at the chapel enjoying games night.

"What 'appens now?" asked Margaret, looking at her beautiful daughter.

"I don't know, Mam," answered Annie. "I'm sorry I didn't tell you about Daniel. I should 'ave told you. I should 'ave trusted you would understand."

"I don't think I do understand," Jacob said, his normally smiling face scrunched into a scowl. "What's young Mr Benton up to? You're a flower painter, Annie. 'E 'as no business inviting you to meet 'im even once, let alone every week, like you're telling us 'e's been doing."

"Dad, it's not like that," explained Annie. "We both feel the same way. I love 'im and 'e loves me. There's nothing sordid or sinful going on. We just walk around the park and talk. Daniel 'asn't even tried to kiss me. I'm angry about all the innuendoes at the factory and the suspicions even my own family 'ave."

"We believe you," Margaret said, putting her arm around Annie. "It's only that this relationship can't possibly work, my dear girl. You'll be 'urt by it, and none of us want that. You've already been 'urt. You've lost your job. Although, in my opinion, they 'ad no right to sack you. This is an example of what you'll face when you mix with the wrong class. It's the way of the world."

"Then it's the wrong way," stormed Annie. "Why can't people accept each other for who they are and not what class they belong to, like me and Daniel do."

Jacob shook his head. Now the young couple had been found out, he assumed Annie had seen the last of Mr Daniel Benton. He wished he could save his lovely girl from the heartbreak ahead. The heavy banging on the front door made everybody jump.

Annie's sister, Helen, stared in disbelief when she opened the door to see Daniel Benton standing in the street.

"May I come in?" he asked.

Helen remained still and silent, her mouth hanging open.

"Is Annie here?" Daniel asked.

Helen opened the door to let him in, indicating he should go through to the kitchen.

The family looked like a painting, frozen in time, not moving or speaking. Only Annie moved. She slowly rose from her chair and held out her hand to Daniel, who swept her face with his eyes before grasping her outstretched hand.

"Good evening," Daniel said, his voice soft and low. "I had to come. I should have come sooner and made my intentions known. The worst kind of cad behaves as I have done. I hope you can forgive me."

"Annie thinks 'ighly of you, young man," said Jacob, rising to his feet. "That's good enough for us. Forgiveness is part of our belief. You'll 'ear no criticism in this 'ouse. Annie's 'appiness is our only concern."

"Then we think alike," smiled Daniel, squeezing the small hand he held.

Jacob frowned his disapproval at the clasped hands and Daniel's face reddened as he let Annie's hand slip from his grasp.

Nobody knew what to say. Everybody stared at Daniel. He seemed so out of place in his grand clothes and his posh accent, which made Annie's family feel inferior and common. Daniel shuffled from one foot to the other before clearing his throat.

"Would it be all right if we went for a walk together?" he asked, knowing that an unchaperoned walk was the cause of all the trouble in the first place.

"Only if chaperoned," answered Jacob. "I think it would be more appropriate if our May went with you. We don't want any more gossip, do we?"

"Right," agreed Daniel. "That's a very good idea. We would be happy to have Annie's sister come with us on our walk."

Daniel looked anything but happy as he headed through the front room to the door. May would probably walk between them the whole way and he had so much to say to Annie which he certainly did not want to share with her sister.

Annie and May dutifully followed Daniel to the front door. The three of them all feeling uncomfortable with the situation, particularly May who had been thrust into accompanying the two young lovers without a choice.

They set off across the recreation ground with May walking, as expected, between them. Once they were out of the sight of Newhall Road and sheltered by the trees of the country lanes, May stopped to tie her boot lace, then fell in behind them at a discreet distance.

Daniel's fingers brushed against Annie's as they walked. It

was enough.

They stopped at a long wooden fence and gazed over the growing wheat field. May walked ahead to pick wildflowers under the hedge.

"My Annie," whispered Daniel with his face close to her hair. "I love you so much."

He glanced up the narrow lane where May had her back turned, stooping to reach the flowers. He risked a brief, gentle first kiss, brushing Annie's lips with his own and tasting the sweetness of her.

It had been a long day for them both. A topsy-turvy day from beginning to end. Now, with Daniel standing close beside her, Annie couldn't have been happier. The laughter that was always bubbling beneath her lips and eyes, escaped in a jubilant crescendo of happiness, as she tossed her red curls and laughed until the tears ran down her cheeks. Daniel joined in, of course. Happiness was contagious, and he laughed until his sides ached.

May jumped up at the sound of their laughter and came hurrying towards them, smiling at the sound of their apparent joy.

"What's so funny?" she asked.

"Nothing is funny, May," answered Annie. "We're laughing because we're so 'appy, that's all. We're laughing because we're together and it's a beautiful evening."

"We're laughing because we are so in love," added Daniel, making poor May blush to her hair roots. "You'll know how it feels when it happens to you."

"It may never 'appen to me. I'm not pretty like Annie," May said.

Annie hugged her sister close.

"You are lovely my dearest May, and you will find some wonderful man who will love you as much as Daniel loves me."

The threesome turned towards home, with May once more in the middle. Somehow Daniel didn't mind. He had kissed Annie for the first time. The first of many kisses. May was his future sister-in-law after all, because he intended to be married to Annie very soon.

James Benton Senior prided himself that he had intervened in his son's infatuation with the flower painter, Annie Jenkins. He had acted swiftly. He had sacked the girl and made it crystal clear to Daniel that the relationship was over. For the past month, nothing had been heard of the messy situation, which made Mr Benton very happy. Granted, his relationship with his son had suffered. Daniel continued to work hard at the factory, only speaking to his father when absolutely necessary, and only discussing business decisions. Daniel was rarely at home for dinner, preferring to eat elsewhere. James Benton took it all in his stride, convincing himself that time would heal the rift between them, knowing that one day his son would thank him profusely for guiding him in the right direction. One day Daniel would meet a girl from his own class. A good Catholic girl, who would make the family proud. Then he would dance at his son's wedding and all this nonsense would be a mere memory.

Daniel spent the summer months working diligently at the factory, burying himself with the details of the latest sales promotion in the capital city of London. He travelled weekly to and from the great city, meeting with buyers in the china departments of Harrod's and Bainbridge's department stores. He avoided his father. He preferred to write reports on his sales trips, and the neatly written papers were delivered to Mr Benton Senior each Monday morning via his secretary. Daniel's work was impressive and impeccable, and his father continued to hold onto his expectations that his son would soon seek reconciliation and return to the family fold.

Annie didn't return to flower painting. Instead she went to work in the confectionary shop where her mother, Margaret, had worked as a young woman. It was still owned by the same kind gentleman, and Annie's mother had maintained a friendship with him, sometimes working a few days when he needed the help. Annie loved the work. She enjoyed meeting the customers and keeping the sweet jars organized and full. Every day she remembered to take home a pear drop for her father—it was still his favourite.

Annie wondered if Daniel would ever ask her to marry him. They still met on Sunday afternoons, when Daniel would pick her up in his horse and buggy and take her for a drive, accompanied by May of course. There had been many kisses since that first one, all of them when they were out of May's sight. Each lingering kiss was filled with the promise of a lifetime ahead, when they would be a couple and be united.

"Annie, I'm going to ask your father's permission to marry you," Daniel began, on one such Sunday afternoon at the end of September. "I want us to be married very soon. It's impossible to wait longer. I have rented a lovely little house for us and I can't wait to show it to you. It will be the perfect place for us to begin our life together. It belongs to my mother's aunt, who recently went to live with her son due to ill health. She was a favourite aunt of mine and I spent many happy hours with her when I was a boy. It was she who contacted me when she knew she had to leave her home. She had heard about my "infatuation" with a working girl and asked if I may consider moving into the house to take care of it for her. I believe it's her way of telling me I have her support, despite what my parents may think."

Annie lifted her face and kissed her sweetheart tenderly.

"It's like a dream," she whispered. "I want to be your wife. You are my whole life."

Jacob knew he should have asked more questions of Daniel. When would they be married? Where would they be married? He was so taken with the plans already laid by the young man, who had already rented a furnished house, that he gave his permission too easily. He assumed too much. If banns were read this coming Sunday at the Chapel, the wedding could take place in as soon as three weeks. Margaret would have a fit if she had to plan a wedding in three weeks. Why hadn't he asked about banns?

With Jacob Jenkins' permission, Daniel took the first opportunity to ask the question of Annie. Allowed time alone, Daniel drove Annie into their favourite country lane where they had walked on countless Sunday afternoons. He stopped the buggy beside the familiar fence where they always stopped to sneak a kiss or two. The field of wheat stood tall and golden in the late afternoon sun, awaiting the harvest. Daniel helped Annie down from the buggy, and in the grass beside the fence, he went down on one knee to pose the all-important question.

"Will you marry me, Annie?"

"You know I will."

"Will you marry me very soon?" Daniel continued. "There's no reason for us to wait is there? Why don't we get married this very Saturday, now I have your father's permission."

"Silly you," laughed Annie. "The banns have to be posted for at least three weeks in the chapel before the wedding can take place."

"Banns posted. What the heck does that mean?" asked Daniel.

"Where 'ave you been living?" said Annie, still laughing. "Banns are the announcement of the marriage and they must be announced every Sunday for three weeks to make the wedding official. Everybody knows that."

"Not me," laughed Daniel. "It isn't going to affect us anyway."

Suddenly he looked very serious and bit his bottom lip. The time had come for him to tell Annie the one thing he had dreaded telling her. He should have told her from the very beginning, but was afraid it would drive a wedge between them. Now, he believed, their love was strong enough to overcome what he perceived as a minor problem.

"Darling, wouldn't you like to marry me this Saturday?" he began. "It would be so easy. No fuss. Nobody interfering. We could be in our own little house by Saturday afternoon. The two of us. Married and together forever."

"You're scaring me now," frowned Annie. "Marry you this Saturday? 'ow? Why? You're not making sense, Daniel."

"Annie, you know my family's feelings about you. I don't have to spell it out for you that the marriage would be frowned upon. In fact, forbidden. I have let you believe it's because you are part of the working class and considered "below" me, but there's another reason. It really is irrelevant to me, because I couldn't really care less about religion, but it's apparently a very big deal for my family. We are Catholic and it's against some stupid church law to marry outside the faith."

Annie was stunned. Catholics didn't marry Protestants. Protestants didn't marry Catholics. They were poles apart.

Catholics were to be avoided at all costs. They were not welcome in any social situations with chapel folk, and they most certainly were never considered as future marriage partners. The list of differences between their faiths was ingrained into church-going people from an early age. Annie could list those differences in her head as she stared at the man she loved.

"Darling," whispered Daniel. "This makes no difference to us. I would never consider marrying in the Catholic Church. It means nothing to me. I know your family go to chapel, and that is fine. I have no problem with you attending services with your family and continuing the practice of your faith. I am in no way threatened by that. I do, however, think your parents would be less than approving of a wedding cere- mony outside the chapel. It will cause them a great deal of anguish if they know we are not getting married there. Please think about this, Annie. We could slip away on Saturday and be married at the registrar's office in Stoke. Your parents will be shocked and upset when we tell them, but the marriage will already be official. They will get over it."

"No, they won't," wept Annie. "My older two sisters 'ad lovely weddings at the Chapel with all the family there to celebrate. If we do this, I won't 'ave any of that."

"I'm sorry, Annie," Daniel said, dabbing her tears with his pocket handkerchief. "I'm asking a great deal of you, I know. Will you think about it carefully, dearest? Saturday we could begin our lives together—it will be so wonderful."

All Annie could see were her parents' faces, full of disap- pointment and sadness. She had thought about her wedding day so many times. A white dress, sisters for bridesmaids, her father escorting her down the aisle and the whole family there to enjoy it with her. She knew it could never happen if the groom was a Catholic.

What was the alternative? She could refuse the offer of marriage, try to move on, and forget Daniel. Impossible! Her family would forgive her, wouldn't they? God would forgive her, wouldn't He?

"I will agree, under one condition," Annie said.

"Anything, darling," Daniel encouraged, looking intently into Annie's lovely face.

"That we go to chapel for a blessing. I cannot agree to marry you without God's blessing, Daniel."

Daniel smiled and nodded. It was such a small thing to ask.

The family was stirring, the young ones eating thick slices of toast, covered in Mam's home-made marmalade, for breakfast, when Annie quietly left. It was like any usual Saturday morning, and nobody noticed that she was wearing her best Sunday dress.

It was a beautiful September day. A day like no other. Annie repeated the date over and over in time to the horses' hooves as Daniel drove her away from her house and onto the high street leading to Stoke.

"September twenty-eighth, nineteen hundred and seven. September twenty-eighth, nineteen hundred and seven. September twenty-eighth, nineteen hundred and seven."

The brick building in Stoke looked cold and uninviting, even on the warm day. Annie's feet felt leaden as she walked up the stone stairs and through the thick oak door. Her shoes echoed on the tiled floor. Every sound seemed more defined, somehow louder than normal. She was aware of Daniel beside her, thankful for the light touch of his hand beneath her lower arm.

Daniel had asked two of his distant cousins to be

witnesses to the marriage. They were sworn to secrecy and they now stepped forward to greet Annie as she made her way along the wide corridor.

"Daniel Benton," the clerk announced.

Daniel ushered Annie and his cousins into the inner chamber to face the registrar.

This was it!

The short ceremony took less than ten minutes. Marriage vows were read by the registrar and repeated by Daniel and Annie. A ring was slipped onto Annie's finger. The appropriate papers were signed and witnessed by the cousins. The registrar shook their hands and proclaimed them "man and wife."

It was done! This was the easy part.

Daniel took Annie's face in his hands and kissed her gently on her lips.

Now they had to face their families.

Annie had asked David Baker to meet them at the chapel at 11.00am, trusting that he would keep her confidence and not tell anybody about the arrangement. David was a respected elder and had known Annie since she was a little girl. He was waiting at the door as they arrived.

The kindly man welcomed Annie with a kiss on her cheek and shook Daniel's hand. He didn't approve of the registrar marriage, but as a faithful, forgiving follower of Christ, he didn't judge them. They came seeking God's blessing on their union and David was happy to oblige. God never turned anyone away; neither did David Baker.

Annie and Daniel knelt at the front of the chapel while David asked for God's blessing. It was a simple prayer from his heart, and Annie was filled with overwhelming joy because of it. For Annie, that was the moment she became a wife.

"Now we are truly married," Annie said, her eyes glistening as she took Daniel's face between her hands and kissed him tenderly.

With trepidation they walked quietly across the street and into number 31 Newhall Road. Margaret was at the kitchen table baking apple pies with the help of seven-year-old Charles, who, standing on a kitchen chair, was covered in flour. Two of the older children were sweeping the yard, and Jacob was mending the leaking tap in the back kitchen.

"Annie, where did you go so early this morning?" Margaret said, looking up from her dough. "Nobody even saw you leave. Were you going somewhere special with Daniel? You're wearing your Sunday best dress, I see."

Annie hugged her mother, despite the floury apron, tears springing into her eyes.

"What is it, ducky?" Margaret asked, concerned now at her daughter's obvious distress.

At the sound of Margaret's voice, Jacob came into the kitchen, taking in the scene before him. Something had happened, and he wasn't sure he was going to like it.

"Mam, Dad, we 'ave something to tell you," Annie began.

"Charlie, you go out into the yard and 'elp your brother and sister," Margaret said.

"But Mam, I'm 'elping roll the dough," protested young Charles.

"Now please, Charlie," Jacob said quietly, sending the boy scrambling off the chair and running into the back yard, flour cascading around him as he ran.

"Well?" Jacob said. "What's going on?"

"There's no easy way to say this," Daniel spoke for them both. "There were circumstances you were not aware of that prevented us from having a church wedding. We were married this morning at the registrar's office in Stoke."

"You were married?" choked Jacob, looking only at Annie.

"Dad, it was the only way," Annie said, tears streaming

down her cheeks as she saw the hurt in her parents' faces. "Daniel is Catholic. You know what that means. I could never be married in a Catholic Church and he could never be married in the chapel. There was no other alternative."

"Yes, there was," Jacob said, his voice trembling with emotion. "You could 'ave broken off your relationship immediately you knew 'e was Catholic. I can't believe what I'm 'earing. Not married before God means you are not married. A registry office wedding is not valid in the eyes of the church."

Margaret had sat in the chair by the fireplace, her legs feeling wobbly and her head swimming. She couldn't believe her daughter would do such a thing—turn against her faith and her family.

"We went to the chapel and David Baker asked God to bless us," mumbled Annie. "I am married. I am. I'm 'ere to collect my things. Daniel 'as a home ready for us. I beg you to accept our marriage. Please Dad, Mam, don't turn us away."

"If you're determined to go ahead with this, Annie, you go pack your things," said Jacob, his face a grim mask. "You must give us some time to get over the shock. Your siblings need to be told what's 'appened. I need to talk to the elders at the chapel and ask for their guidance. I pray you can live with the decision you've made."

Annie realized there was nothing more to be said. She longed to run into her mother's arms, but knew by the dark visage on her father's face that enough had been said.

"I'll wait in the buggy for you, Annie," Daniel said quietly.

CHAPTER 20
HOME

What should have been a joyful ride to their new home was tainted with the altercation at the Jenkins' house. Annie felt so alone, even with her husband beside her. Her family was estranged and the look on her mother's face was burned into her mind. Surely they would forgive her when they had recovered from the shock of today.

As they bounced along the country lane towards the little white house nestled behind a screen of aspens, Annie shook off her unhappy thoughts and made a promise to herself to devote the rest of her wedding day to Daniel and the love they shared. She smiled at her new husband as he helped her from the buggy and escorted her into the house.

Annie's experience of different types of houses was limited. Apart from the row houses of Newhall Road, she had only seen a few other homes belonging to elders in the chapel. All of them were larger than her own house, but were all located nearby and varied only by having slightly bigger rooms and a third bedroom on the second floor.

She stood looking around in awe at the lovely, cozy living

room she had stepped into. The wide windows were framed with flowered curtains, the wooden floors covered with a deeply-piled pale blue carpet, and a deep-seated floral sofa sat before the fireplace with side tables of dark mahogany on either side. Two high-backed armchairs in dark blue velvet were placed on either side of the window, one with a footstool to match, and three framed landscape pictures completed the atmosphere of comfort and serenity. It was the loveliest room Annie had ever seen, and she gasped with delight.

The kitchen was equally stunning, with a large wooden table, four chairs, a dark blue and white tiled floor, a polished grate containing two warming ovens, and built-in cupboards filled with every pot, pan and dish a cook would require. Annie smiled at the thought of her mother managing to cook food for twelve in the tiny kitchen at home.

Watching her mother cook at home was a miracle of maneuverability, as she deftly moved pots and pans and dishes around to make room for preparation and baking. In the back kitchen there was always a pile of dishes in the sink. It was up to the girls in the family to work away at the pile before the next meal. Water had to be boiled in the big kettle hanging over the fire and carried into the back kitchen, then, standing side by side, two girls would wash in the big stone sink and two would dry, piling the clean, dry dishes onto the bench along the back wall.

Annie's new back-kitchen had a large country sink, an enormous gas range, a gas boiler and a long wooden counter, piled with washing bowls and jugs. A wooden rack full of dish towels and linens hung from the ceiling with pulleys. The window over the sink showered the room with light. A door at the back of the room led directly into the water closet, which was indeed a luxury for Annie, as it was normally a trip outside.

The two bedrooms upstairs continued to impress Annie. Both bedrooms were delightfully furnished. Both had double beds, piled with pillows and covered with floral bedcovers to match the window drapes. Soft rugs were placed on each side of the beds and there were wardrobes, dressers and two small boudoir chairs to complete the comfort. Annie thought she had never seen such a lovely bedroom; so big and airy with so much furniture, and a big double bed for just the two of them.

Daniel had always had his own bedroom, furnished with the necessities of life—a wardrobe, dresser, desk, armchair and trouser press. A basin and jug filled with warm water and a fresh pure white towel were placed on the dresser every morning and evening by Leonard, his "man" who took care of such things for himself and his father.

Daniel wondered if the tiny bedroom he was to share with Annie was appropriate; he looked at her anxiously as she gazed around the room.

"Do you like the house, Annie?" asked Daniel, holding his breath.

"Like it?" Annie gasped. "How could I *not* like it? It's the most beautiful house I've ever seen. I can't believe I'm going to live 'ere with you, Daniel. Look at the size of the rooms! Look at the size of this bed—for the two of us."

"I'm looking, and I think we should test it out right now," laughed Daniel, making his new wife blush to the roots of her hair.

"It's only the afternoon, Mr Benton," she said, backing away from him. "Are you making an indecent suggestion?"

"I am," said Daniel, grabbing her arm as she made for the door. "Annie, don't make me wait a second longer. I have dreamed of this moment for more than two years. Now we are married and alone, why would we wait?"

"Because it's still daylight, and you might see me," blushed Annie.

Daniel burst out laughing.

"Annie, are you serious? So you want us to wait until it's dark so I won't see you?"

"Don't laugh at me, Daniel," Annie said. "I'm embarrassed about you seeing me. I don't know what to expect. In fact I really 'ave no idea what being together entails, except for the few remarks I've 'eard from the married women at work. From what I've 'eard, it's not something a woman looks forward to. In fact most of the women really 'ate it."

"Oh, I see," Daniel said, trying to control the smile on his face. "Well, my darling girl, I suppose we will have to learn together, because it's not something I've done before either. All I know is, we love each other, and we'll take our time. I don't want to do anything that may scare you."

He took Annie's hand and led her downstairs. He had packed a basket of food for them before leaving that morning and set it on the table, along with a bottle of his father's best wine.

"Let's eat," Daniel said enthusiastically. "There's one of cook's beef pies here, with cheese and cold vegetables. Even a fruitcake for dessert—our wedding cake."

Annie hadn't eaten all day. They sat beside each other at the kitchen table and ate their wedding feast and drank the wonderful red wine. Wrapped in their own world, the family trouble of earlier in the day faded into oblivion. With a full stomach and a head full of good wine, Annie left the kitchen and climbed the stairs once more.

Daniel carried their bags into the bedroom and discreetlyy left Annie alone, offering to clean up the kitchen and bring the rest of the wine up to the bedroom.

The light was fading and Annie moved around the bedroom, putting away her few items of clothing. She shook out the white cotton nightdress she had bought yesterday and laid it on the bed. With shaking hands and stumbling fingers, she unfastened all the buttons down the front of her dress then slipped out of her layers of clothes until she stood naked beside the bed. The nightdress felt soft and cool against her skin and she shivered at the thought of lying beside Daniel wearing only the flimsy garment.

Covered by the gathering dusk, Daniel stripped down to his undergarments and climbed into bed beside his wife, a glass of wine in each hand. They lay back on the pillows, sipping their wine and watching the last of the light disappear, then, with the empty glasses safely stashed on the table beside the bed, Daniel leaned over to kiss his bride.

The darkness was security for Annie as the kisses grew deeper and longer and she felt Daniel's tongue push her lips apart. It took her breath away and her loins flooded with a warmth which certainly wasn't unpleasant. As promised, Daniel took his time, moving his hands to gently touch Annie's breasts and thighs. Annie sighed and arched her back in response, moaning for Daniel to keep going. The underclothes were discarded and the white nightdress pulled over Annie's head. Now, skin to skin, Annie felt for the first time the thrill of her husband's closeness and the strength and power of him pushing against her. Too late now for Daniel to take his time. The human urge within him overtook every other instinct and he barely contained himself as he sought to enter Annie. He had waited too long. Too many years of loving her. Too many months of wanting her. Too many minutes of moving carefully and slowly not to frighten her. He groaned as he spilled his seed onto the sheets between Annie's legs.

"Annie, I'm sorry," he gasped.

"Why are you sorry?" whispered Annie, kissing his moist forehead and holding him close.

"I made a mess," he muttered. "It was too early. I couldn't control myself."

"Touch me, Daniel," Annie responded. "Explore me. Love me."

Her legs opened at his touch and he felt the soft cloud of hair under his fingers. She was so delightful; so beautiful. He moved his fingers to the rhythm of her hips until her whole body stiffened and a stifled cry escaped her throat, before she collapsed against him, shaking with emotion.

"I love you, Mrs Benton," Daniel said, covering her face in kisses.

"I love you, Mr Benton," his wife replied.

The newlyweds made love often—sometimes before it was completely dark. Annie loved looking at her husband as much as he loved looking at her, and they never tired of demonstrating their love for each other.

From what Annie had heard from married women on the factory floor, hers was a most unusual marriage. Women who had been married for more than twenty years would whisper to each other that their husbands had never seen them without their clothing. They all put on their nightwear before their husbands joined them, and whatever happened in the bed always took place in the pitch dark. Annie feared they would be horrified by the first few days of her marriage with Daniel.

It took five days for Margaret and Jacob to come to terms with their daughter's actions. They set off on a fine dry evening, with some trepidation, to walk the two miles to see the newlyweds. It was a tense meeting for them all at first, but Annie's parents were gracious and loving as they had always been, and soon the four of them were sitting around the kitchen table drinking tea and eating the apple pie

Margaret had brought with her. Annie's eyes filled with tears as she heard her parents profess their love for her and the support for their marriage. She knew it wasn't what they had wanted or expected, and that they were disappointed with her actions, yet they were willing to forgive her and accept Daniel as her husband.

It was a wonderful relief for Annie and as she hugged her mother and father, she felt a huge surge of happiness flood through her. The acceptance from them was the one thing that made her marriage to Daniel complete.

Daniel had taken the week off from his job at Winston Field China, but Monday morning was looming closer and closer and he knew he would have to tell his father and mother about his marriage to Annie. Not a pleasant thought!

After a day of avoiding his father, Daniel found him leaving his office for the night and announced that he would be joining them for dinner.

Unlike the comparative quiet reception of their marriage news at the Jenkins' house, the Bentons greeted the news with horror, voicing their disapproval in loud and volatile voices. Daniel's mother screamed, his father yelled, his sister joined in with hysterical laughter. Daniel stood calmly in the midst of them waiting for the noise to abate. They refused to accept the non-Catholic wedding as legal. They said Annie would never be welcome in their home. They called Daniel selfish and ungrateful for marrying a chapel girl from the working class, making them the laughing stock of the entire community.

"Even so," said Daniel when a lull in the tirade presented itself. "We are married and it is legal. Aunt Mildred has rented us her house on Braxton Avenue and we are idyllically happy. If you insist on banning Annie from your house, then I will assume I am not welcome either. Let me know if you change your mind."

Daniel bowed his head to his mother, turned on his heel and left. There was nothing more to be said. They had behaved as he had expected.

Winston Field China continued to evolve and grow. There was never any question of Daniel Benton leaving his position—he was far too valuable. The orders he had procured in London, Birmingham and Manchester alone had elevated the once insignificant company into a strong competitor in the Staffordshire pottery industry.

Annie worked at the confectionary shop three days every week, and always remembered to take the bag of pear drops to her father every Sunday after chapel.

Daniel wouldn't attend the service with her, but would drive her in the buggy and join her family for dinner afterwards. Sunday dinner was a tradition in England's midlands and north country. If money was scarce, as it often was, families would eat frugally during the weekdays—chips and egg, chips and peas, chips and sausage, chips with bread and butter, bacon and cheese on oatcakes were all favourite meals. Sunday dinner was different. It was a "real" dinner. Usually served at one o'clock in the afternoon, there was always a roast of beef with Yorkshire pudding or a leg of pork, potatoes, vegetables and lashings of thick brown gravy. The meat would be cooked very well and sliced as thin as paper, enabling everybody to have at least a small taste. Most families enjoyed a pudding afterwards. Usually apple pie or a suet pudding, always with custard.

In the Jenkins' household, there were never enough chairs for the whole family, especially with four of the eldest siblings now married and accompanied by their spouses and five small children. Margaret loved all the hustle and bustle of Sunday dinner and managed the meal and the people with a patient ease. The youngest were served first, and sent to find seats in the front room, most of them settling themselves onto floor cushions, their plates precariously balanced on their laps. Seats at the kitchen table were reserved for Jacob, Margaret and the senior siblings, some with babies on their knees. The rest stood around the two rooms helping each other cut meat, or pass salt and pepper, or help with the children. It was organized chaos every Sunday, and Daniel loved every minute of it.

He wouldn't have traded his Sunday dinner with Annie's family with sitting in the austere dining room at his parents' spacious house, being waited on by staff and served with sumptuous food. This was his life now, full of noise and laughter, and people who really cared about each other. A family who struggled to make ends meet financially, but poured all of their energy into each other.

After dinner, Daniel sat with a sleeping baby on his knee in the middle of the kitchen, listening to Annie laugh with her sisters as they cleared the mountain of plates and paraded them into the back-kitchen, where other sisters were up to their elbows in suds at the kitchen sink. Margaret sat at the table drinking her second cup of tea and smiling at the world around her. Jacob sat beside the fire in his armchair, smoking a pipe and nodding as the sleep of utter contentment overtook him.

This is my family now, thought Daniel. I didn't just marry Annie, I became part of something much bigger. Something I would never have imagined. So far removed from the family I grew up in. I want it to last forever.

CHAPTER 22
TWO YEARS OF GRIEF

Despite the denial of Daniel's powerful family to their union and their refusal to accept the marriage as legal, Daniel and Annie remained happy. They loved being together in their cozy little house. They were thrilled when Annie became pregnant, and shared their good news with Annie's family as soon as the doctor confirmed they had a baby on the way. Margaret was delighted to hear she could expect her sixth grandchild and busied herself with sewing a layette and knitting booties and matinee coats, sewing her love into every stitch.

Daniel shared the good news with his family too, but received a wall of disinterest from his father, and a raise of the eyebrows from his mother, who considered the child conceived out of wedlock.

Margaret hurried to her daughter's side the moment she heard labour had begun. Mrs Phillpott was considered to be the best midwife in the area and she accompanied Margaret to the little house in the lane. After birthing ten children of her own, Margaret knew what to expect and was full of eager anticipation as she settled Annie more comfortably into the double bed.

The typical expectant father, Daniel couldn't sit still. He made endless pots of tea, paced between rooms, ran upstairs to comfort Annie, ran downstairs to brew more tea, and finally hurried to the door announcing he was going for a walk up the lane.

Annie's labour was hard and, as with most first babies, very long. The first sign that there was a problem was a gush of blood when Mrs Phillpott checked the progress of the birth. Margaret knew it wasn't a good sign and when the bleeding continued, she hid her tears from her daughter.

A baby girl was born in the early hours of the morning. She had red hair and pure white skin and was perfect. She lay still and silent in Margaret's arms. She had already gone to be with God.

Nothing could console Annie. She thought her heart would break from the agony. Mrs Phillpott used all of her skill and experience to deliver the damaged placenta and stop the profuse bleeding, rescuing Annie from, what had been, a dangerous, life-threatening delivery.

The baby layette was packed away and after staying for most of the following day, Margaret wearily left the young couple to mourn their tiny daughter, who they named Martha.

It took months for Annie to recover, both physically and emotionally. Daniel slept next to her every night, holding her close, stroking her curly hair, rubbing her back, never expecting anything more.

Slowly Annie regained her strength. She hadn't left the house in weeks, but was able to take care of the chores and cook the meals. She looked forward to visits from her mother and siblings, but she started to become concerned that she hadn't seen her father. When she asked about him, her mother would avoid the question or say he had been busy lately, but Annie knew her father would always make time for her and his absence worried her.

"Annie, you need to come 'ome," May said. She had delayed going to Annie's house for as long as she dared, but now the situation was dire and Annie had to be told.

"Dad's sick, Annie," May continued. didn't want me to tell you, but the doctor told us to gather the family together. It's a tumour in 'is liver. 'E doesn't 'ave long."

Jacob's skin was a weird shade of yellow. Annie hurried to his side and took his hands in hers. No need for words. Jacob knew she was there and two tears spilled down his cheeks with relief. Now he had said goodbye to all his children, even Annie. His beloved Annie.

Jacob's death overshadowed everything. He was the head of the family. Their hero, their mentor and advisor, their spiritual counselour and their loving father. The small chapel Jacob had helped build was packed to overflowing for the funeral. His favourite hymns were sung, his favourite scriptures read and Mr Baker spoke about Jacob's faithful life of service to his God and fellow man. Margaret sat with her head held high, hearing the accolades of the community who loved him. How grateful she was for the years they had spent together and for every cherished memory they had made. He had gone before her to meet his Lord, but he would be there waiting for her, she knew.

The house at number thirty-one was never the same. Somehow quieter. People spoke in whispers, and even when the house was full of people, it felt subdued. The space Jacob had occupied for so long couldn't be filled.

Something changed inside Annie too. Her beloved father was gone, but as Daniel comforted her, she lifted her face to be kissed. She needed her husband to love her more than she ever had before. Death was suddenly, for Annie, such a part of life that she clung to Daniel in despair and desire, realizing that only the love they shared would help her through the grief.

Where there are valleys, there are almost certainly mountain tops. Annie welcomed her second pregnancy with quiet jubilation. A second chance. A wonderful miracle.

Margaret was there at the house for the birth of the second of Annie's babies. It was a quick and easy delivery, and another baby girl with red hair was born dead. Another baby to bury in the earth. The grief was immeasurable and Annie swore she would never carry another baby for God to take it before it had a chance to take its first breath.

Daniel returned to comforting his wife, even though his heart was breaking. He had held his little daughter for a long time before Margaret had taken her away somewhere. She looked just like Annie. So beautiful. He had willed her to breathe—just breathe, knowing it was an impossible dream. She would be lain alongside her sister in the tiny grave at the cemetery.

Margaret walked into her house to tell the children the sad news. A cup of tea was thrust into her hand as she collapsed onto a kitchen chair. Her hands shook so much she set the cup down and wept into her hands, the tears spilling between her fingers and splashing onto the wooden tabletop.

"Mam, don't," said May, putting her arm around her mother. "God 'asn't forgotten about us. It's not for us to question why."

Margaret nodded, then raised herself from her chair and headed for the stairs.

"Goodnight," she murmured. "God bless."

She needed Jacob tonight. He would have held her tight and comforted her with his wise words of faith and hope. She lay on the bed she had shared with him for more than twenty five years and wept. Wept for the loss of another baby and for the emptiness in her heart left by him.

"I wish you were 'ere, my love," she whispered into the pillow.

In the morning, when May took a cup of tea up to the bedroom for her mother, Margaret had joined Jacob during the night. The peaceful smile on her face said it all—she had died knowing she would soon be reunited with her husband.

The house filled with people, as family, friends and neighbours all crammed into the tiny space to mourn the beautiful lady of the house. Shock and disbelief on their faces and in their souls at the untimely passing of fifty-year-old Margaret. The three youngest children sat silently in the midst of all the commotion looking stunned. Charles, only eight years of age, huddled between William and Mary-Jane, who were only three and four years older. It had been a tragedy to lose their father, only the year before, but now that Mam was gone they were unable to function.

The two eldest girls, Helen and Sarah, took control of the chaos, thanking neighbours and friends for their kindness, but firmly requesting they leave the family to grieve. When the house was emptied of everybody except the immediate family, Helen brewed tea and buttered bread to bring some semblance of normality into their lives.

"Mam wouldn't want us sitting around crying," Sarah said softly. "She's with our dad now and I bet she's the 'appiest person in 'eaven this morning. She'll be cuddling those two beautiful baby girls by now—one in each arm. Can't you see 'er?"

"I'm the only one who's seen Mam this morning," May said. "I think she would like it if we all went to see 'er. She looks lovely. A big smile on 'er face. Like she could already see our dad waiting for 'er."

"Come on then," Sarah encouraged, taking Charles' hand

and leading the procession of siblings up the narrow staircase.

"I'm scared," whispered Charles, clinging onto Sarah's hand.

"Why would you be scared, our Charlie?" Sarah said. "You weren't scared of our Mam when she was alive, why would you be scared of 'er now?"

They moved to circle the bed, instinctively holding hands. Tears spilled down their cheeks, but there were smiles on their faces. Helen, as the eldest, said a simple prayer, thanking God for their mother and asking for strength for the family to endure the loss of her. Following Sarah's example, each of them bent over and kissed Mam's cheek, murmuring "I love you, Mam," before turning to hug their siblings.

When they returned to the kitchen, the question on all their minds was verbalized by May.

"Who will tell Annie?"

Annie doubted she would survive.

May and Helen had come to her house in the early evening. Annie thought they had come to see the new baby, wrapped in a white blanket and laying so peacefully in a tiny coffin in the front room downstairs, awaiting the funeral.

The words they spoke didn't make sense to Annie. Daniel sat beside her on the bed, supporting her around her waist as Annie's two sisters repeated the news.

Annie didn't remember what happened next, only that she woke up with a cold cloth on her forehead and a glass of water at her lips. Daniel's anxious face came into focus as he tried to get her to drink. Her sisters cried silently from the bedside, causing Annie to remember the reason they had come to see her.

A strangled scream caught in Annie's throat, almost choking her.

"Mam, Mam," she cried. "No. I can't bear it. Daniel, 'elp me."

His face wet with tears, Daniel held his wife close, but

could give her no comfort. The older girls tried to help. Gently telling Annie it would be all right. That Mam had died smiling. That she was with Dad. Nothing helped, and they both finally left the sad house to return to their husbands and their own sad houses.

The funeral for Margaret and Marjorie, the second baby girl, took place at the same time. Grief beyond imagination enveloped the little chapel, as the people gathered there tried to come to terms with their deaths.

Daniel sat in the chapel with Annie's family around him, trying to comfort him in the loss of his daughter, even as they were breaking under the sorrow of their mother's death. Annie lay in bed at home, comatose and unaware of the day when the rest of her family was laying her mother and baby girl to rest.

After the funeral, the family met to discuss how they would move forward. There were still young children at home who needed to be cared for. Despite their grief, there had to be a plan made for the future.

Annie's older brother, John, had married his sweetheart, Rosemary, the same year Annie had married Daniel. He applied to the landlord to become the tenant of number thirty-one Newhall Road, as it was common practice for adult children to take on the tenancy when parents died. John, Rosemary and their two little girls moved into the family house as soon as the paperwork was in order, so that the younger children still living at home were not disrupted. With both parents gone it was the best arrangement for the Jenkins family.

During the following three months, May continued to visit Annie regularly. May was planning to marry a young potter named George in the near future. She hoped that, by the wedding day, Annie would be able to attend and join in their celebration.

Annie felt nothing. She wanted to be left alone. She didn't want to see her family and even found Daniel's presence intolerable. She wouldn't wash or get dressed. Her hair hung in greasy ringlets around her head. She wouldn't eat and only took a drink if Daniel forced her, prying her lips apart and pleading with her.

When May visited, she took a basin of warm water up to the bedroom and bathed her sister, whose body was emaciated, with sores beginning to form on her back and buttocks. May was embarrassed to wash her sister's private parts, but Annie showed no objection, and lay with her legs open allowing her sister to clean her.

A black hole had swallowed Annie, and she could find no way out. In the hole, she saw her babies crying for her. She saw her mother with her arms open waiting for her. She wanted to stay in the hole with them.

Daniel asked the elders from the chapel to come and pray for her, knowing how faithful Annie had been. He thought if anybody could reach her, they probably could. All to no avail. She lay on the bed, staring at the ceiling, while the three elders gathered around her and prayed quietly for her recovery.

Annie knew they were there, but there was a thick curtain between them that prevented her from seeing or hearing them clearly. Only a few words reached her and they seemed meaningless, like a foreign language.

As Annie grew weaker and slept longer each day, Daniel worried more and more. He thought about her all day while he was at work and rushed home at the end of each day to find his wife still prostrate in bed, rotting away.

In desperation, Daniel sought his family's help, something he had sworn he would never do.

While May was at the house one Saturday morning, Daniel drove to his parents' home. He didn't expect a courteous reception, but was willing to endure any amount of criticism and resentment for Annie.

He found his parents in the morning room, sipping coffee. His father reading a newspaper and his mother bent over her needlepoint.

"Please excuse the interruption," began Daniel. "I wouldn't have come if the circumstances were not so dire."

Daniel's mother dropped her sewing when she saw her son enter the room. He looked ghastly. His face was ashen. He was thin and unkempt, his hair disheveled and his face in need of a shave. She forgot her anger as she moved to his side and grasped his hands, leading him to sit in the nearby armchair.

"Daniel, what is it?" she said. "You look terrible. Is there bad news?"

James Benton had seen his son every day and noticed the drastic change in him, but had said nothing to his wife, assuming that the loss of two babies was taking a toll on his young son. He assumed Daniel would be strong enough to put it behind him without any fuss, but now he wished he had warned his wife ahead of time.

"Spit it out, boy," barked his father.

"James, please," Daniel's mother said sharply. "Give him some space. All you ever do is yell at him. Can't you see he's in trouble. Have you no compassion left?"

Daniel's father slumped back into his chair. When Isabel spoke with authority, he usually listened.

"I need your help, Mother," Daniel said, looking into her eyes, where he detected a glimmer of sympathy. "Annie is so sick. I think she is dying. She cannot recover from the deaths she has endured in less than two years. Both her parents, as well as our two baby girls. It's been too much for her. I am here to beg you to help us."

Fighting the tears which threatened to strangle him,

Daniel pleaded with the two people who had never shown the slightest interest in his marriage, or the losses they had suffered.

"I know you have skilled doctors attending you who could help Annie recover. She won't eat or drink. She has shrunk inside herself somewhere and I cannot reach her. Please, if you have any love left for me as your son, help me save her. She is my whole life."

Isabel didn't look at her husband. Despite her strong feelings against Annie and the marriage they had entered into, she focused all her attention on her only son, who was so wretched and unhappy. From the earliest days of marriage, she had been under her husband's domineering thumb, hiding her once gentle and charitable nature under a thick layer of self-preservation. Her cold detached manner met with approval from James and made life easier and free from conflict for Isabel.

"Bring her here, Daniel, so that she can be properly attended. I will summon Dr. Clarkson as soon as she is settled. He will be able to help her regain her health and strength."

"Mother, I cannot tell you what this means to me. I will bring her here, but do so only because she will have no knowledge of where she is. At present she is so far away from reality, I doubt she will even be aware we are moving her."

James Benton never moved from his chair, but didn't object to the plan either. Isabel would have her way. The girl would come into his house and there was nothing he could do to stop it. Maybe she would die. That would solve all their problems.

Daniel hurried away, promising to return the following day with Annie.

Isabel met with her housekeeper, Mrs Frost, to make

arrangements for one of the guest bedrooms to be made ready. She also asked Mrs Frost to arrange for Jenny Black, the chamber maid, to attend Mr Daniel's wife during her stay with them.

Annie was afforded every comfort in the big house. Dr. Clarkson examined her and prescribed several medications, but cautioned the family that Annie had been through an extraordinary amount of grief in her young life and the way out of her despair was not an easy road.

Jenny Black was the perfect caregiver for Annie. She was patient and kind and soon had Annie sipping consommé soup in small amounts. Jenny drew a bath for Annie and helped her out of the bed and into the comforting warm water, where she washed her gently with a soft sponge. Annie's hair was a matted mess, and Jenny took her time washing the curls, then brushing them very carefully until all the knots were untangled.

Annie didn't know where she was at first, only that some-body was taking care of her. The warm water on her skin felt comforting, and the smell of lavender permeated her senses. It was the first time she had felt anything other than sorrow in so long she thought she saw a glimpse of light in her dark hole.

Recovery was slow and painful. Mrs Frost made every easily digested food in her vast arsenal of recipes. Nothing was too much trouble for the young Mrs Benton. She was one of their own—a working class girl.

"Come on now," Jenny Black coaxed, lifting the spoonful of soup to Annie's lips. "This is Mrs Frost's best chicken broth. It'll build you up. You'll soon feel better."

It did make Annie feel better. In fact, she was soon sitting in a chair beside the bed and dipping home-made crusty bread into the excellent variety of soups coming from the kitchen.

Daniel was elated. His hope turned into reality as he saw a daily progress in Annie's recovery. One day it was a small smile when he entered the bedroom, then it was an unsteady few steps towards him, and, by the end of the second week at the big house, he arrived home to find his wife dressed in a simple day dress. She was so thin and pale, but she was getting better.

The black hole began to shrink as Annie gained strength. The light came in slowly, as though through a filter, and lit the edges of Annie's vision. She noticed the smell of the lavender soap Jenny used to bathe her, and the aroma of the leek and potato soup served at lunchtime. She felt the soft touch of the silk nightgown on her skin. She heard the carriage draw up below her bedroom window and knew it was Daniel coming home from the factory.

Soon she would be well enough to go home.

James Benton Senior met with his son to discuss future sales trips for Winston Field China. Business in their own country was lucrative and the owner wanted to expand into North America.

"No question about it," began Daniel's father. "America is the place to be. Donald Jeffreys told me just last week that his sales in New York have surpassed his expectations, and his product is vastly inferior to ours."

James Benton lit his pipe and lay back in his armchair, squinting at his son through the smoke. The so-called "wife" had gained strength recently, and looked like she may recover completely, so there was no excuse for Daniel to remain by her side indefinitely.

"Your promotion and sales plan for the American market was impressive," he continued. "I want you to make plans to travel to New York at the first opportunity. I would trust nobody else with the task. Talk to the owners at The Aynsley Factory and ask permission to take one of their master potters with you, at our expense. He will be able to demonstrate how a lump of clay is turned into a work of art. An in-store exhibition has proved effective in the big cities here, and the Americans will eat it up. I expect you to be ready to go within a few weeks, depending on the availability of a ship's passage."

"I agree the time is ripe for developing the market overseas," Daniel said. "My only worry is leaving Annie at such a vulnerable time. I don't want her to relapse, which she may do in my absence."

Mr Benton Senior sucked on his pipe and tried to remain calm. He knew any outburst about "the girl" would not be helpful.

"She is in good hands now," he ventured. "Your mother and sister will make sure she has everything she needs, and that her health continues to improve. You will only be away for a few months, and by the time you return she will be completely recovered."

There was no point in arguing. Daniel's father had made up his mind.

Annie was devastated by the news. She had planned to move back to their house soon. To try to pick up the pieces scattered by the horrors of the past two years. She hated living in the Benton mansion with the morbid, dark rooms and whispering staff. Her only comfort was Jenny Black, who had become her confidante and friend. Breakfast and lunch were the worst, when she sat at the long dining table in the austere room with silent Mrs Benton. Dinner was somewhat better, with Daniel beside her and Mr Benton and Daniel's sister, Felicity, seated on either side of Daniel's mother. The conversation was dull and forced. Nobody spoke to Annie, except Daniel, and the atmosphere of unacceptability was palpable.

It would be unbearable when Daniel had gone!

"Please, Daniel, don't go," Annie begged. "I want to go 'ome. Can I go 'ome? If you 'ave to go, please take me 'ome first. My sisters will 'elp me. I could manage so much better if I was in our 'ouse."

"Darling, don't ask," Daniel replied. "You need more time before you are well enough to be by yourself. Don't you like Jenny taking care of you? I thought you had made friends with her. Dr. Clarkson will look in on you weekly and be on call if you need him. I would feel much better about going to New York if I knew you were here, safe."

The next few weeks flew by as Daniel prepared for his trip and Annie prepared herself to wait for him to return.

Daniel held Annie tightly. It was early morning and the sunlight filtered through the gap in the curtains, casting a weak light onto the couple lying clasped together in the middle of the bed.

"You know I don't want to go," whispered Daniel. "I would much rather stay here with you."

"How will I manage 'ere without you?" Annie said. "They all 'ate me, even more now than ever. It would 'ave been different if we 'adn't 'ave lost the babies. They would 'ave loved their grandchildren, despite me being the mother. Your father's making you go on this trip 'oping it will end our marriage."

"Well, he would be very wrong if he thinks that," assured Daniel. "I will be back in a few months, in time for spring. You can be brave until then can't you, darling? This promotion trip is so very important for the company, and the Americans asked specifically for me. Macy's Store is the largest in New York and this invitation to assist in expanding their fine china department is unprecedented. I have to go."

"I know you do, dearest man," agreed Annie. "The time will fly by. Promise to write every day."

Daniel nodded, and sealed his promise with a kiss.

The day of Daniel's departure was dull and rainy. He moved quietly around the bedroom, gathering last-minute personal belongings, and tried not to disturb Annie. To no avail. Annie's eyes had popped open at the first tiny rustle, and she followed Daniel with her eyes, watching him dress and prepare for his long journey. When all was ready, he went to his wife and held her in his arms one last time, wishing he didn't have to go. His final kiss lingered on Annie's lips, as Daniel dragged himself away and swept across the room and through the door without looking back. He wanted to remember the kiss and not the vision of his beautiful wife, propped on her pillows with tears in her eyes.

Although it was early, Annie couldn't go back to sleep. She rose and watched from the window as Daniel's carriage clattered away down the driveway in the rain. She dressed slowly, not wanting to ring for Jenny to help her, then sat at her dressing table to write her first letter to Daniel, even though he had only just left. She wanted to reassure him of her love and tell him how she would miss him. It helped to put her feelings into writing.

Jenny arrived shortly after seven o'clock, surprised Annie was already dressed.

"I'll help you with your hair, Annie," Jenny said, picking up the silver-handled brush from the dressing table as she tried to tame the wild red curls.

"I'm going to miss my Daniel so much," Annie said. "It will be difficult to live 'ere without 'im. I wish I could go 'ome."

"Don't fret, now Miss," comforted Jenny Black. "Time will go by quickly, and all of us downstairs are looking out for you."

The breakfast food was laid out as usual on the buffet in the dining room. Mr Benton snorted and raised his newspaper to cover his face when Annie walked in. He quickly finished his tea and marched towards the door, while Annie chose her breakfast food. She was used to being ignored by Daniel's father.

As she sat eating scrambled eggs in the silence of the austere room, Mrs Frost, the housekeeper, quietly entered and coughed discreetly to let Annie know she was there.

"Yes, Mrs Frost," acknowledged Annie. "What is it?"

Mrs Frost moved from foot to foot, and wrung her hands in front of her.

"I've been told to give you a message from Mrs Benton Senior, if you please, Madam."

"Well, what is it?" Annie asked, putting down her fork and giving the housekeeper her attention.

"She would prefer… Well, they would prefer… That is, the Master and Missus… You are to eat in the servants hall from now on."

It was obvious Mrs Frost was extremely uncomfortable with the message she had been told to deliver. Her face flushed and she cast her eyes down, not wanting to meet Annie's gaze.

"I see," Annie finally said. "Thank you, Mrs Frost. Please don't feel badly about it. It's not your fault."

In fact, Annie was happier in the servants' hall. Cook welcomed her with a curtsey and then a big hug, and all the house staff made an extra effort to make her feel at ease. The food was the same as that served to the family, and the conversation was a vast improvement on the frigidity of the dining room.

Annie never saw her in-laws. She was well enough to visit her brother and his now extended family of younger siblings in the familiar house in Newhall Road. Jenny Black accompanied her on the outings and the long walk built Annie's strength and energy. She relished the rolled oatcakes smothered in cheese and the big mug of tea thrust into her hands upon her arrival. How she had missed them all.

A picture of their mother and father took pride of place on the mantle. The photographs captured their images, but the absence of their beautiful souls left a vacant place in the home that could never be filled.

Annie thought she would never laugh again, but her younger brother, Charles, had her giggling with stories of his antics at school. He was a born orator, like Jacob had been, and could tell a story like nobody else.

"You should 'ave seen Mr Boulton's face when 'e sat on 'is chair and one of the legs gave way, sending him sprawling. Serves 'im right for giving us a mathematics quiz every morning. The whole class had two strokes of the cane for laughing at 'im. It was worth it."

"Oh, our Charlie," Annie laughed. "You are better than any medicine, really you are."

With support from the staff at the big house and visits to her family, Annie thought she might make it until Daniel returned. She wrote to him every day, mailing each letter to the address he had left for her in New York. It took weeks for mail to get to its destination, so she wasn't surprised that no return letters arrived.

Robert Johnson, a master potter from the Aynsley Pottery Factory, accompanied Daniel to New York. He was to give practical demonstrations to Macy's customers in the skillful art of pottery making. Daniel liked the strong, quiet man, and after spending ten days together crossing the Atlantic, they became firm friends.

Living and working in New York was like living on a different planet. The two Englishmen spent their first days in the city feeling like two fish out of water. Everything was faster, bigger, louder and infinitely more exciting than their relatively quiet, peaceful lives in Staffordshire. The streets were lined with tall buildings, making it difficult to see the sky. The Singer Building, on Broadway, stood a massive forty seven stories high, and Daniel and Robert rode an elevator to the very top to look out over the city. It was like being on top of the world. There were underground trains, travelling through tunnels, carrying passengers to and from the heart of New York.

The streets bustled with people, horse-drawn carriages and carts, trolley cars, and motor vehicles. Several times every day the two friends stepped in front of oncoming traffic that drove on the right side of the road and didn't seem to follow any particular rules. The horse manure was shoveled and piled on the sides of the streets and left in steaming, stinking piles awaiting removal by an often late or non-existent sanitary system.

It seemed most people living in New York didn't sleep very much—the city came back to life after ten o'clock when Daniel and Robert were thinking about retiring. Theatres offered productions of Gilbert and Sullivan Operas, dramas and comedies. There were carts in the street selling everything from oysters to apples. The two friends roamed the streets wide-eyed and awestruck at the great city and its teeming population from every culture and country imaginable.

Daniel and Robert stood side by side across the street from the impressive Macy's Store on the corner of 34th Street and Broadway. This is where they would be working for the next few months.

"Bloody 'ell, Daniel," Robert gasped. "Look at the size of it. Bigger than all of the shops in Stoke put together."

"Right you are, Bob," Daniel said. "Needs to be doesn't it? There are over three million people living in New York. A few more than back home, right?"

"Aye, a few more," laughed Robert.

Macy's staff greeted the newcomers warmly. The two men were rapidly becoming aware of the one thing most New Yorkers had in common with each other—an overwhelming friendliness. Unlike the British, who rarely spoke to strangers, it seemed everybody they met had a smile and a greeting. They were informal and easy to like. Their drawling pronunciation of the English language somehow enhanced their congeniality, and the Americans seemed to enjoy Daniel and Robert's dialects equally.

Settled into their lodgings in a large Victorian house owned by a jocular middle-aged woman named Mrs Billington, known to all as "Billie," they began life in the Big Apple. Customers poured into Macy's to watch Robert create urns, vases, dishes, jugs and every type of vessel from a lump of grey clay thrown onto a potter's wheel. Sales soared as Daniel personally escorted buyers around the fine bone china displays, helping them choose a dinner service or a tea set to their liking. It was gratifying work in a wondrous environment.

As he had promised, Daniel wrote to Annie every day, telling her about the great city, not aware that his letters were circumvented by his mother, and never reached Annie. He missed her most at night when he crawled into bed. It was always the favourite part of his day, to cuddle into his sweetheart and feel her warm, soft body next to his. He missed her so much it made him ache, and he fell asleep every night with the image of her beautiful face in his mind.

Christmas lights twinkled and glowed from every building in New York City. The two Staffordshire men were mesmerized with the sights and sounds of Christmas filtering through every corner of the Macy's store. Every day was new and exciting as the customers clambered to buy everything "Christmas," including the products from Winston Field China.

Daniel had a persistent cough. He assumed he had picked it up on the ship. It began as an annoyance at night, keeping him awake with the constant tickle in his throat, but as the winter set in and the temperature dropped, the cough worsened.

After checking in with a doctor recommended by Billie, he was prescribed a cough mixture, which he took several times every day. By the third week of December Daniel had a fever and a deep ache in his chest when he took a breath. The cough mixture was certainly not working.

The doctor was concerned when he saw Daniel. He had lost weight and had dark circles under his eyes. He could hear rasping, popping sounds when he listened to his chest, and knew from experience it was probably pneumonia.

"Bed rest for you, young man," said the doctor. "I mean it. Total bed rest, or you'll be in more trouble than you are now."

Robert Johnson was worried about his friend. He shared a bedroom with him, listening to him cough his nights away. There was no relief. Billie prepared hot poultices for Daniel's chest, swearing that her mother's recipe would cure any cough. All to no avail.

Christmas was miserable for Daniel. Spent huddled in bed, with Robert bringing him soup and tea. The biggest comfort was two letters from Annie, which had arrived the week before. Daniel read and reread them many times, picturing his lovely wife writing words of love and devotion to him. He drifted into an uneasy sleep clutching the letters in his hand.

CHAPTER 26

RETURN TO ENGLAND

Frigid wintery weather enveloped England. It was mid-January of 1910 and people hurried about their business, anxious to be indoors and out of the biting wind.

Mrs Benton sat in the drawing room close to the fire, with a warm blanket over her legs and a shawl around her shoulders. She felt the cold badly, and barely tolerated the winter months, wishing she could travel to Spain or Italy during the cold weather, like some of the other factory owners' wives and families.

However, Mr Benton thought being away during the winter a frivolous luxury, and he had no intention of placating his wife.

The telegram from New York arrived mid-morning. It was from Robert Johnson and was brief: "DANIEL BENTON DIED JANUARY 14TH, 1910. STOP"

James Benton couldn't stop shaking. A servant had collected him from the factory, saying only that he was needed at home urgently. He now stood next to his grief-stricken wife, reading the single piece of paper again.

"What is this?" he finally blurted out between clenched teeth. "What is this? It's not true! It's preposterous! Daniel is 22 years of age. Impossible. They've made a mistake."

As James yelled and pounded his feet onto the floor, he knew it was no mistake. Robert Johnson would never send such a telegram if it were not true.

With the realization that his son was dead, James Benton collapsed into an armchair, his head in his hands. Mrs Frost, the housekeeper, was at her wits' end to know what to do. Isabel Benton lay on the sofa, silent and pale with her eyes closed, and the master was inconsolable. The housekeeper quickly poured two large portions of whiskey from the decanter on the corner cabinet and firstly poured some into her mistress's mouth, causing her to splutter and cough, and next held it to her master's lips. The fiery liquid mostly spilled down his chin, but enough trickled into his mouth to bring him to his senses.

Annie sat at the window of her bedroom looking out onto the frosty landscape. She had just finished writing to Daniel, which always made her feel sad. She missed him so much and longed for the day he would return and they could pick up the pieces of their lives.

Mrs Frost interrupted her daydreaming, when she knocked quietly on the bedroom door. She entered the room with a downcast face, and a crease of worry between her eyebrows. Annie's instincts made her fearful of the message the housekeeper carried.

"The Master would like to speak to you downstairs," Mrs Frost muttered, not meeting Annie's eyes. "If you could come right away, please."

James Benton directed all the hurt and anger he felt towards the girl who had taken his son away from his family. He glared at her through swollen, red eyes as she entered the drawing room.

"Pack your things and go back to your family," he ordered. "We don't want you here. We never wanted you here. Our beloved son, Daniel, is dead. You will be a daily reminder of what we have lost. I want you out of this house within the hour. You have nothing to do with us."

Annie's vision receded to a pinpoint, as blackness closed in on her. She regained consciousness to find herself propped up on a chair in the drawing room, where Mrs Frost held a glass of water to her lips. Then Annie remembered the news, delivered to her with venom by her father-in-law.

Daniel was dead! Her Daniel! Her love! Her husband!

She didn't look up at her abuser but raised herself from the chair and stumbled towards the door. Mrs Frost accompanied her, supporting her up the stairs and helping her lay down on the bed in her room. She worried this would return Annie to her catatonic state. The kindly housekeeper ordered hot, sweet tea and encouraged Annie to sip it slowly.

"Within the hour," Mr Benton had ordered.

Jenny Black cried as she packed up her friend's clothing. How could she comfort Annie? It was impossible. She feared the young widow would never recover from this latest devastating loss.

"You'll be much better off with your family, Annie," Jenny whispered, folding the dresses carefully before putting them in the trunk. "The Master and Mistress 'ave never liked you, and your family all love you so much. You need to be with people who love you now."

John and Rosemary Jenkins warmly welcomed Annie into their cramped little house. At first they thought she had arrived for a visit, but one look at her told them this was no ordinary visit, but something very bad. Annie choked out the news that Daniel had died in New York, and that his parents had told her to leave immediately.

"You already 'ave so many people living 'ere, but I 'ad nowhere else to go," she sobbed.

"Where else would you go?" said Rosemary, wrapping her sister-in-law in her arms to comfort her. "You can sleep with your younger sister, Mary-Jane. She 'as a big bed all to 'erself since May and Daisy went to room with our 'Elen, and our Lizzie's staying with Mrs Keay from the chapel who is sickly and needs help. The boys already sleep in the front room downstairs, and the two trundle beds in our room work fine for our two little girls."

"That's all settled then," chimed in John as he pulled his sister into his arms. "You'll survive Annie, with our 'elp. I'll let the rest of the family know what's 'appened. One thing is for sure, if love can 'elp you get through this, there's an unlimited supply of it right 'ere."

Annie felt safe, loved and completely numb. Her family cherished her, comforted her, and nourished her. She sat among them feeling nothing but the great burden of her sorrow. Somewhere deep inside she knew she would overcome this latest grief, and she patiently waited for the darkness to abate, and the despair to lighten its grip on her.

Six weeks after Daniel's demise, Annie's two oldest sisters came to visit with news about the Benton family.

James Benton Senior had been so distraught at the news of his son's death that he had immediately telegraphed Robert Johnson with instructions to have Daniel's body preserved and returned to England for a proper Catholic burial.

The sisters had been informed by the management at Winston Field China that the factory was to close on Thursday afternoon for the funeral.

Annie stared at her sisters in disbelief. How could her in-laws make arrangements for Daniel to be buried in a local church and not inform her? She understood they hated her and didn't accept she had been lawfully married to their son, but to not tell her about the funeral was unthinkable.

"I want to go," Annie said.

"That may not be a good idea, Annie," was John's first reaction. "You wouldn't be welcome by the family. Also, the service is at St. Gregory's Catholic Church."

"What does that matter?" exclaimed Annie. "I'm going anyway. I'm his wife and I should be there. I'll go by myself and sit at the back. Nobody will even notice me."

"I'll go with you, Annie," May offered.

Thursday afternoon at two o'clock, Annie and May walked down the high street to St. Gregory's Catholic Church in Longton. The dark clouds overhead threatened snow or sleet and the two women linked arms and hugged their coats tightly against the penetrating cold. The Catholic Church was an imposing building with brickwork turned black by the smoke of the pottery ovens, the interior dark and cold.

As Mission Methodists, Annie and May had never set foot inside a Catholic Church in their lives. Compared with their own tiny chapel it felt cavernous and scary. The sisters were awed by the gothic pillars supporting the high ceiling, the dozens of rows of wooden pews with kneeling stools, and the high altar set below a stained glass window depicting Christ's crucifixion. They sat at the back beside one of the tall pillars, barely noticed by the other people swarming into the church. The casket carrying Daniel's body was carried in by six pallbearers, who placed it at the front of the church and removed the lid so that everybody could see Daniel.

Annie tried to stifle a gasp, and slumped against May's arm, as she saw her husband, dressed in evening dress, propped up in the coffin surrounded by white satin. Annie felt May's arm slide around her shoulders and was glad of the support. The service was a blur of words echoing off the cold walls and floating around Annie's head without meaning. The Benton family sat at the front of the church, straight and stoic, none showing a sign of emotion. The stiff upper lip of the British firmly in place.

James Benton had done his duty as a father and would bury his son in the family grave at the Catholic cemetery. His tombstone would read *"Daniel William Benton, 1887-1910, Beloved son of James and Isabel Benton, Rest In Peace."*

No mention was made of a wife named Annie.

CHAPTER 27
SWEET SHOP

John and Rosemary Jenkins ran their tiny home with the same love and care of the previous tenants, Jacob and Margaret. William, Charles and Mary-Jane never had to move out of their family home, and the distraction of John and Rosemary's two tiny daughters, Enid and Nancy, filled their days with constant activity. The little girls thrived on the attention they received from a doting group of teenagers and adults, but their favourite was Aunty Annie, who never tired of cuddling, reading, playing and singing with them.

For Annie, the little girls were a life line. She grieved her own baby girls every day, but Enid and Nancy helped fill the abyss in her heart. Rosemary was happy to leave Annie to most of the caregiving. She had her hands full with running the home for so many people and spent most of her days shopping and cooking. John earned a decent wage working as a plate maker, but with eight hungry mouths to feed, Rosemary had to shop carefully and make meals with the cheapest ingredients. She counted herself fortunate that her father had a vegetable allotment garden and, even during the winter months, supplied her with onions, carrots and pota-toes, safely stored in the allotment shed. A pound of cheap stewing beef, with the vegetables added, bubbled in the big black pot over the fire for several hours, turning the concoc-tion into a rich consommé soup. The "lobby," served with Rosemary's crusty bread for dipping, was everybody's favourite on a cold wintry day.

Every Saturday morning Annie visited Daniel's grave at the Catholic cemetery. She took a token with her to mark her visit, something small and insignificant to others, but meaningful to her. A round stone, picked up on the country lane where they met so often; a lock of her hair wrapped in paper and buried just below the earth on the grave; a bead from a necklace Daniel had given her for their first anniver-sary. When spring finally arrived, she gathered wild crocus, bluebells and snowdrops to make a small posy, progressing to colourful summer daisies, cornflowers and columbine. It gave Annie great comfort to take her small gifts to the grave, and eventually she could lay the flowers at the foot of the headstone with a smile, knowing how much Daniel would love them.

May married her sweetheart, George Podmore, at the end of summer. The chapel wedding was a celebration of their union, with wonderful community singing, members of the family reading scripture, and Mr Baker delivering a perfect message. Annie looked radiant, although she shed many tears during the service, thinking of her own wedding only a few years before. She had gained weight and her hair and skin had returned to their healthy glow.

After the service, the bride and groom stepped outside so that all the neighbours from the street could throw rice and shout their words of congratulations. While the men worked inside to move all the pews to the outside walls and set up food tables, the women scurried back and forth from the tiny back kitchen, bringing in the prepared sandwiches and cakes. With all the tables set, May and George returned to loud applause and cheering. May blushed to the roots of her red hair with all the attention focused on her, while George held her hand and looked like the cat who'd got the cream.

When the younger children returned to school after the summer break, and the little girls needed less persistent care, Annie thought she should find a job and help with the household income. She saw the burden on her brother to make enough money to cover the cost of rent and food. He worked six days a week most weeks, and his fingers were stuck in the shape of the plates he made. He never took time off, even when he was sick, for fear that losing a day's pay would impact the ability to meet their expenses.

The sweet shop in Longton still held a place in Annie's heart. Her mother had worked there many times during her life, and Annie had enjoyed the time she worked there too. It was a good place to start looking for work. She pushed open the door, hearing the tinkle of the little bell as she entered. An elderly lady peered at her from behind the counter.

"What can I get for ya?" she asked, wiping the back of her hand across her nose.

"Is the shop still owned by Mr Douglas Cresswell?"Annie asked.

"Cresswell? Dead and buried 'e is. Left the shop to 'is son, Albert. 'E dunna bother with it though. Couldn't care less! Look 'ow run down it is. I can't work full time and 'e pays me next to nothin'. I'm just about ready to pack it in, I can tell ya."

"Do you know 'ow I could contact Albert?" Annie continued.

"Across the road, duck. 'E works at the town 'all. Some kind of office job."

Annie thanked the old lady and crossed the street, going

into the town hall through the double glass doors, her boots echoing on the stone floor in the empty hallway. Albert Cresswell, Town Planner, was the sign on the door at the end of the first floor corridor. Annie knocked on the glass and, on hearing a loud "come in," she entered the large office. Albert looked over his glasses at the young red-haired woman.

"How can I help you?" he asked.

"My name is Annie Benton and I came to talk to you about the sweet shop," Annie said with confidence. "I knew your father. 'e gave me a job when I was younger, and I loved working for 'im. My mother also worked for 'im on and off for many years, in fact she met my dad in the sweet shop."

"Well?" Albert asked, tapping his pencil up and down on his desk, anxious to return to his work.

"The sweet shop is sadly neglected," began Annie. "I spoke to the old woman who works there, and she wants to leave. I would be very interested in running the shop for you. I could turn it around and would be willing to work 'ard to restore it to its former condition. It's a shame it's been left to run down so badly. I'm 'ere to ask if you would consider me for the task of being the sweet shop lady—I can assure you the shop will be profitable when it's clean and well-stocked again."

Albert tried to analyze the talkative, beautiful young woman standing before him. She was short and slender, but feisty and confident in her manner. He guessed her to be in her early twenties, but something about her deep blue eyes made her look older. Her skin was alabaster white and flawless, and whips of her red hair curled around her face, even though she had gathered the rich tresses into a bun at the nape of her neck. Her clothes were obviously stylish and of good quality—this was no ordinary working girl. Albert liked the look of her and, even though he didn't consider the sweet shop worth thinking about, he was curious about her plans for its resurrection.

"Well, Annie Benton," Albert finally said. "It sounds like you have a plan all set out for my father's sweet shop. I have to admit it's not something that interests me, and I have neglected it. If you think you can turn it around, I'm going to give you the job. Mind you, I'm not willing to pay you any more than I pay the old lady to begin with. You'll have to prove yourself. Let's say after four weeks we will review your position, and pay you according to your ability."

"Thank you Mr Cresswell," Annie said. "I won't let you down."

"Well then, why don't you begin next Monday. I will let Mrs Newban know she can leave at the end of the day on Saturday. Then it will be all up to you. I will meet you at the shop on Monday morning at eight thirty to give you a cash float and a key. Any questions?"

"No, I don't think so," answered Annie, flushed with excitement at the outcome of the meeting. "I will see you on Monday morning. I can't wait to begin the transformation."

It took several weeks of hard work to make inroads into the mess at the sweet shop. Annie threw herself into the rescue project with gusto. She often took Enid and Nancy to the shop with her, encouraging them to polish the newly washed sweet jars. They had their own little aprons, and rags for polishing, and loved "helping" Aunty Annie. Any damaged or crushed sweets delivered to the shop were put into a special brown bag to take home later for the family to share. The little girls were in charge of the brown bag and took their responsibility very seriously, frequently taking out the sweets to count, and hoping that the next delivery would produce a few more rejects.

Albert Cresswell was delighted with the progress Annie had made when he visited the shop every Saturday. Even though the renovation was far from complete, Albert gave Annie a generous raise after just two weeks, and a further raise at the end of a month. Annie was delighted to be able to give John a good portion of her wages to help with the household expenses. Rosemary made all kinds of wonderful meals with the extra money: chicken and pork were added to the entrees, strawberry tarts and apple pies were plentiful, and salted bacon was a regular breakfast food.

The bottles of sweets filled the shelves and the display in the pristinely clean window showed varieties of chocolate, salt-water taffy, liquorice all sorts, and the latest product called walnut whip—a swirl of chocolate filled with cream, with a walnut on the top. Customers began to flock into the shop, and Annie, dressed in a starched white apron, greeted them all with a smile and a friendly greeting. Sweets were weighed carefully by Annie, and served in white paper bags. Every child could choose a free sweet from the dish on the counter, and any purchase could be gift wrapped if requested.

Albert contemplated Annie's proposal for a new name for the shop. Instead of just "Sweet Shop," she had suggested "The Pear Drop." It had a nice ring to it, Albert thought. He was so taken with Annie's business sense and success that he agreed whole-heartedly to the new name. Annie never told him it was to honour her dad, who had loved those particular sweets, but when the sign went up outside the shop, she couldn't help but shed a tear, thinking of all the times she had taken pear drops home for her dad.

During the following few years, Daisy married Arnold Copestake, a young man from the chapel, and Lizzie married Mrs Keay's only son, Albert. William was serving an apprenticeship at the printers where his father had worked. Mary-Jane was employed in the office at Foley China. Charles found full time work at The Aynsley Pottery Factory, and Enid was in school. Life at number thirty-one Newhall Road was as sunny as could be. Money was now plentiful with four workers in the family to share the load. The men in the family were all members of the temperance chapel, so none of their hard-earned wages was spent in the pub. Rosemary's life of hardship for so many years, raising three teenagers alongside her own two girls, had moved into a time of comfort. Cooking and taking care of the household with money to spare, was enough to ease the burden of worry when she had managed with so little.

By now Annie was a handsome woman of twenty-four. She had never looked at another man, though several had tried to court her—mostly chapel men. The few years with Daniel felt like a dream, but no man had ever caught her eye, or touched her heart in the same way. She was content with her life. The Pear Drop was virtually her own shop, to do with as she pleased with no interference from the owner, except to praise her. She had countless nephews and nieces, who invaded the family home on Sundays after chapel, as they always had. She was never lonely for company and always surrounded by people who loved her.

The one-armed man, who came into the shop every Friday night and always bought two ounces of wine gums, was polite and quiet. He told Annie his name was Thomas and she reciprocated by telling him her name, emphasizing the "Mrs" Annie Benton. It wasn't until Enid and Nancy were in the shop one Friday night that Annie's marital status was called into question.

"Hello, I see you have help tonight," Thomas said. "Who are these two new assistants, may I ask?"

"I'm Enid, and this is my sister Nancy. She's only three."

"You both look very grown up. I'm sure you are very good at serving sweets," added Thomas, smiling at the two girls over the counter.

Annie caught his eye and smiled as she turned to reach for the wine gums sitting on the middle shelf in their shiny jar. *Thomas was a kind man to talk to the girls—most men wouldn't even notice them.*

"We 'ave always 'elped Aunty Annie," informed Nancy.

"She's our favourite Aunty and she lives with us because 'er 'usband is dead."

There it was! In one sentence from a three-year-old. Annie's cover was blown.

"Ah! I see," said Thomas, not daring to look at Annie. "That's bad news."

"Oh no," chimed in Enid. "It was years ago. Nobody even remembers 'im, right Aunty Annie?"

Annie almost dropped the jar of wine gums she was so flustered.

What is wrong with me? Why should I care what this customer thinks or knows about my life? He's just a nice man with one arm who buys wine gums every Friday night. Pull yourself together, Annie.

"Here are your wine gums, Thomas," she managed to say. "Say goodbye girls."

"Goodbye, Thomas," they chimed together.

That's when it began.

The following Friday Thomas held out a rose when he came into the shop.

"This is from my garden," he said. "I hope you like roses. This one's the first bloom."

"Thank you," whispered Annie. "There was really no need."

Annie weighed the wine gums. The silence was awkward. Neither of them knew quite what to say. Thomas paid for his sweets and left quickly.

It took several Fridays for Thomas to pluck up enough courage to talk to Annie again.

"I wondered if you might meet me sometime after work?" he ventured. "Just for a walk or a cup of tea at Webberley's Cafe."

Annie considered his offer carefully, taking her time to weigh the sweets.

Do I want to go out with him? What would be the harm? He seems a nice man, and Daniel's been gone so long. I don't know anything about Thomas really. I wonder if he's been married too. He's pretty old—probably in his thirties. It's not like I have anything else to do or anywhere else to be.

"Thank you for asking," Annie answered. "Maybe a walk would be nice."

Thomas was overjoyed, and said he would be back in an hour.

It was the first of many walks on Friday nights. Annie found out Thomas Gardiner was thirty-two years old, and worked as an accountant in a large, prestigious pottery factory. He had been born with one arm and felt it had never made a difference to his life. He had never been married, and lived alone after losing both his parents. He enjoyed cooking, particularly puddings and cakes and had recently been experimenting with inventing different kinds of sweets. His dream was to invent a new sweet that would make him a rich man.

"How many more sweets do you think we need?" laughed Annie. "Look how many we already stock in our shop—all of them delicious and popular. I can't imagine people would want more."

"You would be wrong there, Annie," Thomas replied. "I foresee people craving more and more sweets, and I think there's a great future in the industry."

Before the end of the year Annie had introduced Thomas to Rosemary and May, who gave their smiles of approval to the quiet man who obviously adored their Annie.

The newspapers were full of pending war with Germany, and the young Jenkins men could talk of nothing else. Rosemary dreaded the future for her family if England went to war. John was only thirty years of age and would probably be called to serve, along with May's husband George, and certainly William at the tender age of eighteen. Thankfully Charles, at fourteen, was still too young to be involved in the fighting. Rosemary prayed the rumours of war would remain just rumours and not materialize into her husband, brother, and brother-in-law leaving home to fight the Germans.

Rosemary's worst fears came to fruition when England declared war on Germany on July 28th, 1914. Within a matter of weeks call-up papers were delivered to John and William at number thirty-one Newhall Road, and to George, who lived close by.

All over the neighbourhood the young men disappeared from the factories, the pits, the streets, as they reported to the various sectors of the armed forces. Their wives and children were left behind to eke out a living without their bread-winners.

Young Charles worked full time at Aynsley China, helping the kiln men stack the china for firing. It was particularly hard work for a young lad, but paid better than other labourers jobs in the pottery industry. He walked to May's house every Friday and handed her his pay packet. Rosemary had insisted he give his earnings to his sister, because she had nobody to help her now that George had gone. The army pay was so low that it didn't even cover the week's rent, and left May, and her little boy, Harry, with little to live on. Rosemary had Annie living with her who earned a decent wage, so it was only fair that May should have Charles' small wage. Even so, the two women struggled to cover the cost of running their homes. They decided to look for work and found a job at the high street green-grocery store, each of them babysitting the children while the other worked. It was the perfect solution to their budget problems. The green-grocer gave Rosemary and May left-over fruit and vegetables at the end of the day, which they happily shared with their neighbours.

The war brought with it so many hardships, but among those hardships there were also many blessings. Sharing what little you had with those who had less became the normal way to live.

Despite the lack of money, the sweet shop remained busy. Like an oasis in a dessert, the little shop shone with colour and light in a dark and dismal world. Annie dropped the price of boiled sweets and peppermints, and ordered chocolate pieces from Cadbury's factory in Birmingham. Chocolate pieces were rejected, misshapen chunks of chocolate which Annie chopped into small pieces and sold in small quantities. She expanded the inventory to include magazines like John Bull, Punch and Vanity Fair. For the children, she stocked a selection of her own favourites: Black Beauty, Heidi, The Jungle Book, The Tale of Peter Rabbit and several others. Some of the local children, not being able to afford a book, came into the store regularly to read the next chapter of a book they particularly liked. Annie scattered a few old cushions in the corner of the shop, so that they could sit and read in some comfort. Her heart filled with compassion for the youngsters whose lives were filled with poverty and worry. A bag of broken chocolate was shared with a small group each day. The children made sure each of them had an equal amount. Annie smiled as she watched them, not sure if it was the books or the chocolate that was the biggest attraction.

"Can I ask your opinion, Thomas?" Annie said as she closed up the shop one Friday night. "I know you like to bake, and I've been wondering if baked goods would sell in the sweet shop. What do you think?"

Thomas took Annie's arm and threaded it through his own as they walked along the wet streets. How good it felt to have a lovely woman beside him. He gave the question some thought before he answered.

"What kind of baked goods?" Thomas asked.

"Oh, I don't know. Ingredients are so difficult to buy now that I wouldn't know if it's even an option." Annie frowned as she thought of the severe shortage of everything to do with baking. "Maybe currant buns, or biscuits of some kind."

"Why don't I make a few things this coming week and bring them around to the store for the weekend," suggested Thomas. "I have a few bits and pieces in the house and could rustle up some simple products. People may really enjoy having another option other than sweets."

"Would you, Thomas?" Annie smiled. "How kind you are. If it works out I could give you my ration to work with, and probably Charlie's as well. Rosemary and May have some help from the grocer they work for, and I know they wouldn't mind if we shared our rations for your baking."

The following Friday morning, Thomas arrived with two dozen small currant buns and two dozen oat biscuits. By noon all had been sold. Thomas insisted the price be only the cost of the ingredients, and Annie agreed. It encouraged people to look around the shop and spend their few extra pennies for a treat or two.

The following Friday there was a small line outside the shop when Annie arrived. Word had got out that The Pear Drop had the most delicious baked products as well as sweets.

Thomas was enjoying himself. It appealed to his creative personality. He sought out recipes, substitute ingredients, and a myriad of ways to bake without the usual products at his fingertips. The results were amazing, and he delivered more and more of his creations to the sweet shop each week. Currant loaves, sold by the slice, biscuits made with potato flour and honey from a friend who kept bees, Eccles cakes, and even egg custard tarts with a filling of Bird's imitation custard powder instead of real eggs.

The experiment was a huge success, and kept The Pear Drop bustling and viable during the dark days of the war.

CHAPTER 30
SECOND LOVE

The end house in Lower Spring Road was larger than the terraced houses it was attached to and had a fenced side yard. It was cosy and clean inside and smelled of pine polish. The table in the kitchen, covered in a pure white linen cloth, was set with fine china tea dishes, and Thomas busied himself boiling the kettle for tea, and placing a plate of assorted small cakes on the table.

"Sit here, Annie," he said. "Make yourself at home."

Annie felt safe and surprisingly content as she sat in one of the Windsor chairs by the table. She contemplated her situation as she watched Thomas prepare the tea. He was a kind, gentle man, not bad looking, not very tall, lovely eyes with long lashes, and dark curly hair which he wore a little too long. She hardly noticed his handicap because he handled everything he did as though he had two arms. For the first time in many years Annie let herself believe she could have feelings for another man.

The homemade cakes were as delicious as they looked, and Annie savoured every bite.

"I could become addicted to your cakes, Thomas," she

laughed. "Although I can imagine my waistline would expand very quickly in a short time."

They chatted and laughed as they drank their tea. They were comfortable together. Thomas had never met anyone like Annie. His heart thumped like a drum sitting so close to her in his own kitchen. She was the first woman to be invited into his house. He had always been shy around women and had kept to himself. He was self-conscious of his arm and felt he didn't really stand a chance of having a sweetheart, let alone one as lovely as Annie.

He reached out and took her hand. She didn't withdraw it.

"Annie, I'm so glad you agreed to come to my house," Thomas said. "I think you're wonderful and I can't believe you're actually sitting here at my table. I've never had the companionship of a lady before, so I'm a bit unsure of myself. All I know is, I feel very good when I'm with you—not shy at all. I hope you'll come here often."

"I would like that, Thomas," Annie said. "I enjoy being with you too. I never thought I would want to be alone with another man after Daniel, but it's different with you. You are so kind and such a gentleman that it's easy to like you."

Annie's heart sprung back to life. She hadn't looked for it or even desired it, but her love for Thomas grew from a few polite words in the sweet shop, to a deep and loving relationship. They went from eating cakes and sipping tea to holding each other close and exchanging their first hesitant kisses.

Thomas, having no experience, let Annie lead the way as she touched and fondled him and finally led him upstairs. She took her time taking off her clothes, laughing as she watched the expression on Thomas' face. When she stood before him in only her under garments, she began to unfasten the buttons on his shirt, then his trousers until he too wore only his underwear. He couldn't hide the obvious passion he felt and quickly covered himself with his hand. Annie took his hand away and moved closer to him, so that they both felt the impact of being next to each other.

Annie slipped out of her undergarments and crept beneath the sheets, with Thomas following her example right behind her. Now there was no hiding, and somehow it didn't matter. Annie was a willing partner in a beautiful act of love, and Thomas thought he would die from the sheer joy of what he felt. Being inside Annie was like nothing he could describe. She was so warm, so moist, so sweet, and he was overwhelmed by emotion as he moved to the rhythm that came so naturally to him. Annie clung to him and dug her nails into his shoulders. She had almost forgotten what it felt like to have a man make love to her, and she wasn't disappointed.

Thomas lay beside Annie, listening to her breathing as he gently stroked her arm and ran his fingers through her curls. What a gift she was. A gift he never considered he deserved. The light inside him continued to burn until, an hour later he once more clasped Annie's warm body and drew her near, wanting more of her sweetness.

Annie spent more and more time at Thomas' house. She often slept there, snuggled beside the gentle quiet man she had come to love. She lay with her head on his chest inhaling the smell of him and listening to the rhythm of his breathing and the faint bump of his heart.

It wasn't until Annie had missed her second period that she suspected she may be pregnant, and fear gripped her like a vice. She had been through this twice before, and she dreaded the loss of another baby. When she confided to Thomas that she thought she was pregnant, he was full of joy and trepidation at the same time. He knew about the babies Annie had lost and guessed she worried this pregnancy would have the same outcome.

"Try not to worry, Annie," Thomas whispered as they lay snuggled under the bedcovers. "I never thought I'd be a dad. I'm so excited I think I may burst. You're much stronger now than when you were eighteen, and I'm convinced you'll have a healthy baby this time. I'll take care of you so carefully for the next six months, but first we must be practical and get married as soon as we can."

"I'd like that," replied Annie. "I can't help worrying, Thomas, but I know we were meant to be together and nothing can stand in the way."

Chapel banns were read the following Sunday and, despite her already-thickening waistline, Annie had her fancy wedding at the chapel. Although it was the middle of February and bitterly cold, it was every bit as wonderful as her sisters' wedding days, with music and beautiful scriptures and Mr Baker's inspiring message. Three of Annie's nieces were bridesmaids, dressed in borrowed dresses from May's wedding, cut down and made to fit. The chapel was packed with everybody Annie loved. Although Thomas had left his Anglican roots behind at an early age, he knew what it meant to Annie, and happily signed the abstinence pledge. He had always been more interested in baking and inventing new sweets than drinking beer anyway.

Annie tried to hide her anxiety from her husband as the baby grew inside her. Every tiny flutter caused her heart to skip a beat, and brought back the memories of the two babies she had already lost. She insisted nothing should be planned ahead. No crib was to be bought or borrowed, no layette was to be prepared, no baby blankets, nappies, soap or towels were to be gathered.

With Mr Cresswell's permission, Annie hired William's young lady, Florence, to work in The Pear Drop. They had been courting for several months and Annie had grown to like the young, shy girl. Annie worked alongside her for several weeks before declaring her ready to be in charge, and handed over the keys.

Annie's sisters worked diligently behind the scenes filling a small trunk, kept at May's house, with all the necessities for the expected baby. A crib used for Helen's and Sarah's children was outfitted with new sheets and soft blankets. Rosemary knitted a thick blanket and made a soft pillow for the pram she had used for Enid and Nancy. All items were hidden away waiting for the new baby to arrive. The entire Jenkins family prayed every day that Annie's baby would survive.

Thomas continued to boil and cook his concoctions of sweet-smelling goo on the gas stove in the back kitchen. His inventions were tested by Annie's family, some producing smiles of delight, but more often grimaces of disgust. The pursuit of a new sweet was a tedious and difficult task, but Thomas was persistent. He loved the flavours of mint and liquorice mixed together, and held onto the dream of a soft centred sweet with a hard shell, which would become a bestseller one day. If nothing else, the house always smelled absolutely wonderful, except when he burned the sugar.

Annie chose a new midwife, not wanting any bad memories to influence the birth of this baby. Sophie Blenkinsop lived close by and had delivered several babies born to chapel ladies recently. She was young, only twenty-six, but had learned her skills from Mrs Skillon, who was renowned for her forty years as midwife supreme.

Annie would be in good hands.

The Jenkins family gathered at Rosemary's house early on Saturday morning in mid-August 1915. It was a hot sticky day and Rosemary served tall glasses of lemonade to the crowd in her kitchen.

"Well, today's the day," May said, excitedly. "Sophie Blenkinsop was sent for at six o'clock this morning. Thomas said Annie woke 'im at four to say the baby was on its way. God willing, we will be celebrating by the end of the day."

At the Gardner house, Annie's oldest sister, Helen, was by her side, holding her hand and speaking gentle words of comfort and encouragement. She had handed a large black bag full of the secret stash of baby things to the midwife, who was quietly unpacking the treasures. Hand sewn towels, face cloths, swaddling blankets, layette, soap and a practical stack of soft cotton toweling cut into uniform squares for Annie to use in her underwear after the baby was born.

"'Elen, you are so kind," Annie whispered as she saw the contents of the bag being unpacked. "I never let myself believe the baby would be all right. I thought it best that I didn't prepare anything until I was absolutely sure. Now I see you have done my job for me."

"Now, now, Annie," Helen said, her voice cracking as she fought back her tears. "All the sisters 'elped. It's the least we could do. No more worrying now, my dear girl. Soon you will 'ave your longed-for baby and our small gifts will be put to good use."

Although it had been almost six years since the last birth, Annie's labour progressed quickly and without incident. Sophie expertly guided her patient through each stage, assuring her that all was well. Annie pushed the dark images of the past out of her mind, and tried to focus on Helen's smiling face—so much like her mother's. As the baby pushed its way into the world, Annie screamed out, not in pain but in fear—finally letting the anguish of the pregnancy and confinement culminate in the shout against all the horrors she dreaded would be repeated. This was the moment that was locked in her brain. The moment when the baby didn't cry and the small lifeless body was placed in her arms so that she could say goodbye.

The last few days of this pregnancy, although weighed down with worry, had felt different than the first two. The baby had poked and prodded her almost until the moment of the first pang of labour. She remembered the odd stillness before, and the movements gave her hope that this baby would be alive.

The silence seemed endless as Helen and Sophie concentrated on the space between Annie's legs. Then a lusty cry!

Sophie lifted up the baby girl for Annie to see. She was perfect. Long and slender with a very red face. She loudly let them know she had arrived. Sophie wrapped her in a blanket and laid her on Annie's chest. Not a lifeless baby this time, but a squirming, healthy, screaming bundle. Helen cried and cried as she kissed Annie and ran to bring in Thomas from the kitchen where he had drank endless cups of tea. What seemed like an eternity to Thomas was, in reality, less than two hours. With legs wobbling under him, he followed Helen into the birthing room.

As Thomas kissed his wife and took the baby with his left arm, awkwardly cradling her against his shoulder, his tiny daughter stopped screaming, opened her eyes and looked at him as though she knew him already.

"Look at that," burst out Thomas, the joy on his face radiating happiness. Then to the baby, "Hello, little one. I'm your dad. You are the most beautiful baby in the world, because you are mine."

His joy turned to tears as he talked softly to his baby. Her blue eyes never left his lips and a little frown gathered her eyebrows together as she pursed her lips into a bow. He couldn't remember a time when he had felt so overwhelmed with happiness.

Thomas had once given up all hope of meeting a woman who would consent to marry him, let alone becoming a father. His missing right arm had always been a source of embarrassment, even though no task was too difficult for him to master. He had been a good football player and a powerful swimmer, despite his handicap. The opposite sex, however, had filled him with dread. How would he dance with a girl? How would he make sure she was always on his left side so that he could hold her hand? How would he hold a girl, or ever make love to a girl? Girls took one look at him and either tried to pretend he didn't exist or smiled at him in sympathy. Neither reaction encouraged Thomas to pursue a relationship.

Except for Annie, who had never seemed to notice, at least not in his eyes. His left arm was enough for her, and his confidence blossomed as their relationship matured into a fondness, then a deep love for each other. Holding Annie's hand, dancing with her, holding her close, making love to her —all were a natural part of their life together, culminating in the fathering of a child.

Helen carried in a bowl of warm water and set it on a low table beside the armchair, where Sophie sat and took the new baby from Thomas. As the grime of birthing was washed away, the soft red down on the baby's head proclaimed her inheritance. The screaming began again and continued for the entire bath, which only made her mother, watching from the high birthing bed borrowed from her sisters, laugh delightedly at the sound.

"Have you chosen a name for her?" asked Helen.

The new parents looked at each other sheepishly.

"No, not yet," replied Thomas. "Annie insisted we wait until after the birth to even think about a name. Now it will give us the greatest pleasure to choose a name that suits our dear little girl."

They decided on Annie Nora, with the rider that they would call her Nora, so that she wouldn't be confused with her mother. From that day forward she was known as Nora.

CHAPTER 32

HUMBUGS

The Great War raged on in Europe. John Jenkins came home, after a year of bitter conflict in the countryside of France, with a shattered collar bone. He was covered in sores and so thin his ribs could be counted through his shirt. His hair had mostly fallen out from lack of nutrition and his teeth were loose and discoloured. He didn't talk about his life in the army, only to say he'd been with some good chaps, who became his best mates. Lying next to Rosemary on the first night home, bathed and fed, he shook with fear as memories of the dark, wet nights in the trenches haunted his dreams. His wife took him in her arms and held him close, until her warmth and serenity calmed his terrors and eased his troubled mind.

John worried constantly about his younger brother, William. There had been only two postcards from him in the past twelve months, sending his love to his family. *God, keep him safe*, muttered John under his breath.

May's husband, George, was with a cavalry unit somewhere, and John Jenkins knew from his own war experience that the horse regiments sustained more than average death and injury. The days of using horses in warfare were coming to an end as weapons became more destructive—shells exploding into the middle of a group of horses did untold damage to animals and riders alike. May lived in fear every day of receiving news that George would not be coming home.

Slowly John recovered from his injuries and, with the tender care of his wife, gained weight. He didn't have the same mobility in his left shoulder and arm, but returned to his job as a plate maker with a new appreciation of the friendly atmosphere. At home, John was never happier than when Enid, Nancy, Harry and baby Nora were playing at his feet. There had been so many dark nights, filled with fear, when he thought he would never see them again.

Annie walked to her brother's house with Nora several times each week, and John became the number one "tester" for Thomas' sweet creations.

"This is a good one, Annie," John said, sucking heartily on the latest invention. "Lovely texture. The mint and liquorice together are delicious. Wait! There's a soft centre!"

John rolled his eyes and smiled as he chewed on the sweet.

"This is the best Tom's made, Annie," he finally said when he had swallowed the last of the treat. "I'd give this top marks."

When several more friends and family had tried the latest concoction, with very favourable reviews, Thomas asked Annie to take a batch of sweets to The Pear Drop for sale to the public. Annie visited Florence frequently to chat about any upcoming plans for a future with William, and pick up wine gums for her husband. Soon the new sweets were displayed in a freshly washed jar and had a prime place on the middle shelf behind the counter.

Thomas couldn't make enough of the new sweets, now

named Gardner's Humbugs, in the small back kitchen at home. He borrowed money to buy a piece of land facing the Alhambra Cinema, and built a small factory. Thomas left his job at the pottery factory and hired three people to work with him, and soon they were manufacturing five different types of sweets, which were sold in all the sweet shops in North Staffordshire. Annie's experience was invaluable as she managed the sales and promotion side of the business.

"It's the obvious next step, Thomas," Annie said, as they sat in the garden of their new home, enjoying the sunset and watching Nora kick a ball around the large lawn. "It would be a dream come true for me. The Pear Drop was where we met. It's where my mam and dad met. Our family 'as the 'istory of it in our bones. Albert Cresswell still owns it, and 'e always liked me. I think we're in a position to offer 'im a good price for the shop. What do you think?"

"I don't want you working too hard, Annie," answered Thomas slowly. "You already do so much with the factory's business, the shop would be a lot of extra time away from home."

"I wouldn't actually work there," explained Annie. "Florence does a very good job, although we may 'ave to 'ire somebody else part time, particularly on Fridays and Saturdays, when it's busy. It would be a good investment for us, especially as we expand the sweet manufacturing side of things. We could try out all our new products before we supply the other shops."

"Very well," Thomas agreed. "Talk to Albert and make him a reasonable offer of £1,000. That will give us room to move if he counteracts the offer."

Thomas rose from his chair and knelt in front of his wife, holding her hand and smiling into her eyes.

"I know this means a lot to you, Annie. I hope it works out."

He kissed her gently before running across the lawn to join Nora.

Albert Cresswell was more than happy with Annie's proposal and offer to buy The Pear Drop. Since she had left to have her baby, he had been forced to take more responsibility for the supplies and maintenance of the little shop. He counted himself fortunate that Florence was such an efficient employee, but he jumped at the chance to be rid of the management of the shop, for a very decent price.

"What do you think, John?" asked Annie, plopping down a bag of humbugs on the kitchen table in front of him. "We bought the sweet shop from Mr Cresswell. You'll never be short of your favourite sweets now."

"Bought the sweet shop," echoed John. "That's a bit of 'istory, if you like. That old shop 'as been part of our family for many a long year. Our mam will be smiling down on you from 'eaven."

Margaret Jenkins continued to smile on Annie. Within a year, Gardner's Humbugs were in high demand all over the midlands and northern England. The factory expanded to employ ten people, and Annie spent many hours working on promotion, sales and keeping the accounts in order. Nora happily followed her mother around, accompanied by a large red bag full of her favourite books and toys, as Annie spent her days happily promoting Gardner's sweets, as well as supervising The Pear Drop, which was more popular than ever with the addition of the free tastes of "New Creations." Although Britain was embroiled in the fourth year of war, it seemed people always had a few pennies to spend on sweets —treats for the children in an otherwise depressed and dismal world.

Since America had entered the war in April of 1917, the allies had gained ground and now the German army was in full retreat. Signs that the Great War was coming to an end were evident, and every parent, sibling, sweetheart and child who had a loved one in the armed forces prayed for their safe return. A postcard from George in September of 1918 confirmed he was still alive, and May held onto her dream that he would be home soon.

Nobody had heard from young William for more than a year, and the family remained cautiously optimistic that no news was good news and hoped he would be returned to them when the war ended.

CHAPTER 33

HOMECOMING

Early in December 1918, May received notification from George's regiment that they had landed on the south coast of England. She had no idea how long it would take for her husband to make the journey home, but she prepared for his homecoming every day— baking fresh bread, covering the kitchen table with a clean tablecloth, beating the rugs, cleaning the front step until it shone, folding and refolding the knitted blanket on the back of George's favourite chair by the fire.

Little Harry was turning five years old and didn't remember his dad. May showed him the small framed picture of their wedding every day so that the little boy would recognize George when he came home.

It was still dark when May was suddenly woken by a noise in the backyard. She peered through the window through the fine mist of sleet, but everything was in shadows. As she was about to turn from the window, a dark figure crept out of the outside lav and stood under the eaves of the back kitchen roof.

May wrapped herself in a blanket, pushed her feet into

her boots and crept down the stairs. Maybe if she lit a lamp in the kitchen, the stranger would be scared away. As soon as the lamp was lit, May heard a gentle knocking on the back door, and froze in fear. The stranger hadn't been scared away —he was trying to get into the house. May didn't move to answer the door right away, but when the knocking persisted, she cautiously moved to the back door.

"Who is there?" May asked in the strongest voice she could muster.

"Let me in," the hoarse whisper pleaded. "It's George."

May scrambled with the lock in a frenzy to open the door. The icy blast of sleet took her breath away as she flung the door wide to let her husband in.

George almost fell as he tottered into the house. He was soaked through and cold as ice. May helped him into the kitchen and sat him in his chair. She took the blanket from around her shoulders and draped it around George's cold frame before turning her attention to lighting a fire.

Only when the flames were licking the coal and warming up the room did May turn to her husband with her eyes full of tears.

"Oh, George. Look at you," she murmured. "Let's 'ave you out of those wet clothes and get you warmed up."

George sat very still, his eyes never leaving May's face. He was so tired. So cold. So hungry. He didn't know what to say to his wife.

"I have fleas," he finally said. "Best I strip off in the back yard. My uniform should be burnt."

It took a great deal of effort for the soldier to go back outside and take off all his clothes. Leaving them in a pile outside the back door, he wrapped the blanket tightly around his frail body before trudging back into the warm kitchen.

May bustled around the kitchen, making tea and slices of bread and lard for the hungry soldier. She boiled and reboiled the kettle with enough water to fill the wash tub so that George could stand in the warm water and soap himself clean of the mud and fleas. May soaped his back and his hair, not even caring that he was naked. George smiled as he felt his wife's hands on his back and the warmth of the fire and water warming up his body. He was so grateful to be home, away from the mud and death of the trenches in France.

"Tell me 'ow you got 'ome," May said.

"It was a long journey," George replied, towelling himself down and dressing in the clothes May had found for him. "A boat from France, full of soldiers. All of us 'ungry and worn out. Then three trains, still full of soldiers. We 'ad nothing to eat for days it feels like. I got into the station after midnight and walked 'ome. Didn't want to wake you up, so I slept in the backyard."

May looked horrified.

"You should 'ave woken me up, George," she said. "Trying to sleep in the backyard with the sleet coming down on you."

"Better than the trenches," muttered George.

Clean and rid of fleas, George could finally take May, still dressed only in her nightgown, into his arms. He had dreamed of holding her like this for many months and the tears choked his throat as he held her close.

Harry came down the stairs and into the kitchen.

"Mam, Mam," cried Harry running over to cling onto May's legs from behind, fear in his voice as he looked up at his mother and the stranger who held her in his arms.

"It's all right 'arry," consoled May through her tears. "This is your dad, 'ome from the war."

Harry stayed cautiously behind his mother's legs and watched the strange man sit in his dad's chair.

"Look at you, young 'arry," smiled George. "Come on over 'ere my boy. Let me take a good look at you."

"Come on, 'arry," coaxed May, holding Harry's hand and

leading him to face his father. "Don't be shy. It's your dad. He's come 'ome to us."

Harry slowly crept towards the stranger, his eyes wide and his hand firmly holding onto his mother. George reached to touch his son's hair, his cheek, his shoulder. Then both Harry and May were in his lap, hugging him and covering his face with kisses. George held onto his precious family and wept silent tears of joy. The thought of coming home to this had kept him alive at the worst of times. The image of his lovely wife and growing son had filled his dreams at night, only to be disturbed by the sound of shells exploding around him. This was real! This wasn't a dream!

John and Rosemary wrote to William's regiment to try to find him. They feared the worst, having heard nothing from him for so long. The chaos of tracing a missing soldier wasn't an easy task, explained the reply to their enquiry. William Jenkins had been in the battle of the Somme, where casualties numbered in the thousands. Many soldiers had died, some shelled so badly that there was no identification, not even dog tags. Badly wounded men had been evacuated to field hospitals, but records were difficult to keep when the stream of wounded never stopped and the bodies of the dead lay in piles waiting to be buried.

The family continued to wait.

"John," Rosemary called, waving a letter over her head as she ran into the kitchen. The envelope was wrinkled and dirty and the address written in a shaky, uneven manner.

John tore open the envelope. A single sheet of paper was enclosed with very few words written on it.

I am alive. In a hospital in North London. Don't remember what happened to me in France. The doc says I'll be going home soon.

Love, William

John and Rosemary held each other close and thanked God for the good news. They had prayed every day for so many months, and had almost given up hope. Their brother was alive and would soon be home again, and they were forever grateful.

Two weeks later a telegram arrived for John, telling him to meet William at the train station the following Saturday. The entire family gathered at John and Rosemary's house to await the return of their young brother. Annie and Thomas provided enough food to feed a small army, and the sisters busied themselves with dressing up the tiny house with streamers and "WELCOME HOME" signs.

John asked his friend, Arthur Mellor, to drive him to the station in his buggy. He was there an hour before the train was due, pacing up and down as the minutes slowly ticked by.

Soldiers returning home poured onto the platform of Longton Station, met by their loved ones with tears and hugs. John didn't see William among them, but as the crowd moved towards the exit stairs, he saw other soldiers being helped from the train. Men who had been in their prime of life when the war began, were coming home blind, or maimed. John walked along the platform, looking into each man's face. Wives and mothers gathered the wounded young men into their arms and held them close—happy to have them home.

John saw his brother as he was helped down the steps of the train by two strong soldiers. His face was the same, although so much thinner. The soldiers handed him crutches so that he could support himself on his one leg. John swallowed the lump in his throat before running the last few steps to embrace his younger brother, almost knocking him over as he pulled William into his arms. He felt so frail. Yet he was alive, and John was overcome with love for the boy who had gone to war, and the man who had returned scarred and maimed.

There was no way of warning the family who waited at the house in Newhall Road. Everybody bore the shock of seeing William at the same time. Some cried, some were silent, some ran to hug him, some turned away to hide their tears.

"I am so lucky," William whispered. "To be alive and 'ave such a family to come 'ome to."

The Jenkins family ate and drank and celebrated. They thanked God for the safe return of their brother. George had a special reason to be thankful that day—he had returned with no injuries, and he could hardly bear it that his young brother-in-law had lost a leg.

Slowly the two soldiers picked up the pieces of their lives. John welcomed George back to the factory to sit beside him as a plate maker, and William returned to work at the print shop where his father had worked, learning to type set, so that he could sit down. He could travel to work by bus, and only had to walk, with the aid of crutches, the short distance to the high street from his home with John and Rosemary.

Tragedy, however, wasn't saved for only a war. An ordinary day could turn into a nightmare.

Three of the men in the Jenkins family had gone to war, and three had returned. How blessed they felt. Now life would return to the pre-war days.

Rosemary was alone in the house on a fine Monday morning when a policeman came to tell her John had been killed by a bus.

Killed in peace time, innocently crossing the street. Head of the family since Mam and Dad had died, John was the anchor that held them all together. Their refuge in times of trouble. Their confidante and mentor. There was no other sibling to step into his place. None other as kind or considerate as John. He was the eldest son and the family patriarch. His nine living siblings gathered together at the house where they were all born and sat like stones, trying to absorb the harsh reality of losing him.

Annie broke the silence.

"There will be no 'ardship for Rosemary and the girls. Thomas and I will make sure they 'ave everything they need," she said quietly. "William 'as a steady job at the printing company and Charlie is working 'ard at the Aynsley factory. Anything we can do to ease their burden, we will do."

The others nodded their heads in agreement. Even though they all had their own homes and families to tend, and for most money was scarce, they would never see Rosemary, Enid and Nancy struggle.

Although Annie wasn't the oldest sister, she fell naturally into place as head of the Jenkins clan. Her early years of grief had taught her to be confident and empathetic, and her marriage to Thomas gave her an affluence she never dreamed of. She comforted them, listened to them, gave advice, loaned or gave them money to help them over a bad spot. She would never replace John, but she loved her brothers and sisters with a passion, and never tired of their presence in her life.

❦

The Jenkins family changed greatly during the following three years. Annie supervised them all like a mother hen taking care of her brood. She mourned with them as they buried two beloved sisters, Helen and Mary-Jane, who both died during childbirth, leaving two sons to be raised by their fathers. She travelled to Lancashire with Sarah and her husband Ernest, to help them settle into a new home with their growing family of six children; they would have four more in the next five years. She stayed with May during her confinements and helped the midwife deliver, first Frederick and two years later Margaret.

The tradition of Sunday dinner after chapel continued. Annie hosted the ever-increasing numbers in her large, comfortable house, where there were chairs enough for all the adults and a place around the low tables for every child to find a place to squat and eat.

Annie sat in the front pew of the chapel when William married Florence, and helped Charles realize his wedding dream of marrying his sweetheart, Alice.

Annie helped Alice, whose parents were both deceased, plan every aspect of her wedding day. She delighted in buying the wedding dress and a new suit for young Charles. Under Annie's supervision the chapel was decorated with flowers and satin bows, with all the sisters working together to provide enough food to feed a small army.

"A toast to Charlie and Alice," Thomas Gardner boomed, raising his glass of blackcurrant juice to salute the bride and groom. "May they be blessed in their life together."

Charles beamed with delight, and held his new bride close. He was the last of the family to wed, and was keenly aware of the love and nurture his older sisters had lavished on him over the years. He kissed Alice on her lips, before presenting each sister with a single red hand-painted china rose, packed carefully in a silver box lined with soft cotton wool.

As Annie took her rose, she thought about her mother and father. Through all the joys and sorrows, Margaret and Jacob Jenkins' spirits were a very real presence. With the whole family gathered for the wedding celebration, their mother and father were still the invisible force that held them together.

For much of the population, however, life after the Great War wasn't easy. It was difficult and challenging. Work was scarce and wages were low. Many of the pottery factories couldn't keep their workers in full-time work and the work-force struggled to make ends meet. The plate-makers at the Foley factory were cut to four days a week, and further reduced to three days as the recession worsened.

"May, you need 'elp," Annie said to her sister, as she looked around at the sparse food on the kitchen table, and the evidence of the tub of lard beside the home-made bread, which meant there was no money for butter. "Tell George to come to the 'ouse tonight, and ask Thomas for food stamps. I know 'e would be 'appy to help you out."

"George would never ask, Annie," said May quietly. She knew her proud husband well, and even with three children to feed, he wouldn't accept charity, especially from his wealthy brother-in-law. "We'll be all right. I was going to ask if I could get some work at the factory," May continued. "Even a few 'ours a week would be a help."

Although it pained Annie to see her sister in such dire circumstances, she found her work washing bottles two mornings each week, while Harry was at school. May dropped off Frederick and Margaret at Annie's house while she worked. It made the difference between lard and butter.

In 1922 Thomas was elected to city council. The sweet factory was successful and busy, and Thomas hired a production manager to free up his time for council meetings and sales conventions.

Thomas was away from the factory for days sometimes. Official business as a city councillor took up much of his time, especially because he was such a conscientious man, who gave his best to everything he did.

Annie went to the factory on Monday and Friday mornings to open and reply to mail, process orders, and look over the accounts.

From the first day of Isaac Williamson's job as production manager, Annie noticed the resemblance. The image of her first love, Daniel, was burned into her memory, and when Isaac walked into the factory and strode across the room and into the office, Annie felt the breath leave her body. The same colouring, the same eyes, the long eyelashes, the straight nose, the tall, slender build, and the confidant walk.

Annie gathered her senses and looked down at the ledger she was studying.

"Annie, there you are," greeted Thomas from behind his new manager. "Let me introduce you to our new production manager, Isaac Williamson. This is my wonderful wife, Annie, who knows more about this business than I do."

"I'm pleased to meet you," Isaac said, looking into Annie's eyes, as she felt the warmth creeping into her face.

Annie shook the hand he held out and nodded her greeting, before going back to her books.

What is the matter with me? I have to pull myself together. He does look like Daniel, but I've been married to Thomas for seven years. This young man has nothing to do with me. Why am I getting so hot and bothered? I wish he wouldn't stand so close to my chair. I can feel the warmth of him, just like I did with Daniel. Stop this now! Look at the ledger.

Thomas took Isaac on a factory tour, and Annie breathed a sigh of relief.

CHAPTER 35

THE BARN

Falling in love is often a mystery to the person afflicted. Annie loved her husband. She loved her daughter. She loved her life. But she couldn't stop thinking about Isaac Williamson.

Sleep became unattainable. Food unimportant. Annie daydreamed through the days, with the image of Daniel, morphed into Isaac, floating in and out of her mind. She avoided him every time she went to the factory, often taking the ledger books home instead of staying in the office. However, she did have to meet with him occasionally to discuss production. Fortunately, Thomas had been part of those discussions for Isaac's first six weeks.

The city council called a meeting for the first Monday in September of 1922. Isaac and Annie were alone for the first time, and the tension between them was palpable. They went over new orders together and entered them into the factory log, with Isaac working on the schedule for production. The Gardner Humbug was still a favourite product and the orders kept pouring in from all over the midlands and northern England.

Annie had barely spoken a word all morning.

"Excuse me, Annie," Isaac ventured at last, trying to break the tension he felt. "Do you not like me?"

Annie's eyes were guarded as she met his gaze from the desk across the room.

"I like you," Annie answered. "But I don't really know you. We both 'ave work to do, so social conversation isn't appropriate."

Annie quickly returned to answering several enquiries that had come in that morning's mail.

"If we're going to work together, I believe we may as well try to be at least civil to each other," continued Isaac. "It feels uncomfortable to sit in the same room with somebody and have no conversation. Why don't we set our work aside for a while and get to know each other better. I think it may ease the tension."

Annie's heart beat rapidly. She didn't want to know him better. She wanted to leave and go home and feel safe, but Isaac had already laid down his pen and walked over to sit on the edge of her desk.

"I'll start," he said, smiling down at her. "I'm twenty six years of age, born in Cheshire, unmarried, parents still alive, two sisters—one married, one living with my parents. I studied accounting and manufacturing of cloth before working in the rag trade for the past five years. I play football every Saturday with a local team, love to swim, walk and read when I have the time, and I'm nowhere near as scary as you seem to give me credit for."

After his speech, Isaac threw back his head and laughed.

"Now your turn. What don't I know about you, Annie?"

Annie had no intention of giving him a biography of herself. She answered in stilted sentences.

"Married to Thomas for seven years, 'ave one daughter, nine siblings, parents are both deceased."

She met his eyes and held the gaze too long. Her cheeks burned and she rose from her desk to escape, but found herself rooted to the spot, swallowing hard to try to gain control of her emotions.

"What do you like to do in your spare time?" Isaac asked.

There was no way out.

"I read books, I like to draw—mostly flowers, I spend time with my large family, and occasionally, when there's time, I also enjoy walking, especially in the countryside."

Annie shouldn't have agreed to go on a walk with the production manager, but she did. Before the end of September she walked every Monday and Friday after the morning's work, unless Thomas happened to be at the factory. Annie left, as usual, at noon. Isaac left a half hour later for an extended lunch, feigning meetings with customers, or an appointment at the bank. Annie waited at a designated spot for Isaac to pick her up in his automobile, and they drove the few miles until they were away from the town and deep in the country lanes.

For Annie the walks were no frivolous encounters. She felt a physical passion for Isaac she hadn't experienced since her years with Daniel. She loved Thomas dearly, and was riddled with guilt that she was deceiving him, but her desire for Isaac overwhelmed her. He was like a magnet drawing her closer and closer, and she felt helpless to pull back.

Isaac had been in love before, but never like this. This was a dangerous love—the boss's wife! What was he thinking? That was the point—he wasn't thinking. Annie, with her wild red curls, white skin, cherry lips, beautiful eyes and slender figure, had driven away his common sense. Her presence had hit him in the pit of his stomach the first day he saw her, and he risked his job and future to be near her.

They had no opportunity for a walk for almost a month,

with Thomas working in the office. The first Monday the boss wasn't at work they headed into the country. As they walked side by side, they didn't speak and maintained their distance. They sensed their closeness, but didn't touch each other. The few inches that separated them was charged with an energy they could both feel. Rain began with a sprinkling of soft mist, which turned into a steady shower. The dark clouds overhead threatened heavier rain and Isaac took off his jacket and draped it over Annie's shoulders to protect her. There was a deserted barn in the next field and they both made a run for it, splashing through deep furrows. The barn was dry and warm, with straw piled on the floor. The perfect place to wait out the storm.

Isaac and Annie sat on a straw bale watching the rain pour in torrents. They were lucky to have found shelter before the deluge began in earnest. Unable to resist the privacy of the secluded island amid the torrents of water, Isaac knelt in front of Annie and took her hands in his.

"Annie, I have never loved anybody like I love you," he whispered. "You have enchanted me, and I can think of nothing else. It's wrong to feel this way about you, I know, and I feel ashamed. Yet I am compelled to love you."

"Being close to you takes my breath away," Annie admitted. "I shouldn't even be 'ere with you, but right now I would rather be 'ere than anywhere in the world."

She slid down from the straw bale and knelt on the soft straw-covered ground facing Isaac. She brushed his lips with her own, inviting him to kiss her. His lips sealed hers in a passionate embrace, his tongue pressed into her mouth, his whole body tense as he gathered her into his arms. Their clothes were cast aside, and their most intimate desires were fulfilled as their bodies joined together. Annie's back arched with pleasure, as Isaac moved inside her. Over far too quickly, they both collapsed onto the straw, panting for breath, and savouring the warmth that spread over their bodies despite the cool rain outside.

When the rain had abated, the two lovers hurried to Isaac's automobile. He had been gone from the factory for far too long, and Annie had to pick up Nora from school. The reality of what they had done hit them both as they drove along the lanes back to town. Annie, full of remorse for having betrayed her husband, Isaac equally guilty for his part in the tryst. Both with regrets that they had defied their principles and followed their hearts' desire.

On the following Monday morning a letter addressed to Thomas sat in the middle of the office desk. It was Isaac's resignation. He had decided to return to Cheshire and didn't plan to return.

CHAPTER 36
SURPRISE

Love is sometimes a fleeting moment in time. The rainy afternoon in the barn was Annie's fleeting moment, and she treasured the memory of making love in the straw with Isaac. He was so like her beloved Daniel.

Thomas never suspected, but noticed that his wife was unusually quiet and thoughtful, and not responsive to his amorous advances, which were infrequent anyway. He was hopeful that his gregarious, fun-loving wife would overcome this unusual phase soon, and be restored to her former happy-go-lucky self.

Mr Salt, a middle aged man who had management experience with Frys Chocolate Factory in Bristol, was hired to fill Isaac Williamson's position. He moved, with his wife and family of four, to take on the position of production manager at the Gardner Factory.

"Mr Salt seems better suited to our ways, doesn't he, Annie?" observed Thomas Gardner as they sat by the fire after tea. "Isaac was too young and inexperienced. I think that's why he gave notice so abruptly and left without a word. I think he was a bit out of his depth trying to run the factory. Mr Salt has years of experience in the chocolate industry, which is not unlike ours, and I believe we are lucky to have him working for us."

"I agree, Thomas. A much better fit," Annie answered, staring into the fire, which hid the glow on her cheeks.

By the beginning of December Annie was certain she was pregnant. She hadn't had a period for three months, her breasts were swollen and sore, and she had been nauseated most mornings for weeks. How would she convince Thomas that the child she was carrying was his? After Nora was born, she had sought her husband's assurance that there would be no more children, and Thomas had obliged by using a contraceptive on the rare occasions they came together as man and wife.

Annie struggled to remember the last time Thomas had approached her for sex. Surely it was more than three months ago. Certainly not since the rainy afternoon in the barn. It was Isaac's baby she was carrying, and the adultery she had committed would haunt her forever. She would have to tell Thomas about the baby soon, before it was noticed by everybody.

Sitting at the kitchen table on a cold Friday evening, enjoying the hearty beef stew she had made that afternoon, Annie looked at her husband's contented face as he dipped crusty bread into the rich gravy. Nora had been excused already, and had gone outside to play with two of her cousins.

"Thomas, I have something important to tell you," Annie began, hesitating now the time had come to divulge her secret. "Do you remember back in September, when Nora stayed at Rosemary's overnight and we went to bed early and made love? I thought then that there was a problem, because it just didn't feel right afterwards. I didn't say anything at the time, but I worried the condom 'ad broken."

She paused, gulping from her mug of tea to steady her nerves. She never lied, especially not to Thomas. He had paused with the bread half way to his mouth and was staring at her amazed.

"I assumed correctly," Annie continued. "I'm pregnant, Thomas."

"Having a baby? Are you sure?" Thomas asked, dropping the bread into the bowl, and leaning forward to look into his wife's eyes, as though the answer was written there.

"I'm sure," answered Annie quietly.

"Annie." Thomas rose from his chair and knelt beside his wife. "I'm sorry. I know you didn't want another child. I feel responsible."

"No, no, don't Thomas," Annie responded, helping her husband to his feet. "It's all right. I'm not upset, really. In fact I'm quite excited. It will be good for Nora to 'ave a younger sibling."

Thomas drew his wife close to him and kissed her lovingly. It was unexpected news, but he felt a glow of happiness as he absorbed the fact that he was to be a father again. He realized that he and Annie had drifted apart recently, with the factory and the city council taking up so much of his time, but he promised himself that he would be home more and work hard to assure his family that they came first in his life.

Annie leaned her head on her husband's shoulder and sighed with relief. He would never know that the baby wasn't his. Thomas was a dear man, who loved her and she would never hurt him. She was ashamed of her secret tryst with Isaac, yet knew she wouldn't have made a different decision. The physical attraction to him was too great to resist, and she would always hold the memory of it in her heart.

"Well now," smiled Thomas, holding Annie at arm's length. "We have to tell Nora and the rest of the family. What a surprise it will be."

The announcement was made after chapel the following Sunday afternoon when everybody was gathered at the Gardner house. It was the week before Christmas and the children had all been involved in a Christmas Pageant, with lots of singing, costumes and even a real live "baby Jesus."

The sisters gathered around Annie, hugging her and professing they all knew just by the look of her. Thomas glowed with pride, as he stood watching the family shower their congratulations and love on Annie. He was getting on in years, but the anticipation of a new baby gave him a new lease on life, and he felt twenty years younger.

The sweet factory had never been more profitable. The Pear Drop was popular and busy, with everybody buying for Christmas. Gardner Humbugs were in high demand everywhere, even as far away as London. Life for Thomas Gardner was about as good as it could get.

CHAPTER 37
ISAAC'S CHILD

Annie took great pleasure in preparing for her next baby. This time she gathered the layette and confinement equipment together herself, and even managed to sew and embroider a beautiful blanket for the pram. Time flew by and June arrived with a flurry of excitement.

The Gardner house was in turmoil, as a parade of sisters arrived one after the other, followed by Sophie Blenkinsop, the midwife who had attended Annie eight years before. Eight years was a long time to go between babies. Most families had a new baby every couple of years, and each birth became easier and quicker. Not so with this baby. The labour was long and difficult.

Nora was dispatched to Rosemary's house early in the morning to spend the day with Enid and Nancy, her grown up cousins. Neither girl had married, and still lived with their mother in the little house on Newhall Road. May dropped off Frederick and Margaret at the house before hurrying to join her sisters for the birth of Annie's baby.

Enid and Nancy delighted in their young cousins and never tired of spending time with them.

The sisters persuaded Thomas to go to the factory, out of the way. No good having him sitting about in the house waiting. They would let him know when to come home. Thomas didn't need much persuading, as being in the house with so many helpful women was more than his nerves could bear. He would rather make humbugs.

The kitchen was a hive of activity, with sisters making bread, scones and pots of stew to feed the family over the next several days. Many pots of tea were brewed and drank during the long day of waiting. Annie was supplied with every need, as she sat in the birthing bed in the parlour downstairs propped up on lacy pillows as though she were a queen.

After checking how far the labour had progressed, Sophie left to attend another birth a few miles away, speeding along on her bicycle in the warm sunshine, humming a tune to herself. She was doing the work she loved to do, and today there would be two babies to deliver into the world. Mrs Dixon's baby would come quickly, it being her fifth, and she would have lots of time left to speed back to Annie's to help her give birth.

The sisters were having a great time together visiting, baking and taking care of Annie. They took turns sitting beside the bed, holding Annie's hand, rubbing her back, wiping her head with a cool cloth. May was beside her when Annie screamed out in pain. Until then she had been in control of each contraction, breathing through it with gritted teeth, but managing to stay calm. Now the agony was too great and she clutched at May's hand in desperation.

"'elp me, May," she gasped. "It's too much."

Daisy and Lizzie came running into the parlour, worried

frowns on their faces. Rosemary followed them. It had been several hours since Sophie had left.

Rosemary calmly took Annie's hand in her own.

"Annie, dear Annie," she said gently. "Be brave and strong. Your baby will soon be born, and we are all 'ere to help you."

Another terrible spasm of pain shot through Annie, sending both her arms flying above her head to grip the bed railings. The sisters exchanged looks with concern.

"Annie, I'm going to check on the baby, if that's all right," Rosemary said.

There was no response from Annie, only a feeble whimper.

Rosemary pulled Annie's nightgown over her knees and asked her to bend her legs. A circle of wet hair was visible between Annie's legs. The midwife wasn't going to get back in time.

Rosemary, May and Lizzie had birthed babies of their own, but never without a midwife. Sophie had taken her bag with her with all the necessary equipment for cutting the cord, but they could improvise. Rosemary sent Lizzie and Daisy to find scissors, string, warm water, towels and anything else they thought would be helpful.

Rosemary always took charge in stressful situations. She was the oldest, and she exuded an air of quiet confidence, which helped everybody remain calm.

"All right, my dear," she instructed Annie. "The baby is ready to be born. Big push with the next pain. God is with us, and is watching over this little one. Let's do this, now."

The room was still. None of them were breathing, waiting for the next pain—then it was loud and chaotic as Annie screamed and pushed and Rosemary watched for the baby's head to appear. It took five more excruciating pushes to deliver the head, and then a minute later the baby slid away in a gush of water, into Rosemary's waiting hands.

May and Daisy were at the ready with scissors and string and the baby was carefully detached from the mother. May wiped the baby with a clean towel as the first lustrous cries were heard.

"A girl!" May announced, holding her up for Annie to see. "She's yours all right. Look at the mass of red fuzz on 'er 'ead."

Sophie ran into the parlour, soaked from a sudden rain shower, and out of breath from cycling so hard from Mrs Dixon's house.

"I'm so sorry, Mrs Gardner. I thought I'd be back here before now, but it was a breach birth and took much longer than usual." Then as she saw the baby, Sophie was more upset. "Oh my dear! I didn't even make it in time."

Sophie ripped off her sodden raincoat, washed her hands in the warm soapy water, and took the baby gently from May.

"Let me check her out right away. She is wonderful. Well done. She looks and sounds healthy and strong. You were in good hands with your sisters, Annie."

Sophie took over and checked Annie, delivered the placenta, and soon had Annie comfortable and smiling. She then bathed the tiny baby girl and dressed her in her layette, bundling her in a soft blanket and laying her in the crook of her mother's arm.

Lizzie had already gone to tell Thomas the good news, and he soon hurried into the parlour to see his wife and daughter. Annie searched her baby's face for signs of any inherited likeness to Isaac, but with the red hair taking all the attention, it was clear to see this baby had Annie's genes.

Rosemary placed the tiny bundle into Thomas' arm and gave him a hug.

"Here she is, Thomas," she said happily. "Another girl for you. Isn't she a beauty?"

Thomas gazed down at the round face and cherry lips and shock of red fuzz in adoration.

"As beautiful as her mother," he said, smiling at Annie. "I am truly the luckiest man in the world."

"What will you call her?" asked May.

"We already have a name picked out for her," said Thomas. "Kathleen it will be, but we'll call her Kathy. Isn't that right, my love?"

Annie nodded. This would be a very special child to her. Her love child. She would be the child she never had with Daniel. Every day this baby would remind her of the two men she had completely given her heart to. Neither of them her husband.

CHAPTER 38

GARDNER GIRLS

The Gardner girls grew up with every privilege compared with their poorer cousins. They had a large house, a garden to play in, they took piano lessons, they were always dressed very finely, and there was always a plentiful amount of food. Their kitchen had a pantry, where one whole shelf was stocked with sweet jars that the girls could help themselves to whenever they liked, except before tea.

Annie didn't help at the factory after Kathy was born, not wanting to miss one day of her daughter's childhood. She doted on the little girl, spoiling her with toys and gifts, and lavishing her with affection.

Both girls looked like their mother, inheriting her red curly hair, but there was something special about Kathy. She had hazel eyes surrounded by thick lashes, which gave her a surreal quality. Being eight years younger than her sister, Nora, they didn't have a lot in common. Nora resented the attention heaped on her younger sister. She was the talented one, with a gift for music, and played piano effortlessly, yet her mother hardly seemed to notice. As Kathy grew up, she had to be forced to practice and never accomplished the heights of musicality her sister naturally had. Even so, their mother would reward Kathy's efforts with gifts—a new hat, a kitten, a trip to the theatre.

Thomas was mystified by Annie's apparent adoration of their younger daughter. She had adored Nora as a little girl, until Kathy was born. Surely a mother loved all her children equally. Although Annie was never cruel or unkind to her firstborn, and provided for all her needs, she did not nurture her. She didn't sit next to her, or touch her. She didn't tuck her in at bedtime or brush her hair. Thomas convinced himself it was only because of the age difference between the girls. He tried to compensate for Annie's indifference by giving Nora extra attention when he was at home.

Annie was determined Kathy would become an even better pianist than her sister, if she practiced enough. Every day, after school, Kathy would have to sit at the dreaded piano and run through scales and arpeggios until her fingers ached. Mother would sit beside her—encouraging her.

The only relief Kathy had from her mother's watchful, doting eye, was on Sunday afternoons after chapel, when the aunties, uncles and cousins came to their house for lunch, and she was allowed to go out into their large garden to play. If Annie could have had her way, she would have gone outside too, to watch her darling girl, but she had to play the host and entertain her family.

"It's not natural," whispered May to her sister Daisy, as they sat sipping tea at Annie's house. "The way she follows that girl around, buying 'er presents all the time, never giving 'er any time alone. I don't know what she's thinking."

"It's only because she was a surprise baby," answered Daisy. "She didn't think she'd 'ave another after Nora, and don't forget she lost those two babies years ago. I think that plays on 'er mind."

"Maybe that's it," agreed May. "I swear that girl won't grow up normal with all the attention she gets."

The aunties all had an opinion about raising children. Annie and her sisters had watched their mother raise ten children with a serenity of spirit they each strived to equal. Even the women their brothers chose as partners had the attributes of Margaret: loving, kind, caring and nurturing. Every child was treated with respect and given the same attention and opportunity. But in Annie's dealings with her daughters, her mother's examples were ignored, as she became more and more besotted with Kathy.

"I'll only be a minute," Annie said, heading for the back door into the garden. "I'm just going to check on the children. See if they need anything."

"Annie," May said in a calm but firm voice, "They are fine. I can see them through the window running around and 'aving a fine time. The older girls are out there playing with them. Stay in 'ere with us and leave them alone."

"Well," hesitated Annie, "I don't feel good about leaving them outside without an adult to supervise. You never know what they'll get up to out there."

"Come on, my dear," Rosemary said, taking Annie's hand and leading her back to the table. "'ave another cup of tea. They're good children. They're only playing. Don't worry so much."

Annie sat and sipped her tea with one eye on the window, following the red curls as they bounced back and forth across the garden, watching her daughter's face as she laughed and squealed. Her thoughts wandered to the man she had loved.

I wish you could see her, Isaac. She's so beautiful. She has your hazel eyes, though nobody seems to have noticed, and your lovely thick, long eyelashes. She will be tall, like you. She is so splendid in every way and I treasure her beyond everything else. Every day she reminds me of how precious love is, even a brief encounter like ours. Then I think back to Daniel—the all too few years we spent together. My first love; my forever love. Somehow when I look at Kathy, Daniel is always there in the background.

Annie shook her head to scatter the daydreams and put down her cup and saucer before her sisters could see the tremor in her hand. Her nerves were always on edge if Kathy wasn't in close proximity.

During the week, when Kathy was in school, Annie would linger around the school after dropping her daughter off in the playground to line up with her class. She had gone through the same ritual every day since Kathy began class one at the Uttoxeter Road Primary School. Annie walked up and down outside the wall that divided the playground from the public pavement, watching Kathy's class file into the building. Once inside, Annie stood at the railing gazing at the big brown brick building, imagining her little girl sitting at her desk, her chubby fingers curling around her stick of chalk as she worked to form letters on the slate before her.

Several times, during those first few months, Annie had gone into the school to peek into the class through the glass panel in the door, only to be escorted out of the building by the principal, who assured her that her daughter was in good hands.

At the end of each day Annie was always the first mother at the school—sometimes a whole hour before classes ended. Most of the children had no parent waiting for them, but ran home with groups of friends, all laughing and chasing each other down the street. Kathy always came out of school with her head bowed, and quietly walked up to her mother, who took her hand for the walk home.

Kathy wished and wished that her mother would stay at home so that she could run down the street with the other children.

CHAPTER 39
ALL THAT JAZZ

As the years went by, Nora grew more and more estranged from her mother, and by the time she was sixteen she was ready to leave home. She applied to the London College of Music and left to study piano in the autumn of 1931.

Thomas was devastated about his daughter's decision to leave home and move to London. The capital city was no place for a young girl with no experience of life. He begged her to reconsider, but Nora's mind was made up. She could no longer live in a house where every waking moment was spent watching her mother lavish all her attention on her younger sister.

Thomas stepped in to find her a respectable place to live with a colleague's aunt, who lived only two tube stations from the college. The colleague owned several sweet shops in London, and Thomas had known him for over ten years. His Aunt, Mrs Winters, was a woman in her sixties who lived alone, and was delighted to have Nora as a student lodger. It gave Thomas at least some peace of mind.

Thomas looked forward to each letter Nora wrote, full of

news about college and London and all the friends she had made. At the end of the first year of college, Nora decided to stay in London over the summer instead of returning home.

"What do you think, Annie?" Thomas remarked as he stood reading the letter in his hand. "Our Nora's joined a band. She's having the time of her life, playing jazz with a group of other musicians she met at the college."

"Jazz!" exclaimed Annie. "What kind of music is that? I thought she was supposed to be practicing to be a concert pianist. We didn't spend all that money on lessons, and money for 'er to go to London to play in a jazz band. What is she thinking?"

"Now, now, luv," Thomas said, trying to calm his wife's tirade. "I think she's doing it on the side. She's still studying piano at the college, but these young people don't stand still these days. It sounds like they're playing on the weekends for parties and such. I'm happy she's enjoying herself and making friends."

"Well, if you say so," grumbled Annie. "Jazz indeed. Where will it all lead to?"

"You never know," was Thomas' final comment.

He intended to find out for himself, and planned to visit London at the earliest opportunity to see what their eldest daughter was up to.

Nora was the youngest member of the jazz band, yet so talented and adaptable that the other musicians welcomed her into their group as a permanent member when they heard her play. Jazz was her new love. So much flexibility. So much creativity. It was as though all the years of piano lessons and even the first year of college had been a preparation for this wonderful thing called jazz. Nora's fingers flew up and down the keyboard as she experimented with different rhythms and notes; none of them written down, but all in her head.

During the summer months the band performed regularly in London's West End. After closing time, a few clubs stayed open, albeit illegally, and welcomed the new music genre whose musicians jammed in exchange for free drinks.

Change came in 1932, after the American jazz musician, Louis Armstrong, performed in several reputable clubs in London, followed by the Duke Ellington Orchestra. Suddenly jazz had arrived and the London club patrons couldn't get enough of it.

Nora's band, The Five Cool Cats, was suddenly in high demand, and not for free drinks. Clubs were offering contracts worth real money, and the music students had a big decision to make: would they go back to college, or continue to play jazz in the clubs? Nora knew what her answer would be—no more college for her. She was hooked.

Thomas stepped off the train in London on a drizzly Friday night in November. He was more than a little concerned that Nora hadn't returned to college, but was continuing to play in a jazz band. She was a headstrong girl, now almost eighteen, but Thomas still saw her as his "little girl" and he had journeyed to the capital city to persuade her to return to college, or return home with him.

The address on the back of the envelope was still the home of his colleague's aunt, which gave Thomas some comfort. At least Nora had a base and wasn't living rough somewhere with her jazz friends. The taxi driver found the address easily near Oxford Circus in the great city, and Thomas stepped onto the drenched pavement, gathered his bag from the back seat, and hurried up the narrow pathway to the front door.

Thomas had written to Mrs Winters informing her of his intention to visit and had given her the date and time he expected to arrive. She now opened the door and smiled at him through the rain.

"Come in, Mr Gardner," she welcomed. "What a nasty night it is. The kettle is on in the kitchen. Come through and have a cup of tea. Here, let me take your wet raincoat."

Mrs Winters prattled on, fussing over the wet traveller, and leading him along the hallway into a bright, warm kitchen. Seated at the kitchen table, Thomas sipped the hot, comforting tea and sunk his teeth into the generous slice of apple pie set before him.

"Nora doesn't get home until the early hours of the morning," Mrs Winters said "The clubs keep very peculiar hours. She's a good girl. Always polite and considerate. I make sure she has a good meal when she wakes up about noon. It's a funny life for a young girl, I must say."

She blushed as she realized it was Nora's father she was talking to.

"Not that I'm judging her, you know," she nattered on. "She's very talented, and loves being part of the band. I wouldn't worry about her, Mr Gardner. This old city isn't all bad, you know."

Thomas looked over the top of his glasses and smiled at Mrs Waters.

"I'm happy she's living here," he said. "It does give me and my wife some peace of mind. If you don't mind, I'll go on up to my room and call it a night. I won't wait up for Nora."

Mrs Waters had a room all ready for her guest on the third floor. She felt sorry for the man, who seemed weighed down with worry about his daughter. She wished him goodnight and left him to rest after his long journey. Tomorrow he would see for himself that Nora was doing well, and some of the worry might be lifted from his shoulders.

Thomas' fears for his daughter's well-being were somewhat calmed the next day, after spending a wonderful afternoon in Hyde Park. Nora was full of excitement and enthusiasm for her new venture, and talked with great animation about the friends she had made in the band, and their early days of jamming for free drinks. She skipped along the tree-lined walks, her red curls bobbing around her small pale face, alive with youth and vitality.

"You have to come with me tonight, Dad," she said. "We're playing at the Metro Club in the West End. It's one of the most fashionable clubs in London, and we have a month long contract. Our band is becoming well known, and we're making some serious money now. I think I'm the only girl playing jazz, so I'm pretty unique. Isn't that crazy?"

Thomas had never been inside a night club. He felt conspicuously out-of-place as he followed Nora down the dimly lit staircase, which led to an equally dimly lit, low-ceilinged room. But there he was, seated at a table in a cellar in the middle of London, watching the other tables fill up with young, obviously wealthy, well-dressed people. Nora ordered a bottle of champagne for her father, even though he would have preferred a cup of tea. Breaking his pledge of abstinence from alcohol was a serious step. Nevertheless, he sipped on the sweet fizzy drink in the odd-shaped glass, as the band wended their way through the maze of tables and onto the low stage.

Nora gave him a wink from her stool at the piano. Apart from the hymns in chapel and the brass band concerts in the park at home, Thomas had only heard his daughter practicing piano. He had no idea what to expect from this strange group of musicians. What kind of sound would such a group of weird instruments produce? Nora on piano, he could envisage, but a set of drums, a guitar, a double bass, a saxophone and a trombone! What a mishmash of extraordinary music makers it was.

Thomas prepared himself for the worst, and was ready with his "encouraging face" for Nora's sake.

The music was low and soft at first, caressing and gentle,

yet full of passion. It followed no pattern, but swept the listeners away with its harmony and tempo. The audience was totally absorbed by the rhythm and creativity of the young musicians, and danced, clapped and swayed through the night as the jazz expanded into full-blown swing music.

Thomas was mesmerized by it all. He peered through the smoke-filled room to catch glimpses of his daughter as her fingers flew on the piano keys. If he needed any further proof that Nora was happy with her chosen life, he only had to see her face lit up with delight, her red curls dancing, her whole body involved in making music.

In the early hours of the morning, when the club finally cleared and only the band was left, Nora introduced her father to her friends. She called them her "music buddies," who were as crazy as she was about the genre in which they had immersed themselves.

On the train home, Thomas was relaxed and content. He would never be able to explain to Annie what the jazz music sounded like, but it was enough that he knew their daughter was happy.

"You should have seen her, Annie," Thomas said, pacing up and down the living room, his face beaming with pride. "She was marvelous. I never heard anything like it—jazz I mean. Nothing like you would imagine. Our Nora's fingers flew up and down that piano, and the other band members can't say enough about how good she is."

"Well, well," Annie smiled. "All that practice came in 'andy then. I must 'ave been mistaken thinking she was going off to the London College of Music to pursue classical music."

"No, luv," Thomas interrupted. "We both thought the same thing. We knew nothing else, don't you see. This new music thing was as much as a surprise to Nora as it was to us. She's found herself in this music. I think we can forget the classical training, and embrace the new life Nora has with jazz band."

"Nothing surprises me about that girl. She's always shown a disrespect for our views, and 'as an independent streak in 'er that borders on insolence. 'Owever, if you're 'appy with what you saw and 'eard in London, Thomas, then I will be led by you in this. I can't imagine what the chapel folk will think when they 'ear about this music called jazz."

"They won't think anything, Annie," Thomas said quietly. "We will tell them how happy Nora is, and they will be happy for her. You know that. Now don't you go telling it any other way, particularly not to your sisters."

Annie pursed up her lips and glared at her husband. It wasn't often he told her how he expected her to behave, but when he did, she knew better than to argue the point. She would double her efforts with Kathy. She would make her practice more, and she would become a classical pianist. Then "little Miss Nora" would see that choosing jazz was a big mistake.

Annie's plan was destined for failure from the beginning. Kathy had never liked practicing the piano and had thrown tantrums from an early age when her mother insisted. As Annie applied pressure for her youngest daughter to practice more, Kathy was defiant and refused to co-operate.

"No, no, no," Kathy had insisted, slamming the lid down on the black and white keys she had come to hate. "I will not play another note. It makes me feel sick. I don't care what you do or say, I'm not playing it ever again."

At twelve years of age, Kathy was as tall as her mother, and as feisty. She marched out of the living room, through the kitchen and out into the garden. She kicked at the grass, sending clods of earth flying in all directions. She wished she lived with Aunty Rosemary and Enid and Nancy. Or Aunty May, whose youngest child, Margaret, was close to her age.

Annie watched her through the window, leaning her head against the cool glass. She wanted Kathy to succeed at everything, to be the very best, to reflect the drive, sacrifice and love which Annie had poured out on her since she was born.

Hot tears stung Annie's eyes as she tried to come to terms with her daughter's independence. What did she have left in life if Kathy wasn't at the centre of everything?

Kathy had gone to a private girl's school when she was eleven, rather than the local school where her cousins attended. She had begged her mother not to stay outside the school during class, as she had done so many times when Kathy was in both infant and junior school. Annie drove her to Brownhills Girls School every morning in her shiny new Austin motor car, and waited until she saw her daughter enter the building. Kathy insisted her mother wait on a side street after school, so that the other girls wouldn't see her.

Kathy was about to begin her second year of high school and still felt the suffocating presence of her mother.

"Why don't you come back to the factory and work in the office, Annie?" Thomas asked as he watched his wife straighten the cushions on the sofas in the living room for the sixth time. He had arrived home in the middle of the morning to change his clothes before attending a council meeting.

"You spend the entire day in this house on your own. You could continue to drop Kathy at school and pick her up every day, as you do now. You were always so good at keeping the books."

"I don't just sit 'ere doing nothing all day," retorted Annie. "I visit my sisters often. I keep the chapel accounts in good order. I shop and cook."

"I appreciate all you do, dear," Thomas said quietly. "I only want what's best for you."

"Then leave me alone," Annie snapped, turning her back on Thomas and hurrying into the kitchen before the tears of frustration spilled down her hot cheeks.

Thomas shook his head and left for his meeting. He

wondered at the change in his loving wife. They had drifted so far apart since Kathy was born. Their second daughter had consumed Annie's life, leaving Nora and himself on the outside of her affections. They were always well fed and their physical needs were met, but Annie's heart was only for her baby girl. Thomas couldn't remember the last time they had made love—maybe two years ago? Even then it had been uncomfortable and embarrassing for them both. The following day Thomas had moved into a different bedroom. It was the easiest solution. The passion they felt for each other had long since died and they were left with companionship at best.

Annie sat in the kitchen sipping her hot tea and thinking about her conversation with Thomas. She could never go back to the factory, but she knew he was right in suggesting she find something to do while Kathy was at school. She had a housekeeper to do all the cleaning, her own car, and more than enough money to buy whatever she needed. The weekends were wonderful because Kathy was at home. The weekdays were dismal and dragged into eternity, because she was not.

How had her life veered off track and left her in a wilderness of dark thoughts? Where would she go to pick up the pieces? There was only one place. It came to her in a flash. The Pear Drop. She still owned it, although she rarely visited. Dora Lawrence, who had taken Florence's place managing the store when Florence and William had their first baby, now ran the store. Annie paid the bills, but that was her only task. The thought of seeing the shop again gave her a small jolt of excitement, as she remembered how much she had loved renovating the neglected little shop. What was it like now?

The following day, after dropping Kathy at Brownhills,

Annie drove into Longton and parked at the curb outside The Pear Drop. The windows were clean and shining and the display of sweets and chocolates looked delightful and tempting. She smiled to herself as she pushed open the door and heard the familiar ding of the bell.

The tiny shop was spotlessly clean inside. Dora was standing on a step stool returning a shiny jar of liquorice comfits onto the newly dusted shelf.

"Hello, Mrs Gardner," she said over her shoulder, before stepping down and moving to the front of the counter to greet Annie. "'Ow nice to see you. Can I get you anything?"

Annie smiled. She liked Dora, and had every confidence she ran the shop very well. Dora's hair was swept into a neat bun at the nape of her neck. She wore a spotless, starched apron over her long-sleeved blue dress, and black boots with a small heel, which added height to her tiny frame.

"I may take some of the famous pear drops with me when I leave," Annie said. "I was curious to see for myself 'ow the shop looks, and I must say I'm pleasantly surprised. You are doing a fine job of managing it."

Annie strode around to the back of the counter, her eyes scanning the rows of jars, all polished and in perfect alignment. The chocolate trays on the bottom shelf contained rows of delicious milk and dark chocolates, which made Annie's mouth water. Beside the cash register stood three different piles of white bags and three different sizes of small white boxes, ready for packaging each shopper's purchases.

A small twinge of disappointment ran through Annie as she acknowledged the well-run shop. Part of her had hoped there would be some fault to find, so that she had a reason to step in and deal with it, but nothing here was amiss.

"I'm glad you stopped by, Mrs Gardner," Dora said. "I was going to write to you to ask for a meeting anyway. I don't know 'ow to begin really."

"What is it, Dora?" encouraged Annie, noticing the girl's obvious concern.

"Well, you see," Dora stuttered. "I'm getting married, and my young man lives in Manchester. I love my job 'ere, but I won't be able to stay, 'cause I 'ave to live with Joe once we're married, I mean."

"Dora, that's wonderful news. Congratulations. When is the wedding?"

"October 21ˢᵗ at The Central Hall. I've gone there since I was a little girl, so it means a lot to me to be married there, and Joe agrees. I 'ate to leave you without 'elp like this, but I was going to ask if I could finish 'ere the week before. To get everything ready, you know."

Annie could hardly believe her ears. This was her chance to be part of the shop again.

"Of course you can leave the week before," Annie answered. "I'm planning to be more involved in the shop now that my daughter is in 'igh school, so it works perfectly for both of us."

The Pear Drop had always come to the rescue. It was like a security blanket for Annie, as it had been for her mother. It fell into place so easily, as it had throughout her life. She was suddenly overwhelmed with emotion at the thought of being here, in this sanctuary of sweetness, every day.

Thomas was overjoyed to hear the news. He saw the

difference in his wife immediately, as her face lit up telling him about her visit that morning. How many years had it been since he had seen the glimmer of a long-forgotten radiance on Annie's face?

Each morning Annie drove Kathy to school before opening the sweet shop. She closed the shop at three each afternoon so that she could collect Kathy from school and take her home. On Saturdays, mother and daughter spent the day together at The Pear Drop, an arrangement that Kathy embraced; Annie was occupied with customers, and not focused on her daughter.

Although Annie had not succumbed to a catatonic state as she had earlier in her life, she realized, as she became more involved with daily life in the sweet shop, that she had spent years existing in a vacuum, where only her love for Kathy kept her alive. As she immersed herself in the atmosphere of the tiny shop full of memories, she allowed love for life to seep back into her. She felt her mother's quiet presence, and her father's gentle spirit. She remembered the rose Thomas had given her over the counter, when she had needed it so badly. She polished the jars, swept the floors, and greeted every customer with a smile of welcome. She wrapped their chocolates with care and offered them a taste of the latest Gardner products.

Thomas began to drop Kathy off at school, and if he had a council meeting close by, he picked her up too. Her mother's vice-like grip on Kathy's life had relaxed, so that she began to tentatively explore her own world. She made friends at school, and met her cousin Margaret to walk to the park on Saturdays. She joined the choir at school and stayed for field hockey practices every Monday and Wednesday. She enjoyed her father's company more and more, and realized that she hardly knew him—a wonderful man who had been living in the same house since she was born, but had become invisible under her mother's dominance.

Kathy blossomed like a spring flower as she gained confidence. Her mother no longer laid out her clothes for the next day; no longer issued orders about who she was to be friends with, or which books she should be reading; no longer picked fault with the way she walked with her toes turned in, or ground her teeth at the dinner table. The freedom was life-changing for Kathy, and she found herself to be happy for the first time in her life.

Nora came home for a visit, wearing the latest London fashion and looking prosperous and beautiful. She played jazz on the piano when the family came to the Gardner house after Sunday Chapel, with Kathy leaning on the lid and watching her sister's fingers fly over the keys in awe. The aunties and uncles listened to the strange music, and purported it to be "interesting." Annie, however, stood entranced as she listened, and when Nora finally rose from the piano stool to her family's applause, her mother hurried over to embrace her daughter with tears of joy in her eyes.

"Nora, that was so beautiful," Annie said, hugging her tightly. "I am so proud of you."

Nora held onto her mother, thinking how many times she had longed for a sign of affection from her over the years.

"That means so much to me, Mam," Nora whispered. "You have no idea how much."

Thomas watched from across the room, thankful that his family was at last together. Even though Nora would return to London the following day, the years of separation were healed with that one embrace.

CHAPTER 42
WEDDING

The summer Kathy turned fourteen, Nora arrived for a rare visit with a handsome young man beside her. His name was Norman Wells, and they had met at the jazz club. He was tall and slender, with black hair and moustache, and he obviously adored Nora. He worked at the City Bank as an investment broker, and looked the part in his immaculate grey suit.

"Don't let first impressions fool you," laughed Nora, as the family gathered for the evening meal. "Norman has a dual personality—London businessman during the day, and cool jazz fanatic at night. We watched each other every night for weeks at the jazz club, before 'e 'ad the courage to talk to me."

"Nora, you are exaggerating," Norman said. "It wasn't weeks, just days. I couldn't take my eyes off your wild red curls, and when you looked up and caught my eye I was completely smitten."

"I wanted you all to meet my 'andsome young man," continued Nora. "E asked me to marry 'im, and I said 'yes.'"

Kathy jumped up from the table clapping her hands as she ran to envelope her sister in a bear hug.

"A wedding. 'Ow wonderful! When? Where?" the questions spilled from Kathy's lips.

"Let me catch my breath," gasped Nora, as she untangled herself from her sister's arms. "The wedding will be next month, August 4th, and it will be in London. Sorry Mam. Sorry Dad. I know you would want the wedding at the chapel, but it doesn't make sense to either of us. I left that life behind many years ago, and our 'ome is London now."

"Don't worry about us," Thomas assured her. "We'll be there no matter what. It will be a grand day out for the whole family. Wait until your aunties hear about it. Planning for a wedding in London will be exciting for everybody."

Thomas rose from his seat and shook Norman's hand.

"Congratulations to you both," he said. "You've got yourself a grand girl, young man. Speaking for Annie and myself, we wish you every happiness."

"Thank you, sir," Norman said. "Nora is indeed the most beautiful, talented woman ever. I'm a very lucky man."

"I'm the lucky one," blushed Nora. Then turning to her sister, she asked, "Would you like to be my bridesmaid, Kathy?"

A scream issued from Kathy's mouth, as she danced around the table.

"Would I?" she squealed. "Yes, yes, yes. What colour dress? What length? 'Ow will I wear my 'air? How about shoes?"

"Stop, stop," laughed her sister. "All in good time, darling. Mam will 'elp us take care of all the details, won't you Mam?"

Until now Annie had sat quietly taking in the scene before her. She had no words to express the joy she felt watching her two girls laugh and talk about the upcoming wedding. There had been times when she could never have imagined such a scenario. Times when Nora almost disappeared from her consciousness and Kathy consumed every moment of every day. Now she saw the fine young woman

Nora had become despite the rejection she had faced at home. Annie admitted to herself that she could take no credit. It was Thomas, who had visited her in London and had written to her faithfully every week, who deserved all the accolades.

"I'm so 'appy for you, Nora," Annie finally said, rising to her feet to embrace her daughter. "Welcome to our family, Norman."

The couple travelled back to London the next morning, leaving the family to make plans for the big day. As predicted, the aunties were overjoyed with the prospect of a trip to the capital city for the wedding, and the chatter was at fever pitch as they all gathered at Annie's house after Sunday Chapel.

It was proposed, after much discussion, that all the aunties would attend along with the female cousins. The uncles and male cousins were happy to be left out of the arrangements. They would prefer to go fishing or to a football match on Saturday afternoon anyway. Annie and Kathy were to travel to London the week before, so that they could shop for Kathy's dress, and help with any last-minute details. Thomas would escort the aunties and cousins by the early train on August 4th, which would have them in London in plenty of time for the wedding ceremony.

Mrs Winters, who had been Nora's landlady for almost six years, bustled and fussed around the family from Longton. The three bedrooms on the second floor were at their disposal, so that they could change and freshen up from their train journey.

"Up you go, ladies," Mrs Winters chatted as she shooed them up the stairs. "There'll be a fresh cup of tea for you waiting in the kitchen when you're ready."

Thomas stayed out of the way, and joined Mrs Winters in the kitchen.

"My wife's sisters are a force to be reckoned with, Mrs Winters," he explained. "Never stopped talking all the way down here on the train. I'm worn out just listening to them."

The kindly housekeeper placed a steaming cup of tea in front of the weary traveller, along with a generous slice of lemon cake.

"You get this into you, Mr Gardner," she said. "Weddings are always more fun for the ladies."

Thomas rolled his eyes as he listened to the squeals of laughter echoing through the house from the upstairs bedrooms.

Annie and Kathy were in the thick of all the preparations, as aunties Rosemary, May, Lizzie, Daisy, and Florence, along with cousins Enid, Nancy, and Margaret, all helped each other look their very best. They all agreed the results were wonderful, as they left the bedrooms in their finest dresses, hats, gloves and shoes that pinched their feet, but looked so stylish.

Nora had insisted on dressing herself in her tiny bedroom on the top floor. She didn't want anybody to see her until she arrived at the church, except her father, who waited patiently downstairs until it was time for them to leave.

Nora had ordered taxi cabs to take the aunties and cousins to the church, and they paraded out of the house in their finery, along with Annie, Kathy and Mrs Winters. Suddenly the house was silent. Thomas stood still, remembering his daughter as a baby, a little girl, a teenager, and the first time he had seen her in the jazz club. He remembered the feeling of awe and wonder that he had become a dad so late in life, when he had given up all hope of even meeting or marrying a girl. Now his hair was grey and he was too thin, but he counted himself as truly blessed to be here on his daughter's wedding day.

A soft step on the wooden stairs caught Thomas' attention, and he looked up to see Nora smiling down at him. A vision of white tule from head to toe, with that wonderful halo of red curls circling her face. Thomas gulped back the lump in his throat and blinked away the stinging in his eyes.

"Ready?" he asked.

"Yes, Dad," she answered.

Norman arrived at St. Mary Abbots Church on Kensington High Street an hour before the wedding. His best man, and best friend, Charlie Kent, tried to keep the groom relaxed by telling him a series of funny stories and jokes, until Norman begged him to stop.

The entourage of Nora's family arrived in a flourish, filling two pews on the bride's side of the old church. Kathy waited in the narthex, dressed in pale blue silk and carrying a bouquet of white roses and baby's breath. Her cheeks were flushed with excitement, and she shuffled from one foot to the other listening for the taxi that would herald her sister's arrival.

All eyes were on Nora as she walked down the centre aisle of the beautiful stone church towards the man she loved. The aunties all cried and the cousins giggled. Annie thought about her first wedding in the registry office, with no family present. She also noticed how old and tired Thomas looked, despite his new suit and the smile on his face.

Nora's jazz band friends had organized a celebration meal for everybody at the ritzy Blue Room Club, complete with accompanying music.

The aunties agreed it had been a perfect day, despite their sore feet.

CHAPTER 43
GOODBYE

Nobody noticed the slight discolouration at first, not even Thomas. He shaved every day, using the mirror in the bathroom to trace the lines of the razor as it slid through the foam on his face. He rarely looked at his eyes, moving his attention from chin to head, as he combed his still-full head of hair into place.

As he caught a passing glimpse of his eyes that particular Monday morning in the late spring of 1938, he paused to take a second look. There was a definite yellow tinge in the whites of both eyes. Thomas put it down to too much good food the day before and not enough water. He'd remember to drink plenty of water today. That would fix things.

He didn't feel like eating breakfast, but went directly to the factory to go over the weekly production with Mr Salt. He sipped a cup of hot sweet tea as he looked through the orders, but set the tea aside as a wave of nausea swept over him.

Should have eaten breakfast, he thought.

Thomas struggled through the day. A council meeting in the evening left him drained of all energy and he arrived home looking and feeling miserable. He headed to bed, with apologies to Annie, saying he had a headache and needed to sleep.

The following days became more and more difficult for Thomas. His skin took on the same dull yellow hue originally only in his eyes, and food was an instant cause of distress and nausea. Annie insisted he see Doctor Keats, and feared for her husband, who had always been so strong and resilient. The stark memory of her father loomed before her —the same skeletal frame, the same taut yellow skin stretched over his cheekbones. Annie knew before the doctor said anything that she would lose Thomas.

Annie and Kathy sat together, holding hands, as Thomas struggled to breathe. It had only been six weeks since the first visit to the doctor. Six weeks of watching the man they both loved succumb to the cancer that had invaded his body. Now it was near the end and Nora was on her way from London.

Annie barely recognized the shadow of her husband lying in the bed. His yellow skin stretched over the bones like a coat of paint, and his once thick hair reduced to a few strands. Yet in his eyes was all the love he had always had for Annie, and he spent every waking moment looking at her. The moments of wakefulness were rare now, but Annie was always beside him so that he could see her when his tired eyelids opened for a moment.

Nora arrived later in the day, heavy with her first baby. She had wanted it to be a surprise, but wished now that she had come earlier, so that Thomas would know he was going to be a grandad.

Doctor Keats came every evening on his way home.

"Mrs Gardner, you should stay with him. Say what you need to say to him. Hearing is always the last of the senses to leave, so he can possibly hear you, even though he is unconscious. I'm sorry I couldn't do anything to help him. Send for me if you need me."

The doctor quietly let himself out, knowing he would probably be coming back very soon.

"Thomas, dear Thomas," Annie said, close to her husband's ear. "I 'ave always loved you. I love you still. It's so 'ard to say goodbye, but rest now and don't worry about us."

A single tear oozed out of Thomas' left eye and rolled down his cheek. He had heard his wife's voice. Annie, Nora and Kathy each held his hand as he drew a deep breath, and once it was released he didn't take another.

Annie remembered laying her head on his thin chest. She remembered her daughters lifting her and helping her into a chair. She remembered the bedroom full of people—her sisters were there, Doctor Keats, her brothers giving her something to drink, Kathy sobbing, Nora white-faced sitting on the bed still holding her father's hand.

Then—nothing!

Doctor Keats provided a powder from his bag and gave it to May.

"See that Mrs Gardner takes this right away," he advised. "It's a sedative and will help her sleep."

May quickly mixed the powder into a glass of water and forced it between her sister's lips until most of it had been consumed. May remembered other occasions in Annie's past when she had succumbed to life's tribulations, and she worried that this would be too much for her to bear.

Annie's house was full of caring people as preparations were made for the funeral. Nora's husband arrived by the afternoon train from London, worried about his wife's pregnancy in light of the grief she now faced. May took Kathy under her wing, taking her to sleep with Margaret overnight and staying close beside her during the long days at home.

"What's the matter with Mam?" Kathy asked. "Why is she still in bed?"

"She's resting," explained May. "She'll feel better soon, but for now it's best if she stays in bed."

Rosemary assumed her usual position as nurse to Annie, spending most of her days in the bedroom trying to feed Annie soup or get her to drink a few sips of water. She bathed her forehead and rubbed her hands and feet. She lovingly fluffed up the pillows under Annie's head and put an extra blanket over her cold body. She talked softly to her sister-in-law, or sang hymns in her quiet, lovely voice. Rosemary had seen all of it before. The catatonic state after the babies died so long ago, and again when Daniel died. She knew Annie's mind was fragile, but didn't know how to help her.

The day of the funeral came and went, with the little chapel filled to overflowing. Annie wasn't there.

Norman persuaded Nora to return to London, even though she didn't want to leave her mother. Their baby's birth was imminent and arrangements had been made for Nora to go into a private maternity hospital. The nursery was ready in their little house in Kensington, with everything laid out for the new baby. The aunties joined Norman in encouraging Nora to go home. They would all be taking care of her mother, they assured her.

Mr Salt from the factory stepped in to help. He dropped Kathy off at school and picked her up each day. She was going into her final year at Brownhills and, despite the chaos at home, she wanted to finish school and move onto college next year. May suggested she live with them for the time being, at least until Annie recovered.

As the days turned to weeks, Annie's sisters took turns staying with her. Doctor Keats was at a loss. He could only keep repeating that "time would heal." Meanwhile, Annie grew emaciated and pale. She didn't seem to hear anything or see anything. She allowed her sisters to bathe her and change her nightgowns and bed linens. She sat in a chair by the window with a shawl around her shoulders and stared at nothing.

Inside her head was nothing but comforting darkness. Sometimes she would see a flicker of light, but then it was gone. Images crept into the darkness sometimes. Almost as dark as the darkness. A man walking across the room, turning as he reached the door—Daniel smiling at her before going through the door and closing it behind him. Always a door that she couldn't reach, and a man she couldn't follow. Thomas opening the door and coming into the room towards her, only to disappear before he reached her. A red-headed baby girl sitting on her bed, but as Annie tried to touch her, an older red-headed girl snatched her away and ran out of the room, slamming the door behind her.

CHAPTER 44
ALIVE AGAIN

Soft singing. Annie definitely could hear somebody singing. It was a hymn she knew. She tried to see who it was, and caught the faint glimpse of a kind face bending over her, lips moving.

"Annie, do you see me?" asked Rosemary, as she watched Annie's eyes focus for the first time in weeks. "Do you see me, my dear?"

Strong, warm hands stroked her head, and Annie smelled lemons and lavender. Her eyelids fluttered open once more and a tiny smile of thanks curled her lips.

It was such a small thing. A tiny smile. But Rosemary rejoiced in it. After weeks of caring for Annie, it was the first sign she had seen that Annie was still with them. Buried somewhere deep inside her ravaged body, the spark that was Annie still smouldered, and Rosemary cried tears of relief.

Annie knew somebody was washing her face with a soft warm cloth. Somebody was brushing her hair, carefully and slowly. Somebody was washing her feet and drying them on a soft towel. Annie felt the love through these simple acts of caring. The darkness inside her head wasn't so suffocating.

She could see so much when she opened her eyes, although what she saw didn't make sense to her. She knew the woman who was bathing her, but couldn't remember her name. She had a kind face and a lovely voice. Annie felt comforted and warm.

"There you are, Annie," Rosemary said. "You are much better today. Would you like to sit in your chair for a while?"

Rosemary supported her sister-in-law as she slowly moved from bed to chair. She covered her thin shoulder with a shawl and placed another over her knees. A vase of fresh flowers sat on the table beside Annie's chair and immediately took her attention. She remembered flowers. How beautiful they were. How delicate and perfumed. She remembered picking them in the hedgerows with Daniel.

Rosemary warmed chicken broth and brought it to the bedroom, praying that she could manage to feed some to her poor patient. Seated beside the window, distracted by the flowers, Annie allowed her nurse to gently scoop up the warm nurturing liquid and feed it to her.

One week later, Annie was so improved that she could get out of bed by herself and asked for her clothes so that she could get dressed. She remembered Rosemary's name, and the names of her sisters, and was anxious to see Kathy. She didn't talk about Thomas and the sisters wondered if she remembered he had died. Should they tell her? Would it be a setback for her? They decided to leave it for the time being. Maybe she would talk about it when she was ready.

Kathy held her mother closely, shocked to see such a change in her, but happy she was recovering.

"I stayed with Aunty May while you were sick, Mam," Kathy explained. "I'm doing well at school, to make you proud of me."

"I don't need a reason to be proud of you, my Kathy,"

Annie said. "You are and always 'ave been the biggest joy in my life."

When Annie thought about Thomas, it was as though she saw him through a fog. She knew she had lost him, but somehow he was still there with her. It was better that way. After all, Daniel had always been there too, in the background.

The factory had continued under the supervision of Mr Salt, but he needed to meet with Annie about the future. The Pear Drop, likewise, was doing well. Alice had agreed to take care of everything until Annie's return. After years of hoping for a baby, Alice and Charles finally were blessed with a daughter. Maureen was three years old, and enjoyed being at the sweet shop with her mother. A corner of the shop became a play area, not only for Maureen, but for the customers' children. The whole family donated items: books, puzzles, blocks, paper, pencils, trains and cars. Alice was delighted with the opportunity to earn extra money, and worked hard to keep the shop in good order.

As Annie's strength returned, Kathy went home to live with her. Nora and Norman came for a weekend to introduce Christopher Gordon to his grandmother and Aunty Kathy. It was wonderful to have a baby in the house again and Annie visibly glowed as she bounced him on her knees.

Look, Thomas. Look at your grandson. What a wonder he is to be sure. I wish you could hold him. I know how proud you must be. I can see a little of you in his eyes when he smiles.

While Nora was visiting, Annie sat down with her two daughters to discuss the future of the factory and The Pear Drop. Nora was all for selling them both, leaving her mother to live comfortably for the rest of her life. Kathy thought it wise to wait until her mother had given it careful consideration, knowing how involved she had been in both ventures. It was ultimately Annie's difficult decision.

The Gardner Sweet Factory had gained recognition throughout the country and had made Thomas Gardner a wealthy man. Annie considered the factory to be part of her husband's history, and she was loath to sell it to a stranger. She sought advice from her lawyer about offering shares of the company to Mr Salt and the workers.

The company was set up as requested, with Annie owning fifty one percent of the shares and the rest were bought, at a ridiculously low price, by the manager and workers. It was an offer the factory employees could barely believe, and they borrowed from friends and family to buy shares. Now they would be co-owners and the profits would be shared by them all. They had Mrs Gardner to thank.

Alice worked at The Pear Drop, with input from Annie for orders and new product, and agreed to stay at the shop for the foreseeable future. Everything fell into place so well, and Annie could concentrate on keeping her fingers in all the aspects of home, factory and shop.

Kathy graduated from high school with honours. Another proud day for Annie as she sat with the other parents to watch her daughter receive her diploma.

"I'm considering applying to Manchester or London for college," Kathy said, as she sat down with her mother for a late dinner. "They are both good colleges. What do you think?"

"College?" questioned Annie, avoiding her daughter's eyes. "Why would you want to go to college? You 'ave a good life 'ere with me, don't you? Now you don't 'ave school we can spend more time together."

Kathy stopped with her fork in midair. Memories of the years spent under the suffocating, domineering presence of her mother flooded into her mind. She couldn't bear the thought of reliving those years, with no father to intervene.

"I thought London would be a good idea," Kathy said,

ignoring her mother's last comment. "I could visit Nora regularly, and I would enjoy spending time with Christopher."

"I will not 'ave it," Annie snapped, slamming her knife down onto her plate. "You will stay 'ere with me, young miss. I 'ave nobody else, except you. I need you to be 'ere with me, not gallivanting off to London. As for your sister, she 'as 'er own life and doesn't need you interfering, pushing your nose in where you don't belong."

"You 'ave your sisters, Ma," Kathy replied, "They all love you and care about you. Look at 'ow they nursed you back to health after dad died. You will never be alone. You don't need me to stay with you."

"Enough," Annie yelled, jumping up from the table. "You will stay 'ere with me. That is my decision. Do not talk to me about this again."

The door banged behind Annie as she marched out of the room and up the stairs. Kathy sat at the table in shock.

CHAPTER 45
ANOTHER WAY

Patience was never a trait of the young. Kathy was no exception and longed to break free and go to college. On the advice of the aunties, she bided her time and stayed with her mother.

"You're still young, my dear," counseled Aunty Rosemary. "Your mam will come around before too long. She needs some time, that's all. I would guarantee you will be away at college this time next year. Try to be patient, and wait it out. Me and the other aunties will talk to Annie and encourage 'er to let you go."

Time seemed to stop for Kathy, as she spent her days as companion to her mother. Wherever Annie went, Kathy was with her. Trips to the factory or The Pear Drop were made regularly every week. The aunties were visited, pots of tea were consumed, scones and jam were served, as Kathy sat on her best behaviour, a reluctant participant.

"Sit up straight, Kathy."

"Change your gloves, dear. Those 'ave a small stain on the back."

"You 'ave kept me waiting five minutes. Tardiness is a bad 'abit."

"I wish you would play the piano, Kathy. It sits there gathering dust every day."

"Don't sniff, dear. It's so unladylike. Use your 'andkerchief."

The criticism continued day after day, with Kathy biting her lips until they bled rather than cause an argument. The aunties seemingly had no influence over their sister, even though they constantly reminded her how lucky she was to have her daughter giving up so much to be with her.

All hope of attending college in London disappeared as rumours of another war with Germany heightened. Nora decided to leave London with little Christopher and move in with Norman's mother, who lived in a small town near Colchester in Essex. The capital city was in a frenzy of fear as gas masks were issued to the population and air-raid shelters were allocated in each community. Norman accepted a commission into the Grenadier Guards and began his service in the war rooms in Westminster, where he worked in the map room preparing reports for the Prime Minister and the heads of the armed forces.

"I am so thankful you stayed at 'ome," Annie said, placing her hands on Kathy's shoulders. "If you 'ad gone to London, you would 'ave been in such danger. You're safe 'ere with me."

On September 3rd, 1939, Neville Chamberlain, the British Prime Minister, announced war with Germany. Every family gathered around their radios to hear it firsthand. For many, the memories of the first war with Germany, just twenty years before, still lingered in their minds. That one had been named the war to end all wars! Not so! Now the young men would leave their homes again to fight the same enemy.

The following Sunday the family gathered for a meal at

Annie's house after Chapel as usual. They all knew that conscription papers would be issued soon and their young men would go to war. May sat silent and still as she gazed at her son, Frederick, who at nineteen would be one of the first to be called up to fight. She remembered George fighting in the mud-filled trenches before Fred was born, and prayed her son would return safely as her husband had. Maybe this war would be over quickly.

War affected every part of society, as the country mobilized its youth for the conflict ahead. Five of the confectionary factory workers were called to serve, leaving Mr Salt scrambling to keep production going. The worry about maintaining production was soon a moot point, as sugar became scarce and the remaining five workers were more than sufficient to keep the factory going. They experimented with using sugar substitutes for some of their products, but without much success. The decline in demand also took its toll and the already depleted work force struggled to earn enough to live on, as their hours were cut to four days a week.

Annie looked for ways to keep the small factory going, and began bottling and packaging saccharin tablets. It proved to be a good decision, as the artificial sweetener became the sugar substitute for everybody. The small amount of sugar allocated to each family was reserved for baking and not sweetening cups of tea.

Every family was issued with a ration book for sugar, meat, tea, jam, butter, milk, cheese, eggs and more. Petrol was also rationed, and Annie carefully worked out how many gallons she would need to keep her car running to and from the factory and the sweet shop.

With sweets on ration, each family was only allowed four ounces of sweets each week. Despite the drastic decrease in sales for The Pear Drop, many families tried their best to keep life as stable as possible for the children. The sweet ration was precious and each child came into the shop, wide-eyed and eager to buy an ounce or two of their favourite sweets.

Another blow came when Alice told Annie she was pregnant again, and would have to give up her job at the shop because her feet were swelling so badly. Annie didn't trust a stranger to take care of her shop. Who would keep everything in order, polish the jars, clean the windows, display the chocolates? There was only one person she could think of who could step into Alice's shoes—herself!

Kathy enjoyed working in the shop with her mother, despite the constant and persistent chatter from Annie, who lectured her continually on the best way to do the chores. At least they were out of the house and meeting other people. Annie excelled in customer service and was at her best when she was serving the myriad of people who came to buy. She treated everybody equally, from the ragged, dirty little boy with a ha'penny to spend and no ration book, to the gentleman dressed in top hat and dark suit, who exchanged his ration coupon for six chocolates placed in a white box and tied with a red ribbon.

The little shop's quiet, calming atmosphere seeped into Annie's soul once more, and she relaxed her obsession with Kathy's small and insignificant shortcomings. Life for mother and daughter was restored to a tentative normal.

Kathy itched to get away and help the war effort like her cousins. The boys were scattered all over England in different regiments, preparing for the fight ahead. The girls had been conscripted to work in the Swynnterton munitions factory.

Many of the trained, experienced troops had left England as soon as war was declared and were encamped on the border of France and Belgium. Their numbers grew as different regiments were deployed to join in the allied defence against the Germans. The strength of the German army was vastly underestimated. The British Army suffered through a cold miserable winter living in the fields of France. When the German army invaded Belgium, Holland and France in the spring, all three were occupied by the enemy within a few weeks. The allied troops were forced farther and farther towards the English Channel, until more than 330,000 had their backs to the sea near the small town of Dunkirk.

What was known as "the miracle of Dunkirk" began at the end of May in 1940, when hundreds of boats of every description crossed the channel to evacuate the soldiers waiting on the beaches of France. Many brave men were lost as they battled the enemy during the evacuation, but the vast majority of troops were saved by the heroic efforts of the armada of fishing boats and small private craft who braved the choppy waters and the bombardment of German guns to rescue the soldiers.

Kathy listened to the news reports on the radio every day, wishing she was old enough to help in some way, and a few weeks later when she turned seventeen, she visited the recruiting office in Stoke and filled out the application form to join the Women's Land Army. She had to lie about her age, but the recruiting officer only briefly glanced at her ID card. If she noticed the lie, she didn't react—Kathy wasn't the first under-age girl in the Land Army and wouldn't be the last.

She didn't say anything to her mother. She would tell her when she received official notification, and knew where she was to be stationed. She received a letter two weeks later, which asked her to attend an interview and medical examination, and once completed, another letter confirmed her acceptance and information on where to report.

"You can't go," was Annie's reaction when her daughter

told her the news. "I won't let you. You are needed at 'ome. You are needed in the shop. You won't make any difference to the war. You're just a girl. You're not even old enough to be in the Land Army. I'll report you to the Army for joining up at seventeen. Why would you even want to go off with a bunch of strangers to goodness knows where?"

"I am going, Mam," Kathy said, standing her ground in front of her irate mother. "I've been accepted into the Land Army and will be leaving next week. I'll be working on a farm in Cheshire, which isn't far away. You 'ave absolutely no say in this."

"We'll see about that, my girl," shot back Annie. "You've always been delicate. You catch cold easily and 'ave no strength to work on the land. They'll make you do all kinds of 'eavy work, like tossing 'ay bales, mucking out cows, driving tractors and the like. Look at you, with your white skin and beautiful curly hair, and 'ands that are smooth as silk. 'ow long do you think you're going to last on a farm?"

"You will 'ave to find somebody else to 'elp in the shop," answered Kathy. "One of the aunties would be 'appy to fill my shoes. None of them 'ave youngsters to look after and would be glad of the extra money. You 'ave to face the fact that I'm leaving, Mam. I'm grown up, and you can't 'old onto me forever."

Annie stormed and cried. She shouted and raved. She threatened to collapse and take to her bed. All to no avail.

Kathy was determined to escape.

KATHY

1940

Cows were big and scary creatures. They produced massive amounts of manure, which covered the inside of the milking sheds, as well as the fields. If you didn't move quickly, a cow could crush you between its massive body and the side of the milking stall. If you didn't keep out of the way when you were hand milking, a hefty kick could leave a bruise that would for days.

Kathy had never been near farm animals. She doubted she would ever get used to working with them. The farm to which she was allocated had twenty Land Army girls working there, and Kathy was billeted with three others in the local vet's house.

"Don't worry about the animals," Fanny said, as she scooped a pile of clothes from the unoccupied bed in the corner of the room. "You'll get used to them. We all had to. Here's your bed. Two uniforms are in the brown paper bag on the chair. Make yourself comfortable. You can put your stuff in the bottom drawer of the chest over there. Not much room, I'm afraid, but we manage."

"Thanks," Kathy said.

She looked around at the loft bedroom, with its sloped roof and small windows. It was stark and cold, with wooden floors and walls. The four beds faced each other on either side of the room, leaving space in the highest part of the roof to dress and undress without bumping your head. The chest in question sat at the end of the room, facing the doorway on the other end. It had four inadequate drawers, and various toiletries and items of clothing were spread over the bottom of the beds and on the four wooden chairs set beside each bed.

Kathy wished she had brought less clothing with her, but for now she crammed what she could into her drawer and left the rest in her suitcase under the bed. The uniforms consisted of two pairs of brown corduroy breeches, two pairs of knee-length woolen socks, a pair of serviceable brogue shoes, two beige shirts, a green pullover, a raincoat and a cowboy-style hat.

Not the height of fashion, thought Kathy, laying the items across the chair.

The other two girls, Myra and Josephine (called Jo), were both from Liverpool and were happy to be in the Cheshire countryside away from the constant bombing of the Liverpool dockland. They were cheerful and friendly and welcomed their new roommate with tales of horror about the farm.

The farmer, Mr Graham, was a hard taskmaster. He didn't care for the Land Army girls, who were supposed to replace his two sons and his healthy, strong young farmhands. Bunch of weak lassies was how he regarded them all. He deliberately set out workloads that were impossible to accomplish, and sneered at them when they failed. They were supposed to work eight hour days, but Mr Graham insisted they be at the farm by six every morning and work until their tasks were complete, which often meant working into the evening hours.

Farm workers were allowed extra rations, and nourishing food was supposed to be supplied. The farmer's wife believed in cutting corners and usually provided a six o'clock breakfast of thick bread and a slice of cheese. Mrs Graham rang the gong for lunch at noon, when she served the soup she had made that morning, with another slice of bread. Supper was more substantial, especially when chickens or a small pig had been slaughtered. Corned beef hash and eggs were common substitutes if there was no farm meat available. Occasionally Mrs Graham baked pies or rice pudding to sate the hungry girls.

Farm work was grueling for all the girls, but particularly for Kathy as the new girl, who had known only a soft, easy life until then. She was partnered with Myra for the first week of work so that she could learn the ropes, but she was slow and awkward and scared of all the animals, particularly the cows and the giant mother pig. At the end of each day there was no hot bath to soak in, or fragrant talcum powder to dust on her skin. The water in the wash house was cold and Kathy shivered her way through washing the parts of her body she could expose without embarrassment in front of the other girls. They didn't seem to mind, and stripped off their clothes, including underwear, and scrubbed away with their washcloths and carbolic soap until the stench of the animals, the muck and manure, was eradicated from their bodies.

"Don't worry, Kathy. Wash those nooks and crannies or you'll never get rid of the smell."

After struggling to wash with a towel wrapped around her for a few days, Kathy finally succumbed to the conditions she found herself in and, with her face glowing beet red, dropped the towel. Soon it was a non-issue and she joined the other girls, as they washed each other's backs and rinsed each other's hair.

After a few months at the farm, Kathy's hands became callused and her arms and legs strong and defined with muscles she didn't know she had. Her cheeks were rosy and her eyes bright. The long summer days, when the heavy trousers were set aside in favour of shorts, were spent outside, herding cows, spreading straw, feeding pigs, weeding Mrs Graham's vast vegetable garden, and hand-milking the cows twice every day.

On her day off, Kathy slept late and walked into the village to buy "real" food with coupons from her ration book in hand. She ate her two ounces of cheese on the way back to the farm, along with a delicious currant scone from the bakery. She laughed to herself when she thought of the dainty little scones, clotted cream and strawberry jam her mother would serve for tea in the afternoons. *What would Mam think if she could see me now*, Kathy thought, as she trudged along the muddy country lanes in her boots, with a fat currant scone in one hand and a chunk of cheese in the other.

Away from her family for the first time in her life, Kathy had never felt happier. Despite the grueling work on the farm, every fiber of her being felt alive and free. Even with her head leaning on the side of a smelly cow while she pulled and squeezed the teats, sending a spray of full rich milk into the bucket, her nose filled with the smell of fresh cow muck, she hummed a song to herself. No mother to criticize, watch over her shoulder to tell her what she was doing wrong, nag about sitting up straight or walking with her toes pointed forwards. No mother to tell her to practice the piano.

With her head held high, watching the clouds part and the sun come pouring through, Kathy turned the corner into the mud-caked driveway at the vet's house. Leaning against her car stood Annie, arms folded across her chest.

CHAPTER 47
CONTACT

"Well, 'ere you are at last," Annie said, standing her ground with her toe tapping out a beat in the mud.

"Mam," gulped Kathy. "What are you doing 'ere?"

"Doing 'ere?" replied Annie. "I thought I'd better find out if you were alive or dead. I've been sitting at 'ome these last many weeks, wondering if I'd ever see you again. Wondering if you'd bother to visit or at least write."

"I've been really busy, Mam, learning about the farm and the animals. We 'ave no time to spare. We work long hours and are so tired by the end of the day, all we want to do is sleep."

"Looks like it," Annie retorted with a smirk. "Walking about like you don't 'ave a care in the world. Where were you today, then? Doesn't look like you were doing much work to me."

"It's my day off," Kathy answered, feeling the old tension rising in her throat as she came under her mother's scrutiny. "I walked to the village to buy food. 'ow did you find me?"

"I went searching through the file you left on your bedside chest. The farmer's wife gave me the address of your billet. I drove 'ere to take you 'ome. This is no place for you, Kathy. You are too thin, and your 'air looks wild. Look at all this dirt and muck you live in. Pack up your things right now. I'll wait in the car."

"What? Do you really think I'm going to leave with you? I can't leave the Land Army, even if I wanted to—and I definitely don't. I'm doing an important job for the war effort. The men who usually work 'ere are in the army, and there are twenty girls 'ere doing their work. Would you rather I work on a munitions factory like Margaret? Or I could get my driver's license and drive an ambulance, or work in a military 'ospital. I chose the Land Army, Mam. You can't make me leave."

"You stubborn girl," yelled Annie. "You've always 'ad your own way. Why couldn't you do munitions work like May's girl and live at 'ome? Rosemary's girls are both still at 'ome with 'er. I'm the only sister whose daughter's gone off to work in the Land Army, miles away. I'll write to the war office and tell them you are only seventeen and I want you 'ome, that's what I'll do."

"No you will not," Kathy said quietly, realizing her mother was close to hysteria. "Mam, it's all right. I like working on the farm. I've made some good friends, and the fresh air suits me. I'll come and visit you when I have a two-day pass, I promise. Please, Mam, go 'ome and take care of things there. I'll need a good 'ome to come back to when the war is over."

Annie's eyes filled with tears. She felt so helpless.

Kathy put her arms around her mother's thin frame and held her close, remembering how frail Annie's mental health was. She didn't want to be the cause of another breakdown, and searched for the right things to say to waylay Annie's fear and anxiety.

"Let's get you a hot cup of tea," Kathy said, taking her mother's arm. "Drive me back to the farmhouse. Mrs Graham always has the kettle boiling, and I bet she's made scones this very day. I'd like you to meet the farmer's wife properly."

Conversation was strained between them as Annie reluctantly drove the half-mile back to the farm. Kathy knocked on the kitchen door and stepped inside, greeting Mrs Graham and reintroducing her to Annie.

Mrs Graham, always hospitable to strangers, had tea, warm scones and butter on the table in a matter of minutes.

"Nice of you to visit your girl," Mrs Graham said, sitting at the table beside her guest. "Kathy's learning the ropes, and works hard. Of course these girls can never replace our sons or our young men, but they do their best. We're glad of the help. The farm would never keep going if it wasn't for the Land Army girls."

"I was concerned my daughter was being looked after properly," Annie said primly.

Kathy rolled her eyes, and tried not to look at the farmer's wife.

"Oh, we take good care of the girls. I spend my whole day cooking for them," assured Mrs Graham.

Full of tea and scones, Kathy escorted her mother to the car, hoping some of her questions had been answered and that she could go home in a better frame of mind.

"Well then," Annie said as she climbed into the driver's seat. "Looks like you've made up your mind to stay."

"I'll come and see you soon," smiled Kathy, trying to sound positive. "Drive safely, Mam."

The country lanes were narrow and lined with hedges, which forced Annie to drive slowly and with care. Her mission had failed, and Kathy wasn't coming home with her. She would continue to live in the big house by herself, rooms echoing with voices from the past, and the shadows of Thomas and Daniel in the corners. She would close up the rooms that were never used, and keep only Kathy's bedroom ready and waiting. She was determined that she would fight the urge to hide under the covers in her bed and stay there forever. Her sisters had nursed her back from oblivion three times during her life and she wouldn't be the cause of more grief for them. She would continue to work in The Pear Drop and go over the books of the factory every week. She would meet with her sisters for tea and talk about the war and their boys who were in the army. She would host Sunday lunch after chapel every Sunday, smiling and pretending all was well.

On the other side of the lane the driver in the army truck slammed on his brakes as he turned the bend and saw the car in front of him. There was no reaction from the woman driving the car. She didn't brake or steer the car into the hedge, and the car hit the front of the truck full force.

Annie lay still, wondering if she had died.

No, she decided, *I am alive.* She could feel a sharp pain in her right lower leg and her head throbbed to the beat of her heart. She could hear voices, and looked up to see faces at the side window of the car. Soldiers opened the door, asking her questions, lifting her. She cried out as they moved her leg. Gently, supporting her leg, they moved her out of the car and onto the grass under the hedges. Annie felt the shame of wetting her knickers in front of the young soldiers, who didn't seem to notice or care. Warm sticky blood ran into Annie's eyes to join the tears spilling down her cheeks.

The soldiers showed such kindness as they waited for help to arrive. They covered Annie with an army blanket, all itchy and scratchy, but warm. A soldier held her head on his lap and wiped her eyes with his handkerchief, then kept it firmly pressed against her forehead.

The ambulance took Annie to Macclesfield Hospital.

Nobody was expecting her home.

Nobody knew she was missing.

CHAPTER 48
INVALID

Annie's handbag had been tucked in beside her by a thoughtful soldier as she was being loaded into the ambulance. Kathy's name and the address of the farm were retrieved by hospital staff, and a policeman was duly dispatched to inform her about the accident. Farmer Graham himself drove Kathy to Macclesfield and dropped her off at the hospital.

With her leg in a cast and her head bandaged, Annie was released the following day. Kathy phoned the factory and asked Mr Salt to drive to Macclesfield to pick them up, then she contacted the Land Army to let them know she had left the farm to attend to a family emergency.

Within minutes of them arriving home, the aunties arrived en masse with soup, scones, and Annie's favourite ginger snap biscuits. The invalid lay on the sofa in the living room propped up on pillows, and feeling very sorry for herself, but enjoying all the fuss as her family gathered around her. The accident had worked out very well—a risk worth taking. She could put up with a cast on her leg and a bit of a headache. She had achieved her goal—Kathy was home!

The official letter from the Land Army stated: "Compassionate leave had been granted to Kathleen Gardner to care for her elderly, sick mother."

Kathy viewed her compassionate leave as a step backwards in her attempt to be independent. She decided she would stay with her mother only until her leg was healed and the cast removed. The Land Army informed her that Mr Graham, owner of the farm in Cheshire, had agreed to allow Kathy to return to the farm when she was free to do so.

Life at home was almost intolerable for Kathy. Stuck inside for days on end, catering to Annie's every whim. She missed the outdoors—even the cows— and the mother pig would be giving birth soon. The girls would all be there to watch the piglets being born, counting them as they arrived, and she would miss it all.

"Are you there, Kathy?" called her mother from the living room. "I need you."

"Yes, Mam, I'm right 'ere," answered Kathy, appearing from the kitchen with a dab of flour on the end of her nose. "I'm making Yorkshire puddings to go along with the beef for dinner."

"Oh, that's nice, dear. Could you bring me a glass of fresh water, and run upstairs and get a different book for me, this one's boring."

Kathy did as she was asked, and no sooner was she in the kitchen mixing batter again, she was interrupted for the umpteenth time that day.

"Kathy, come in 'ere." Her mother's whining voice cut through her like a knife. "Bring me a nail file will you dear? I don't know 'ow I've managed to break a nail while I'm just lying around. Put the kettle on while you're about it. We'll 'ave a cup of tea, and make sure there's strawberry jam for the scones this time. I didn't like the blackberry jam yesterday. It gave me 'eartburn."

Annie wrote pages of instructions to Mr Salt at the factory, and asked him to bring the books to the house every Friday morning while she was convalescing. She dispatched Kathy to The Pear Drop to find out if Jennifer James, one of the chapel ladies who had stepped in to run the shop, was doing her job and keeping everything in order.

"Check all the jars and make sure they've been dusted," Annie said. "Tell 'er you will be at the shop on Saturday evening to count the money and do the bank deposit. You will also report to me on what stock is low and needs reordering. We can't leave that up to Jennifer. She'll 'ave no idea what to do."

On and on and on the constant demands went all day long, until, after three weeks of it, Kathy was at breaking point. She waited until Annie was having an afternoon nap, and ran along the street to Newhall Road to seek out Aunty Rosemary.

"You 'ave to 'elp me, Aunty," she gasped as she fell into a chair in the tiny kitchen. "I can't stay with 'er any longer. She's driving me mad."

"Oh, Kathy," Rosemary commiserated with her young niece. "You'd 'ave to be a saint to put up with our Annie when she gets like this. Catch your breath now and we'll try and sort things out. Me and the other aunties should 'ave come to the house more. We shouldn't 'ave left it all up to you."

"It's not the work," explained Kathy. "Mam is so demanding and never leaves me alone. I want to go back to the farm. I want to go soon. I won't make it for another month. I swear I will run away before she gets her cast off."

"It won't come to that," said Rosemary, passing Kathy a cup of steaming tea. "I'll get the aunties together tonight and we'll make plans to take over from you. Go 'ome and take care of your Mam for now, but please don't worry that you 'ave been abandoned by us."

Rosemary kissed the top of her niece's head before she left.

"Go on now," she said softly. "We know 'ow to 'andle your Mam."

When it came to issues with Annie, her sisters were used to coming to the rescue. Rosemary, May, Lizzie and Daisy met at the house in Newhall Road and made plans to alleviate the pressure on poor Kathy. Before the second pot of tea was finished, they had drawn up a roster for the days ahead, each taking a day to devote to the invalid.

"It's not like we 'aven't done it before," smiled May. "When Annie needs our 'elp, we're always there. She's 'elped us all out over the years. That's what sisters do."

The sisters nodded in agreement. Now, maybe, Kathy could go back to the Land Army sooner than she thought. Annie would kick up a fuss, of course, but May offered to talk to her the next day and persuade her it was the right thing to do. Kathy had her own life to live and her own path to follow.

Mr Salt drove Kathy to catch the train to Macclesfield and Mr Graham met the train in answer to Kathy's telegram informing him of her return. She had only been away for a few weeks, but her roommates greeted her as though it had been many months.

"Kath, we missed you," Fanny babbled, as all three girls pulled her into a group hug. "How's your Mam? The mother pig had fourteen piglets. They're adorable and smelly. The old collie, Jasper, died two weeks ago. Mrs Graham cried for days. Jo was kicked in the knee by Mildred, the big cow with the white face, while she was trying to milk her. The biggest news—an entire battalion of soldier are camped on the other side of the village."

Fanny paused for breath, and Myra and Jo filled in all the details of the camp full of soldiers. They all ended up lying sideways across Kathy's bed laughing, as they planned various outrageous plans to meet the soldiers.

Kathy was so happy to be back at the farm. She had left her mother hysterically crying and imploring her to stay at home, or she would die. The aunties were all at the house to supervise Kathy's departure and take over the care of Annie. Aunty May put Kathy's suitcase into her hand and pushed her through the door towards Mr Salt's car waiting outside.

"Off you go, my duck," smiled Aunty May. "Don't you worry another minute about your Mam. She'll be all right with us. She's making a big fuss to make you feel guilty about leaving. You go on now, and do your farming work with the other girls. We're all proud you're 'elping with the war effort."

Kathy thanked her Aunty May as she walked towards the car. She knew her aunties all had worries of their own, with loved ones in the armed forces. Not knowing when the call would come to cross the English Channel and begin fighting.

As she lay in bed that night, staring at the wooden roof of the attic room, Kathy thought about her mother and how trying and difficult she had been. She had no intention of going home for a visit. In fact she had no plans to go home at all.

The Land Army girls from Graham's farm all walked to the village together, giggling and chatting, dressed in their best civilian clothes and ready to dance. The village council had decided to hold dances every Saturday night to help make the soldiers in the tent camp feel welcome.

It changed the girls' lives completely. Young men had vanished from every community since call-up began, and now there was an overabundance of them waiting in the Village Hall, lining up to dance with the all-too-few girls. Partners were switched many times, as each soldier jostled for a chance to put his arms around a girl for a few minutes.

Five men from a colliery band in a nearby town travelled to the village every Saturday to play the latest dance music—their way of supporting the lads in the army, helping to give them a good time. The ladies from the Women's Institute stood behind tables on one side of the hall, serving punch and homemade biscuits. All very civilized.

Kathy never sat down, but danced all night with dozens of different partners, all dressed the same in their khaki uniforms. Whether short, tall, fat, thin, clumsy or elegant, they were all polite, well-behaved, and so happy to be dancing with her.

After four Saturday dances, the girls had their favourite partners picked out. Kathy liked one soldier in particular, and always scanned the crowd standing around the sides of the hall to catch his eye. Robert Stevens was a quiet, handsome young man, who lived in Oxford and had been studying veterinary medicine at The Royal Veterinary College in London before the war started. He was instantly drawn to the girls from the farm, enjoying the stories they related about the animals they tended. He particularly liked Kathy, with her red curls, rosy cheeks and bubbly personality, and he made a beeline for her every Saturday night.

Intimate contact, such as kissing or holding a partner too close, were frowned on in the Village Hall, but the row of horse chestnut trees at the back of the hall became known as "kissing copse," and the soldiers took full advantage of the privacy the huge trees provided, if they could persuade a girl to step outside with them.

Kathy took no persuading when Robert led her outside for a "breath of fresh air." She knew they were headed for the chestnut trees, and felt the tiny butterflies inside anticipating her first kiss. They spent the rest of the night behind a massive tree on the outskirts of the copse. The first tentative kisses led to the wonder and delight of lips parted, and long deep kisses that left them both breathless and wanting more. With their bodies pressed together, Robert fought to control himself, but was increasingly aware that he was losing the battle, particularly with Kathy's back to the tree, and the bone of her pelvis pushing into him. He reached for her breast, and groaned as he felt her nipple hard against the middle of his hand. With superhuman strength, Robert pushed himself away from her and gazed into her beautiful eyes.

"Enough, Kathy," he murmured. "I'm sorry, I shouldn't have done that. I had no intention of staying out here so long. It was just meant to be a few kisses, but you're too lovely, I was carried away. It was wonderful, but I think we should go back into the hall now.

"I wouldn't mind staying out 'ere," whispered Kathy, embarrassed that she was even saying such a thing. "I loved your kisses, and everything else. I could feel 'ow much you wanted me."

Robert blushed, knowing what she meant.

"Let's meet again next Saturday, and come out here to our tree. I'll think about you every minute while I'm away from you, Kathy. Don't let's complicate it by going too far before we're ready."

The "kissing copse" became a regular haunt for the two young lovers. They could barely wait for Saturday nights when they only danced the first couple of dances before scurrying off to their tree.

Kathy had never felt anything like this feeling she had for Robert. He consumed her every waking moment and filled her dreams at night.

She did venture home on a four-day pass at Christmas, but didn't tell Annie about her young man, preferring to keep her relationship with him a secret from the prying questions that would come from her mother.

Annie was out of her cast, and, although she still used a cane to help her balance, she was back to working in The Pear Drop, even though the The Government had banned the use of private cars. Annie had swallowed her pride, walked to the high street, and stepped onto a bus for the first time in her adult life.

The house seemed dull and dark to Kathy, and she

noticed many of the upstairs rooms had been closed off. Even the dining room downstairs had dust sheets on the furniture and had a musty, empty smell. She would be spent time airing out the old house and putting up decorations. Nora, Norman and Christopher were coming to spend a few days with them, and the boy cousins were coming home on leave. It would be a grand Christmas.

It was, indeed, a great Christmas for the whole family. Annie's house sparkled with Christmas lights and shone with newly polished furniture and clean windows. Bedrooms were opened up for their visitors and the dining room put into full use for a Christmas Eve party with the entire family. The little chapel on Newhall Road was full to overflowing for the Christmas Day service, with the soldiers on leave reading the scriptures and Mr Baker saying special prayers for their safety.

Kathy loved being with her extended family during the Christmas break. Each Land Army girl was only allowed to take off four days on rotation, and Kathy counted herself lucky to be at home from December 23rd to December 27th. Throughout the hectic days Kathy thought about Robert, and confessed her secret to her sister before she returned to the farm.

As the new year began, Kathy shivered through her chores on the farm. The loft bedroom at the vet's house was ice cold, and the girls chipped in and shared the cost of buying a paraffin heater to take off the chill. Mornings were the worst, when the first milking of the day left the girls chilled through to their bones. Mrs Graham made volumes of porridge for breakfast to warm them up.

While the Saturday dances were on hold until the spring, Robert and Kathy met at the village pub instead, surrounded by soldiers and Land Army girls. The wintry weather kept them indoors, so no visits to the chestnut tree. A quick walk around the village green, a sweet kiss in the moonlight, holding hands and sharing a beer were precious shared times together.

Throughout the winter and into the spring, regular bombing missions over Britain by the big German planes filled people with fear. London was hit the hardest, with much of the East End and docklands bombed out during the blitz, but many other great cities were bombed and badly damaged, from Liverpool to Southampton, Manchester to Glasgow. All over the country lay the ruins left behind after the air raids.

Nothing was secure or permanent in the lives of the people of Britain. Troops were moved and relocated to continue training—among them Robert's regiment, which left the village in April bound for Scunthorpe in East Yorkshire.

Kathy and Robert wrote to each other every day, but knew there would be very little chance of seeing each other in the foreseeable future. He would head home to Oxford to see his parents when he had a three-day pass, and Kathy would visit her mother.

The farm flourished despite help from "a bunch of bloody girls," as farmer Graham often called them. The mother pig produced another big litter of eleven babies. Myra left the Land Army and joined the Women's Royal Air Force. She was replaced by Linda, a girl of eighteen from Manchester, who had six younger siblings and was used to hard work.

Kathy went home for Christmas once more, filling the bleak house with her energy and warmth. Annie relished every moment her daughter spent with her, following her from room to room to be near her, talking to her and touching her. Kathy kept her good humour knowing she would only be at home for a few days, and smiling at the secret she was keeping for Boxing Day.

Despite Nora's absence, Christmas Eve at Annie's house was joyous, as the sisters and their families gathered for a feast. Army life had turned May's son, Fred, into a tall strong man, and they were all introduced to his girlfriend, Dorothy, who was a real beauty with her dark hair and eyes. Kathy smiled at her cousin Fred, who was so shy, as he put his arm around Dorothy's slender waist. Aunty May frowned her disapproval as she looked Fred's girlfriend up and down. Aunty May didn't approve of lipstick, high heels and smoking, but the frown didn't bother Dorothy.

The Boxing Day secret arrived at noon. Kathy had been on edge all morning, willing the time to move more quickly. She flew to the door when she heard the quiet knock and threw herself at the young man standing on the doorstep. He responded by pressing his lips onto hers and holding her close, as Annie appeared in the hallway.

Robert was ushered inside, Kathy still clinging to his arm and smiling up at him.

"Mam, this is Robert Stevens," Kathy said, looking at her mother. "'E's my boyfriend, and I 'aven't seen 'im since 'is battalion moved away in the spring. We 'ad this whole thing planned, so that we could see each other this Christmas."

"Please to meet you, Mrs Gardner," Robert said in his low quiet voice. "I've heard so much about you."

"More than I've 'eard about you, young man," Annie declared. "Kathy kept you very quiet I must say. Boyfriend are you? She's never 'ad a boyfriend before. You'd better come in and tell me all about yourself."

Satisfied that she had all the details, Annie went to change into her new blue satin blouse. She was meeting her sisters for tea at Rosemary's tiny house in Newhall Road. A quiet time for the elderly ladies amidst the turmoil of the celebrations. Kathy couldn't wait for her to leave, and she fell into Robert's arms the minute the door closed behind her mother, and held him close. For the next hour they loved each other with their kisses and caresses, trying to make up for all the months they had spent apart. When Annie returned she peered at them both suspiciously, noticing their red cheeks and shining eyes, and was left with no question about what they'd been doing.

Robert took the last train back to Scunthorpe at the end of the day. Mr Salt, now a close family friend as well as the factory manager, drove him to the station, with Kathy clinging to his arm in the back seat. When would they see each other again? Would Robert be deployed to fight soon? They both had the same thoughts, knowing that their relationship, like all others during war, was tentative and temporary. There were no guarantees.

"Write to me every day," Robert whispered in Kathy's ear.

"I promise. Every day," Kathy replied, moving her lips to meet his, even with Mr Salt seeing their reflection in his mirror. She didn't care, it may be the last kiss.

CHAPTER 50
WAITING

The winter days at the farm were always difficult. Every chore seemed to sap energy and take longer, especially handling the cows, who somehow seemed bigger, wetter and considerably more stubborn. Mucking out the milking shed was particularly onerous, and the girls kept their sense of humour by making up mucky words to popular songs. "Somewhere over the cow shed, shit will fly," was a particular favourite, as they mimicked Judy Garland in the Wizard of Oz.

The Japanese had bombed Pearl Harbour in December, 1941, resulting in a full commitment from the US to join their allies in the war against Germany.

The Americans began pouring into the country, causing quite a stir, particularly among the young ladies. The abandoned army camp on the other side of the village was designated for an American infantry division and news spread quickly around the village and into the surrounding farms that they had arrived. With their superior uniforms, money, drawling speech and confident manner, they were an instant hit with the farm girls. Saturday nights at the pub took on a whole new atmosphere, as the girls giggled and made eyes at the US soldiers. For their part, they lived up to expectations, carrying chocolates, chewing gum and even nylon stockings with them as gifts for the deprived British girls.

A few of the more gullible girls believed the stories some of the GIs told them, and were wide-eyed with wonder that they were friends with Clarke Gable or Cary Grant, that they lived in Hollywood, that they were millionaires. The more sensible girls, like Kathy, heard the truth and enjoyed the company of farmers, teachers, carpenters, husbands and fathers, who were far away from home and missing their families.

The country was packed with troops and equipment. The trains, buses, streets, towns and villages were jammed with men and women in uniform. All assembling, training and preparing for a strike against the enemy who now occupied most of Europe. Next time it would not be a "Dunkirk." They would arrive in France ready to push the great armies of Germany right back into their own country.

Kathy managed to see her Robert several times over the next few years. When he had a three-day pass he headed to Cheshire and stayed at the village pub to be near her. Many soldiers were getting married to their sweethearts, wanting to have at least a few days together as man and wife while they could. Kathy's cousin, Fred, married Dorothy in September of 1942, and her cousin Sam married his sweetheart the following spring.

Robert and Kathy decided they would marry when the war was over. Although Kathy was a chapel girl, she had always had an independent side, which didn't always fall in with her family's view of life. She was the one who suggested spending the night with Robert at the pub. If they were waiting to be married, it didn't mean they couldn't sleep together. Robert didn't put up a fight. His dreams were always full of making love to Kathy. He even had condoms provided by the army.

The proprietors at the pub turned a blind eye when Kathy followed her soldier up the winding wooden stairs.

"Lovely young couple like that should have some time together," the landlady smiled. "It's all right with me, how about you Billy?"

"You know me," answered Billy with a chuckle. "Anything to help the war. He'll fight all the better for getting his end away."

"Oh, be quiet," his merry wife laughed.

The room upstairs was cozy, with a fire smouldering in the grate and a gas light flickering on the wall above the bed. The young couple undressed without talking, with their backs to each other. Kathy slipped into her long flannelette nightie and Robert left on his army underwear. Like their first hesitant kisses, they didn't know where to begin, but tucked into bed beside each other their nervousness quickly melted away, and they were soon wriggling out of their clothing. How wonderful it felt to be so close. Robert tried his best to take his time and enjoy touching and kissing his beautiful red-headed sweetheart. They both laughed and lay back on the pillows after the quick first encounter. They had all night together to try again. Making love in the early hours of the morning, they savoured each moment and clung to each other in ecstasy.

"Thank you, Kathy," Robert whispered. "I love you more than you can ever imagine. This is the most wonderful night of my life. To me, you are my wife already."

"It was wonderful," Kathy said. "I feel the same way. You are and always will be my dearest 'usband."

"I probably won't get leave again for three months. Will you come and stay here with me again?"

"Every time you visit I will come 'ere to sleep with you. Even if the war lasts for ten years."

"If it lasts for ten years, we'd better change our minds about being married, I think," laughed Robert. "Why don't we make plans that if the war is still on next spring, we'll get married anyway?"

"That's a good plan, darling. 'ow can the country keep going on like this? Just waiting and waiting."

"They want to be well prepared," Robert stated. "The high ups are slowly moving all the troops to the south of England. It may be more difficult to visit you after this, because I'm sure my unit will be transferred south very soon. Who knows where we'll be sent to."

"Then this makes our night together even more wonderful," smiled Kathy through her tears.

Kathy was in the milking shed, spreading fresh straw. It was an overcast, cloudy day at the beginning of June and her tummy was rumbling, letting her know that she needed lunch. One of the girls who had been working in the kitchen garden came bursting into the shed, trying to catch her breath as she motioned for Kathy to come quickly.

"Come on, Kathy," the girl shouted. "There's news about the war. Mrs Graham's got the radio on in the kitchen."

Girls came running from all directions and gathered in the kitchen, while Mrs Graham shushed them to be quiet so they could all hear.

The announcer, in his sombre war-time voice, said that this was D-Day and a military force of British, American and Canadian troops were invading the beaches of Normandy, with air and naval support. The waiting was over.

"God go with them," said Mrs Graham.

The girls all murmured their own similar prayers.

Now it would begin. The battle they had been preparing for for years. The Americans joining the war had made all the difference. They had the men and the equipment to make sure victory was a possibility for the allied troops.

The letters from Robert were sporadic, but he wrote hopeful and optimistic words, assuring her of his safety and never-ending love. Then nothing for more than a month. Kathy knew what that meant. She would wait. Wait for news. News she dreaded.

A letter arrived for her in late October. It was from Private Graham Dougherty, who served with Robert. He had promised to write to Kathy if anything happened to his friend, and something had happened. Their unit had been fighting for control of a bridge. The details were difficult to read as there was so much of the letter blacked out. It was apparent that Robert's unit had been overpowered and had been ordered to retreat. When they regrouped, Robert was not with them. His family had been informed that he was missing in action. His friend thought he should let Kathy know.

Missing in action. What did that mean?

Kathy was distraught, and Mrs Graham told her to ask for leave and go home, because she was no good to them, moping around the farm and not getting her work done.

Annie was at The Pear Drop when Kathy arrived home. She had ridden three buses from the farm, knowing her mother and Mr Salt could no longer use their cars. A complete ban on petrol had been issued for all civilians, except farmers and doctors.

The house was locked and she went to the back door and looked under the brick in the flower bed to find the key. Inside, the house was cool and damp and silent. So different from the house she remembered growing up in, when her father was alive and Nora was still at home. The rooms were always so full of light and there were always bowls of fresh flowers scattered around to perfume the air. Now the air was stale and the rooms were dark, with the curtains closed to keep out the light.

She found cheese and bread in the kitchen pantry and made herself a cup of tea. Dreams of a future spent with Robert danced through her head as she sat at the kitchen table eating. It was a lovely dream. A dream though. Only a dream.

Aunty May was bringing the washing in off the line when Kathy came through the back gate into the yard, making her Aunty jump in fright.

"Kathy, what are you doing 'ome?" May asked, giving her niece a hug.

"I'm taking a leave for a few days, Aunty May," answered Kathy. "Robert's missing in action and I needed some time to think about that."

"Oh, my dear girl," May said. "Come on into the 'ouse. We'll 'ave a cuppa. What bad news. The news none of us wants to get."

Tea and tears. That's what life was sometimes. There were never tears without tea.

"I didn't want to stay in the 'ouse. I expect Mam is working at the shop, and the 'ouse is so quiet and sad. I really don't know 'ow I'm going to talk to 'er about this. We don't really get along these days."

May sipped her tea and didn't answer her niece. Annie had thrown herself into keeping The Pear Drop running. It was the only thing she had left. She had become a bitter, lonely woman, despite the efforts of her sisters to intervene. They had asked her to join the ladies group at chapel, or the choir, or even volunteer on the weekends with the Salvation Army who made tea and passed out food to families in need. The answer was always the same. She had enough to do running the shop, without getting involved with useless activities.

Kathy picked up fish and chips on the way back to the house. She would surprise her mother with a meal, and hopefully their visit could begin in a positive way. She opened up the curtains in the living room and also opened some windows to let the fresh air fill the room. She found a tablecloth in the linen cupboard and covered the kitchen table, then went outside and picked a bunch of late-flowering dahlias which were still in bloom down the side of the house. Setting the flowers in a vase in the middle of the table made the kitchen feel warm and inviting. Lastly, she put the kettle on to make the ever-present pot of tea, and waited for Annie's arrival.

The shop always closed promptly at six o'clock, but Annie now had to wait for a bus to take her home. She hated riding the bus. She didn't like sitting beside strangers when she was cold and tired. Her feet were never warm and her eyes smarted from the thick cigarette smoke on the bus. She arrived home tired and hungry, not expecting her surprise visitor.

"Mam, surprise, surprise," Kathy chirped, walking to the door to greet her mother.

"Well, well," Annie said, accepting a kiss on her cheek. "What brings you 'ome in the middle of the week? Did you kill one of the cows, or something?"

"Let's go into the kitchen," Kathy said, avoiding the questions. "I've picked up fish and chips for us and the kettle just boiled for tea."

"Flowers and a tablecloth as well," noticed Annie.

"Let's eat before we talk," persuaded Kathy, not wanting to jump in with her news about Robert right away. "I've kept the food warm in the oven."

The two women sat opposite each other, nibbling on their fish and chips. Annie was, in fact, enjoying every bite. She hadn't eaten like this for weeks, and to have company to eat it with gave her great pleasure, but she wasn't going to admit that to her daughter.

Kathy put the plates into the sink and hugged her warm teacup in her hands.

"I've taken a short leave, Mam," she explained. "I had a letter from one of Robert's mates in the army. Robert is missing in action. I have no idea whether 'e's alive or dead."

Tears spilled onto Kathy's cheeks, as she muttered the news to her mother.

Annie thought back to losing Daniel so many years ago. How devastated she had been. But this was different. This wasn't Kathy's husband—just a casual boyfriend. They'd hardly spent any time together over the years since they met; an odd weekend leave here and there. No, it wasn't like losing a husband as she had.

"Don't take on so, Kathy," her mother said. "There are lots more soldiers, for goodness' sake. The country's exploding with them. I daresay you'll be sweet on another young man before too long."

"Stop it," Kathy said in a monotone voice, trying not to get immediately angry. "You 'ave no idea of the relationship between me and Robert. We love each other, just as if we were married. Don't look at me like that. It means exactly 'ow it sounds. 'E is no casual acquaintance, Mam. 'E is the love of my life and I know I won't meet anybody like 'im again."

"Kathy, I know you're upset now, but it will pass believe me. You stay 'ere with me and you'll soon feel better. It's always the best to be at 'ome with your Mam."

Kathy looked at her mother's smiling face. She had been wrong to come home. She should have stayed in the village, at the pub, in the room where she had stayed with Robert.

CHAPTER 52
NO OPTION

Somehow Kathy forced her way through the leave, spending time with the aunties and as little time as possible with her mother. Fred's wife, Dorothy, had given birth to a baby girl and they were living with Aunty May. Fred was somewhere in France fighting with the Welsh Guards. The baby was a distraction for Kathy and she spent hours holding her and talking to her, watching the crooked smile turn her lips into a lopsided bow.

When Kathy returned to the farm, she found the address of Robert's parents stuck in the back of her sock drawer. She had forgotten he had given it to her. It had been during the winter when she had worn her boots and thick socks, and the scrap of paper was with those same socks when she dragged them out on a cold autumn day. She wrote to them, explaining who she was, and asking for any news they may have about their son.

She waited every day for the postman to deliver the mail to the farm, then hurried into the kitchen to ask Mrs Graham if there was anything for her.

"Don't keep coming in here every day, Kathy," Mrs

Graham said. "I'll let you know if you get a letter. You're driving me crazy with your constant mithering."

After weeks of waiting, a reply arrived. It was from Mrs Stevens, Robert's mother.

Dear Kathy,

How lovely to hear from you. Robert told us all about you on his last leave, and we know how much you mean to him. We have no news of our son, but pray he is safe somewhere. His ID dog tags have not been found, which gives us hope that he is alive. The army will be in touch with us when they have some definite information to pass on, at which time we will write and let you know.

Sincerely,
Gloria Stevens

Kathy read the letter several times. There was hope. The dog tags were proof that he was still alive, weren't they? She would wait for more news. She would wait and wait until she knew where he was and what had happened to him.

Not wanting to go home, she spent her next few days of leave with Nora in Colchester. Norman remained in London, busier than ever in the war rooms. Their little flat in London had escaped the bombing, but Nora was grateful of the safety she and little Christopher had found with her mother-in-law. Norman's mother lived in a large house and there was plenty of room for Kathy to stay with them. Colchester was such a beautiful town, with its ancient castle and tree-lined walks. Flowers and grass grew everywhere, unlike the barren streets of Longton, where industry had taken its toll on most natural spaces. Long walks with Christopher were a joy for Kathy, and for the first time since she had joined up, she didn't want to go back to the farm in Cheshire.

She was twenty-two years old when the war ended. There had never been news of Robert. He was one of the missing, who had never been found, and she had waited every day for nothing. She had never mourned him, because she truly believed he was alive, and had refused to give up hope. She still refused to stop hoping. Maybe now the war was over, they would find him.

England was once more overflowing with troops as the Americans, Canadians, British and many other nations' military forces gathered to be demobilized before returning to their respective countries of origin. Slowly, young men began to reappear into society and try to pick up the lives they had left behind six years before. Many didn't return, lost or injured in battle, changing the world forever and leaving the economy and workforce in shreds.

The Gardner Sweet Factory slowly started to recover. With the gradual return of sugar into the country, the old recipes were dusted off and put into production. Although the purchase of sweets still required a ration coupon, it was easy for shops selling sweets to slip in extra goodies, and the soldiers waiting to return to their homelands were good customers. Mr Salt welcomed back Joe Worden and Sidney Byron, two young men who had survived the war—after all they were still shareholders. The families of the three men who didn't come home were compensated for the shares their men had owned.

Annie struggled with a difficult decision. She had kept the factory going because of Thomas. He had started it all and had been so proud of his humbugs. In recent years she cared less and less and wanted to be rid of the responsibility.

She decided to discuss her predicament with Mr Salt and the two other shareholders.

"Gentlemen," Annie began. "I want to be completely 'onest with you. I no longer want any dealings with the factory. I want to sell my shares, or the factory. The question I put to the three of you is: One, would you be interested in buying my shares? Or, two, would you prefer I sell the factory and pay out your shares from the sale?"

Mr Salt didn't answer immediately. Joe and Sidney just stared at Annie.

"Mrs Gardner," Mr Salt finally said. "Could we have some time to consider what you've told us? Speaking for all three of us, we really love this little place, and the boys here have come through five years of hell. We will have to talk it through before we make a decision."

"Of course," agreed Annie. "Let's meet on Monday morning next week."

Annie shook hands with the three men and bided her time with her own decision.

When they met again the following Monday, Mr Salt was the spokesman.

"Mrs Gardner," he said. "All three of us are of one mind. I have a good number of working years ahead of me, and these two men even more than me. We have no idea how we would raise the money to buy your shares, or what the factory is worth, but we all want to at least give it a try. We all think, now the war's over, that this little factory will grow and be profitable again. We're all willing to take that risk. It's just the money that will be the issue in the beginning."

"That's all I need to 'ear," smiled Annie. "My 'usband would be 'appy to know it will continue. I will seek my lawyer's advice and let you know about the value of the company and the share prices. I sincerely 'ope and pray we can make it 'appen."

Mr Salt, Joe and Sidney could think of nothing else while they were waiting to hear from Annie. None of them had the kind of money it would take to buy her shares, and they knew it as well as she did. The two young soldiers both had young families to support and knew they were lucky to have come home to a job, but now the future seemed unsure. They dreaded being out of work, when there were no jobs to be had.

The next meeting between them was called for Friday afternoon after the day's work was done.

Annie's lawyer accompanied her, and looked over his glasses at the three men as they came into the office. A stack of papers sat in front of him and he shuffled through them as Annie invited the men to take a seat.

"I will speak for Mrs Gardner," the lawyer said in a firm voice. "She has made her intentions known to me and I have drawn up the necessary papers for your signatures. That is, of course, if you agree to the terms."

The men looked at each other, all colour drained from their faces.

"It doesn't matter how much the factory is worth, or what Mrs Garner's shares actually cost. She is willing to offer you her fifty-one percent of the shares in The Gardner Sweet Factory for one pound per share." The lawyer was obviously not impressed with Annie's decision. Joe, Sidney and Mr Salt however jumped out of their chairs and all tried to grab Annie's hands at the same time.

"Ahem!" the lawyer coughed. "If you agree to these terms, the papers are here for your signatures. May I add that you are three very lucky men."

Annie had no regrets. The factory had provided her and her family with everything they needed and more. She had enough money to live well for many years, including a generous inheritance. The Pear Drop was another story. Could she bear to part with it?

Kathy had no option but to return home. She had stayed at the farm until the Graham boys, who had both survived the war, returned. She had no idea what to do with the rest of her life now that her life in the Land Army had come to an end. Her plan had been to marry Robert and find a job in London while he finished his studies. The endless days of being with Mother stretched before her like a prison sentence.

"I don't know why I didn't think of it before," began Annie, bursting into Kathy's bedroom while she was unpacking her suitcase. "Now you're back to stay, you must run the shop for me. I'm getting too old to keep up with the work, but you can take it over. I'll teach you everything you need to know. Oh, Kathy, it will be such fun. You and me together again, just like it used to be."

Annie turned and left the room as abruptly as she had entered it, leaving Kathy staring after her. Run the shop. Was that her lot in life? It could be worse. It would give her something to do. She was convinced she would never marry. She would be a spinster, poor Miss Gardner—the old maid.

Kathy felt stripped of all emotion. She had become used to the routine of the farm and had moved through each day automatically taking care of the chores. She never went into the village with the other girls at the weekend to drink beer with the Americans. She read and reread the few letters she had received from Robert and the one letter from his mother.

Bottles filled with sweets didn't replace cows or pigs. The confines of the tiny shop felt claustrophobic compared with the freedom and fresh air of the farm. The lack of physical activity made her squirmy and impatient, and the constant, overwhelming presence of her mother drove her crazy.

"Why don't you go 'ome, Mam," Kathy encouraged her ever-present mother. "There's nothing to do 'ere. I don't need you to keep me company. Go 'ave tea with Aunty May and Dorothy. Go buy a new dress."

"Don't tell me what to do, young miss," replied Annie.

"There's plenty to do 'ere if you know where to look. The windows could do with a polish, and the outside window sill needs washing again. It's a daily job to keep things clean around 'ere with all the smoke and soot from the factory kilns."

"Well, I'll get both those chores done right away," Kathy said between clenched teeth. "That means you are free to go. I enjoy being on my own. I'll see you after the shop's closed. You were going to pick up meat and make a meat and potato pie for tonight's meal, remember."

"I did promise you that pie," agreed Annie. "If you're sure you'll be able to manage on your own."

Annie finally succumbed to her daughter's persuasion and put on her hat and coat.

"See you later," called Kathy, as her mother left the shop.

Every day seemed a battle of wills between the two women, until Rosemary stepped in with a suggestion that made life easier.

"Why don't you share the work?" Rosemary asked as they sat down for lunch on Sunday at Annie's house. "You could work a day each. That way you'd both 'ave a day off every second day to do whatever you wanted. The shop doesn't need two of you there all the time—except maybe Saturdays. Petrol is available on ration again, so you can drive your car, Annie."

Annie, of course, didn't agree. But she never did. Kathy thought it was an excellent idea and, after much discussion, her mother gave in. They set up a roster to work alternate days, with both of them at the shop on Saturdays. Kathy was forever indebted to her Aunty for her insight. She still had the evenings and weekends to struggle through, but with five days by herself, she felt she would cope quite well.

Preparations for Christmas began early that year. It would be a Christmas of celebration for the entire country.

Many of the service men and women were already home and those still waiting for release were granted a week's leave. Fred would be home with the family, and the chapel would be filled with all the young men and women who had been absent from their midst for six years.

The Pear Drop sparkled and shone with Christmas ornaments, tinsel and candles. A small tree, covered in red bows and white angels, sat in the corner opposite the door. A silver bowl full of colourful sugary treats rested on the counter by the till, ready for each child to choose one as a treat. Extra chocolates adorned the front window display, and red, green and white Christmas boxes and bags were at hand to gift wrap the selected goodies.

Kathy had decorated the house similarly, adorning every surface with cascades of ivy and holly, and erecting a large fir tree in the hallway, complete with coloured glass balls, silver bells and candles. Although it was weeks before the big event, she forced herself to get into the spirit of the season, particularly as her cousins would be home from the army, and Christmas Eve would be celebrated at their house. She would play her part, and help her mother host the special annual feast to celebrate Christ's birth, despite the ache in her heart that it would be another Christmas without Robert.

A wintry blast of cold rain followed Kathy into the house. She stepped over the letters strewn on the floor beneath the letterbox, blowing on her fingertips and throwing the bag of groceries onto the floor. She gathered up the letters and saw, among them, an envelope addressed to her in faintly familiar handwriting. She picked it out of the other envelopes and turned it over. She had seen the handwriting before, many months ago. The return address was in Oxford.

Kathy sat down on the chair in the hallway, not trusting her legs would hold her if she read it whilst standing.

My dear Kathy,

I apologize for not staying in touch with you. It was too painful to write to you with no news of our dear son Robert. We never gave up hope, but as the months dragged on, we had to face the fact that he may be lost forever.

At the beginning of August, we received a letter from an army official that Robert's name had appeared on a POW list. We felt it unnecessary and probably cruel to inform you. We didn't want to raise your hopes. The next correspondence confirmed Robert's capture in October of 1944, and his transfer to a camp in Poland. He was transferred to a different camp several months later, but the British army were not sent the list of POWs from the camp. It was only after liberation, when lists of the prisoners were found, that the details of Robert's internment were uncovered.

Records are difficult to follow during such chaos, and the army was not able to find any other knowledge of Robert after February of 1945. God alone knows what happened to him.

I'm so sorry this is not the news you or we hoped for. We felt we had to let you know. We hope you can find peace,

Sincerely,
Gloria Stevens

The letter lay on Kathy's lap, her fingers gently stroking the words written there. She would put it with the other letters in the box in her room. She would read it often to remind herself that he hadn't died on the battlefield. He'd been taken prisoner. Was that better, or worse? Had he died in the prison camp? If not, where was he? With her mind in a turmoil, Kathy decided not to share this latest news with her family. It was a private, personal letter that only she could possibly understand. Everybody was excited about Fred and Sam coming home. They didn't need reminding how lucky they were, and that many thousands of people, including her Robert, would not be home for Christmas.

The letter safely stashed away, Kathy came down the stairs to find her mother wrapping gifts on the dining room table.

"Come and 'elp me with this, dear," Annie said. "It's a gift for Fred and Dorothy's little girl, Ann. I saw it in the market the other day and couldn't resist buying it for 'er. A real little kitchen, with pots and pans, spoons and plates. She's going to absolutely love it."

Kathy went to hold the paper while her mother tied the bows with red ribbon. She was happy her mother was distracted enough not to notice her daughter's red eyes and pale face.

"I wish you could play the piano, Kathy," her mother prattled on. "You could if you would practice. Why don't you try some easy Christmas carols, then we could all gather around the piano and sing on Christmas Eve. If only Nora was coming for the holiday things would be different. Now there's a good piano player. Why don't you give it a try? You 'ave little else to do when you're not at the shop."

Kathy didn't answer. The piano had been held over her head as a threat, or a reward since she was a girl. She wouldn't play that piano if her life depended upon it. She hated it with a passion.

Gloria Stevens' letter was only the first of two to arrive that week. The second sat on the mat below the mail slot all day while Kathy was at the shop and Annie was at Rosemary's house making mince pies.

Kathy was home before her mother, who had decided to stay at her sister-in-law's for a meal and join her at ladies group at the chapel, to help put up the Christmas tree. The letter on the mat stared up at Kathy as she slowly bent to pick it up. Another letter from Robert's mother. This time she carried it into the kitchen and placed it gently on the table while she filled the kettle with water to make tea. She didn't want to open it. She dreaded what it might say. She made the tea first and sat at the table before reaching for the envelope.

. . .

My dear Kathy,

I should have waited before writing to you a few days ago. We never expected to hear further news so soon. The POWs are slowly being repatriated. They are arriving from camps all over Europe and are of all different nationalities, so it has taken some time to complete records, or even produce an accurate list.

We were informed only yesterday that Robert is among these soldiers. His port of entry was Dover. His condition is unknown at present. He is just a name on a list. We know that if he was able he would have contacted us in some way, but that hasn't happened. We assume he may be injured or sick. But HE IS ALIVE!

We will be in touch with you the instant we hear more.

Affectionately,

Gloria Stevens

Kathy sat like a statue at the table, not daring to move, hardly breathing. Alive! Robert was alive! She reread the letter slowly, making sure she had it right. The cup of tea was left untouched as Kathy ran upstairs, pulled her suitcase from under the bed, and began throwing her clothes into it. She had to get to Oxford right away. To Oxford where Robert's parents lived. She had to try to find Robert.

By the time Annie arrived at the house, Kathy had her suitcase in the hallway and was putting on her warm coat and boots.

"Kathy? What's going on? Where are you going?" questioned Annie.

"I'm going to Oxford, Mam," answered Kathy breathlessly. "Robert is alive and I need to be with his parents and try to find 'im. The army has informed them he is on a POW list. That's all I know. I'm running to Mr Salt's 'ouse to ask 'im to drive me to the station."

"Wait, you can't just run off to Oxford," Annie said grabbing her daughter's arm. "Think first, girl. It's almost Christmas. You can't abandon me at such a time."

"Don't try to stop me," Kathy said, snatching her arm away from her mother's grip.

She was out of the door and running down the icy street before Annie could say anything else. As she ran, trying to keep her feet from sliding away from her on the thin layer of ice covering the pavement, her thoughts crowded her head with questions she couldn't answer. She skidded to a stop as she reached Mr Salt's house. She had left in such a hurry she hadn't thought about money for the train fare, or for other expenses. She banged on the door, and by the time Mr Salt opened it, she already knew where she could get the money she needed.

"What is it, lass?" Mr Salt asked, noticing Kathy's worried frown and disheveled appearance.

Kathy explained what had happened, and asked Mr Salt for a ride to Stoke station.

"Let me get my coat and car keys," Mr Salt said. "We'll set off in a minute or two."

The car engine took some encouraging to get going, but once they were on their way, Kathy asked Mr Salt to take a detour.

"Could we swing by the The Pear Drop on our way?" she asked. "I need to pick something up."

The spare key to the sweet shop was tucked deep inside Kathy's handbag. Once inside, she headed straight for the cupboard tucked into the far corner. The cash box was hidden at the back of the bottom drawer. Kathy reached inside to find the envelope full of cash, and tucked it into her handbag. She scribbled a note of confession to her mother, and left it in the cash box. Her problem solved, Kathy rejoined Mr Salt and continued her journey to the station.

Kathy took a train from Stoke Station and changed at

Crewe, before going onto Oxford. The train was jammed with people trying to get home before Christmas, and Kathy squeezed herself into a small space by the corridor door. Her mind was in a turmoil, not knowing what to expect when she arrived in Oxford. Worried that she wouldn't be able to find Robert, or that he was blind or badly wounded.

She arrived in Oxford too late at night to consider finding the Stevens' home, and asked a taxi driver to recommend a small inn or hotel she could stay in overnight. The White Swan Inn had a room available, and Kathy thanked the taxi driver for his help as she paid the fare.

The hotel must have been used to patrons keeping late hours, because there was still food available in a small room adjacent to the bar, where Kathy ordered tea and a sandwich. The rain had turned to sleet outside and she shivered as she looked out into the empty street. Where was Robert this night? Was he safe and warm somewhere? Tomorrow she would begin her search to find him.

CHAPTER 54
SEARCHING

Mr and Mrs Stevens were having breakfast when the doorbell rang. Frowning, Mrs Stevens went to answer it. The young woman standing outside was a stranger to them. Her clothing and shoes were wet from the constant sleet-filled rain that had persisted all night and into the morning.

"'Ello," she said. "I'm Kathy."

Mrs Stevens let out a small cry, then took Kathy's hands in hers and pulled her inside.

"Oh, my dear girl," Gloria Stevens cried. "You're here. I told Mr Stevens you would come, and here you are. Come in out of the cold. Let me take your wet coat."

Gloria Stevens was tall and slender. She had greying hair pulled into a bun at the nape of her neck. She wore a grey woolen skirt and a pale blue blouse, with matching cardigan. A gentle waft of rose water whirled around her as she took Kathy's arm and led her into the kitchen.

"Donald, this is Kathy."

"Kathy? You mean Robert's Kathy from the midlands?"

Mr Stevens asked, standing up and taking Kathy's cold hand in his two warm ones. "Gloria said you would come."

Like his wife, Donald was tall and slender. The similarity to Robert was striking. The same eyes and mouth, and the same deep smooth voice. Kathy gulped back the tears that threatened to spill down her cheeks.

"Come and have some tea and toast, dear," Gloria said. "We are delighted to meet you. We feel we know you, because Robert never stopped talking about you when he was last on leave."

Gloria's eyes misted with tears as she mentioned Robert, and she quickly wiped them away, as her husband reached for her hand.

"I'm 'ere to find Robert," Kathy stated. "There 'as to be a way to find out where 'e is. Where do I even begin my search?"

"I don't know what to tell you, my dear," Gloria interrupted. "There are probably all kinds of rules and regulations about tracing soldiers who have been lost for so long."

"I won't know until I've tried," Kathy said. "And I'm going to try. Rules and regulations won't stop me. I need to see Robert with my own eyes. I'm going to Dover to begin my search."

Donald and Gloria exchanged glances. This young woman was determined, but they feared she would be stopped in her efforts to find their son. The army was doing their best, in a time of chaos, to ensure the soldiers were reunited with their families as quickly as possible. They would probably not be tolerant of civilians who barged in making demands.

The weather had improved by the time Kathy had finished her tea and toast, and with her clothing dry, Mrs Stevens offered to drive her to the station. It had been wonderful to meet Robert's parents, and Kathy wondered why Mr Stevens hadn't offered to go with her on her quest. She would have welcomed a companion, but realized as soon as he reached for his walking stick, and slowly limped to the door, that he wouldn't have tolerated the journey.

It took all morning to travel to Dover, as Kathy had to change train stations in London, which meant trying to cross the city by bus and tube. London was filled with people and traffic, and was a maze of confusion for a girl from the midlands who had only been to the capital city years earlier for her sister's wedding. Finally she arrived in Dover, grateful that she had taken the week's cash from the shop for expenses. A moderate hotel would serve her needs and she didn't expect to be there for long. She caught a bus outside the station, which took her to the Clarendon Hotel near the sea.

The hotel staff was a mine of information. The repatriation camp was only a few miles away and the chaps were always in and out of the hotel bar, making up for the lost months, even years, as prisoners. There was nothing quite like a pint of English beer to drown the memories and lift the spirits.

"You won't get far going to the camp, luv," advised the middle-aged lady at the hotel desk. "You're better going to the army headquarters in the main road. That's where all the records are, and they're the ones who have the authority to send soldiers home. Most of them have gone by now. Only a few stragglers left who are helping clean up the camp."

Kathy frowned as she went to her room. A few stragglers? That didn't sound good. Where was Robert? First thing the next morning Annie went looking for answers.

Her shoes echoed on the marble floor of the imposing city building, requisitioned by the army for military service. Notices hung on every pillar in the vast entrance, with arrows giving direction to various departments. Kathy didn't know where to start. She scanned the words quickly, searching for a helpful sign.

WAR OFFICE DIRECTORATE
BRITISH EXPEDITIONARY FORCE
MIDDLE EAST
CENTRAL MEDITERRANEAN
WEST AFRICA
MEDICAL SERVICES
SPECIAL SERVICES

A dozen other arrows scattered further into the hallway. Then she spotted one....

P.O.W. INFORMATION

She quickened her step, following the arrow pointing down a long corridor to her left. Army personnel scurried back and forth, intermixed with civilians on a mission, like Kathy. She stopped outside a large double door marked P.O.W. INFORMATION and took a deep breath before pushing both doors open at once.

A chaotic crowd of people filled the room. Some waiting in line, some filling out forms, some sitting in the cramped waiting area clutching papers and files. Kathy joined the shortest line behind an elderly woman who shuffled from foot to foot impatiently waiting for the line to move forward. There were more than twenty people in front of her, and the line moved as slow as a snail towards the harassed soldier sitting at one of the fifteen desks lined up along one wall of the cavernous room.

It took several hours for Kathy to navigate the army bureaucracy. She finally sat opposite an army advisor with the forms she had completed in front of her. He read through the information carefully before going over to search through the banks of filing cabinets along the wall. Kathy never took her eyes off him, as he opened drawers and shuffled through the thick wads of paper.

"Well, you are in luck," the soldier said as he sat facing Kathy. "Here it is. Robert Stevens ended up in Stalag three in district two, situated in East Germany. Looks like he was moved a number of times, which is maybe why you didn't hear he was a POW right away. But we have him now. Came in on a hospital ship. He's in the Royal Herbert Hospital in Greenwich. Transferred there two weeks ago. I can't imagine why his family weren't notified."

The young soldier wrote down Robert's information and handed it to Kathy with a smile, elated that he had been able to help the pretty young woman. For many of the people waiting in that room, the search for their loved ones didn't turn out so well.

After a quick detour to pick up her bag, Kathy was on her way to the station bound for London. She would find Robert by the end of the day.

CHAPTER 55

HOME SAFELY

The Royal Herbert Hospital in Greenwich was easy to find. Kathy had left her bag in a locker at Victoria Station and taken the tube to Greenwich, where the impressive hospital building stood on the south side of Shooters Hill situated on Woolwich Common. It was a park-like setting in South London and Kathy skipped through the fallen leaves as she made her way to the main entrance.

Her stomach in knots, she approached the "Enquiries" desk and gave Robert's full name to the young woman smiling up at her.

"Ward twelve. Third floor, then turn left," were the instructions.

Kathy hated the smell of hospitals. Carbolic soap and bleach, mixed with some underlying odour she would rather not think about. Ward twelve proved to be under the supervision of an austere nursing sister, who stopped Kathy at the door to the ward with an expression of instant distrust.

"Visiting time is from six o'clock until eight o'clock and is strictly adhered to," she informed the red-headed young woman, who looked like she had been blown in by a strong wind. "No visiting outside of those two hours."

"Please," pleaded Kathy. "I've come to look for a soldier. I've travelled half way around England looking for 'im. Could you please make an exception for me—just this once?"

"Exception!" the nursing sister hissed. "No, I could not. If I let you in, I'd have every other patient's relatives and friends lined up at every hour of the day trying to get in here. You'll have to come back at six."

With that, she entered the ward and closed the door behind her firmly.

It was almost four o'clock. Kathy walked slowly back the way she had come and down the two flights of stairs. Two hours to kill. She looked around the wide entrance foyer and noticed an arrow pointing along the corridor to her left, with the word "cafeteria" written below it. Afternoon tea would suit her very well. She was instantly cheered by a bright, sunny room where the aroma of tea and buttered crumpets welcomed her. She was very aware, as she sat eating and drinking, that two floors above her Robert was lying in a hospital bed with unknown injuries. The minutes ticked by slowly as she waited for visiting hours to begin.

At six o'clock, Kathy was the first visitor outside the door of ward twelve. She was joined by several other visitors before a young nurse, with blond hair and a nose sprinkled with freckles, opened the door widely and welcomed them in.

There were forty-two beds in the ward—twenty-one down each side with a walkway between them. Kathy walked slowly down the centre of the room, her heart pounding, looking at the men in the beds on either side. Some of them winked at her, and she looked away quickly, embarrassed. She didn't see Robert anywhere, and felt panic rise in her throat. She turned at the end of the long ward. Had she missed him?

On her right hand side, the third bed from the end, Kathy saw a soldier lying still, his eyes and head covered in bandages. She approached the foot of the bed and stooped to read the name on the chart.

"Robert Stevens."

Tears choked in her throat, as she quietly crept to his bedside and gazed down at the injured man who had been her strong, healthy soldier; the man who had danced with her, kissed her and made love to her.

"Nurse?" Robert murmured, sensing there was someone standing beside his bed.

Kathy took his hand and bent to kiss the dry, cracked lips, the escaping tears dripping onto the thin unshaven cheeks below her.

"Not a nurse then," Robert said, his hand grasping Kathy's arm, pulling her towards him.

"No, Robert. Not a nurse."

They lay holding each other. Neither spoke. It was enough to be in each other's arms.

When the tears had subsided, and their breathing had slowed, Kathy sat on the side of the bed looking at her poor brave soldier. He was so thin. She could see the bones in his arms and deep crevices on either side of his collar bones. The bandages covered his entire scalp and both his eyes.

"I've been looking for you, Robert. I knew you were alive somewhere, and I 'ad to find you. Oh my love, I am so 'appy. Your parents will be overjoyed when I tell them you are found."

"My parents?" Robert formed the words slowly and with difficulty.

"I 'ave been to see them in Oxford, and I told them I

would find you. Robert, you are safe now. 'ome in England. You survived, darling."

Kathy kissed his lips, moistening them with her own.

"Look at me, Kathy. I'm good for nothing. I may not recover my sight and I have a head injury that makes me slow and clumsy. My original battle injuries were insignificant compared with these. There was a fire at the stalag camp I was in, and we all panicked. Thick smoke surrounded us as we fought to get outside. I remember the roof caving in and when I regained consciousness, I was lying outside in the dirt screaming in agony."

Robert clung onto his sweetheart's hand, choking on the tears as his memories overcame him. Kathy kissed the back of his hand as she cried along with him.

"I'm not the soldier you fell in love with any more. Only a shadow of him. The memory of you kept me alive through all the horror, but being alive isn't enough if I can't pick up the pieces of my life."

"Not another word, Robert Stevens," Kathy said. "You are alive, that's all that matters. You'll soon be fit and well again, I know it. It may take time, but we 'ave all the time in the world now the war is over. If the memory of me kept you alive, then let the love of me make you strong."

The two hours of visiting time was over far too quickly for the young couple clinging to each other in bed number three. The pretty young nurse came over to remind Kathy that visiting time was over and she had to leave. Kathy gave Robert a final kiss and squeezed his emaciated body in one final hug, promising she would be back the next day.

As the two young women walked out of the ward, Kathy asked the questions she couldn't ask Robert.

"What are 'is injuries? Will 'e recover? Is 'e blind?"

"You should talk to the sister really," the nurse said. "But she's off duty now, so I don't mind telling you what I know, just don't mention anything to her, or I'll be for it."

Kathy nodded her agreement.

"Your young man had a pretty bad head injury, which affected his speech and motor skills. He'll probably be moved to a rehabilitation ward once he's stable, and they'll work on helping him to walk. His eyes are bandaged because of burns. They're waiting to see how well they heal on their own, but he may need skin grafts later on. He'll see an eye doctor in a week or two to take a look at what can be done. I'm sorry, luv. You've seen how packed the hospital is with soldiers. All of them brave young men hoping to get their lives back. They deserve all the help we can give them after what they've been through."

"Thank you for telling me about Robert," Kathy said. "I'll be back tomorrow, and every other tomorrow until 'e's well again."

Taking the tube into London, Kathy was in time to catch the last train to Oxford to give the good news to Robert's parents. She would find a place to stay near the hospital tomorrow, so that she could be near him until he was discharged.

CHAPTER 56
A NEW REALITY

Annie waited for word from her absent daughter. Christmas was almost upon them, and Kathy had only written once to say that she had found Robert. Surely Kathy would be home before the holidays, and not leave her mother to face the season on her own.

A second letter arrived, asking Annie to send money so that her daughter could stay with Robert until he was able to leave the hospital.

Wasn't it enough that she had taken the entire week's shop cash with her when she'd run off to the south of England? Now she was asking for more money, while Annie was left taking care of everything at home.

Despite her reluctance to help Kathy, her mother sent money by return post. If Kathy needed money, then her mother had no decision to make—she had to help her.

Annie asked Alice to once again step into the breach and run The Pear Drop while Kathy was away. Alice's girls were both in school, and she welcomed the chance to work at the shop.

Kathy had no intention of going home while Robert was

struggling to regain his strength. She had promised him she would be at the hospital every day, and she never missed. She was there when he was transferred to rehabilitation, and obtained permission from the therapist to go into the ward every morning for several hours to help Robert with his exercises. She learned how to massage his legs, improving the circulation, before he began the hard work of learning to walk. She followed the therapist's direction and held Robert's feet while he pressed into her hands. Slowly he graduated to walking between poles for support, with Kathy cheering him on, to walking with the aid of two canes. Every day he gained strength and confidence.

Robert's eyes were still bandaged, but there were definite signs of healing and the doctors were optimistic. In the darkness he lived in, he imagined Kathy's beautiful red curly hair, and her plump rosy lips, and couldn't wait for the day he would see her again.

The week before Christmas, the eye bandages were removed and

Robert had his first blurry vision of the red hair, and wept tears of joy.

"There you are, my beautiful redhead," Robert murmured into the soft curls, as he held Kathy close. "I never stopped seeing these red curls in my dreams, Kathy."

Plans for Christmas had been put on hold waiting for Robert's recovery. The doctors were optimistic and encouraging, but cautioned their patient not to rush his rehabilitation and give his body the time it needed to recover and gain strength.

Robert would not be going home for Christmas.

Mrs Stevens had made the trip into London to visit her son several times and, although disappointed that he would remain in the hospital over the holidays, she planned to be with him on Christmas Day. She had a special surprise for him, and shared the secret with Kathy.

"Promise not to tell," she began. "I've arranged for a hired car to bring both me and Mr Stevens down to London. It will be the best Christmas present for Robert and for us."

Kathy agreed. She knew how much her dear soldier had missed his father, and how he worried about him. She couldn't wait to see them all together.

Two days before Christmas, as Kathy helped Robert into the exercise room, he brought up the question that had been looming in Kathy's mind for days.

"Why don't you go home for Christmas, Kathy?" Robert asked, taking her hands and looking into her eyes through his dim vision. "One day here is much the same as the next, and Mother will be here for most of the day."

"No, I don't want to leave you," was Kathy's emphatic answer.

"Please, darling," Robert continued. "Go spend a couple of days with your family. It would mean so much to them."

Everything in Kathy's head screamed, 'I don't want to.' She would much rather stay in London and spend the day with Robert and his parents than make the journey to Longton and face her mother.

She finally relented, and after kissing Robert a tearful goodbye, made the long train journey home on Christmas Eve.

She was grateful to find two of her aunts at the house when she arrived. They both came scurrying into the hall to hug her, bringing warm slippers and her old woolen cardigan to fend off the chill inside the house.

"Merry Christmas, Kathy," Annie said in a stifled voice. "I'm so grateful you could spare the time to come and see me."

Kathy put her arm around her mother's frail shoulders and kissed her thin cheek.

"Lovely to be here, Mam," she murmured. "I bring best wishes from Robert and 'is parents."

"Well then, that makes everything all right, doesn't it?"

Annie shrugged off her daughter's arm and stalked into the living room, back to her chair by the fire.

"Did you 'ear that, May?" she continued. "Best wishes from Robert and 'is parents. Is that supposed to make me feel better for not seeing my daughter for weeks on end?"

"Let's 'ave a drink of ginger wine," May said, ignoring her sister's comments. "It's going to be a wonderful Christmas now you're 'ome, along with all the boys."

May poured glasses of her celebrated non-alcoholic ginger wine and handed them to her sisters and Kathy.

Before the wine was half finished, family arrived en masse and filled the hallway with laughter and chatter. Pots of warm food were dispatched to the kitchen, along with plates of cake and a large bowl of trifle. Kathy was soon in the middle of her cousins, caught up in the joy of the first Christmas of peace for six years. Everybody wanted an update on Robert. Everybody except Annie.

In the silence of her bedroom, when all the guests were long gone and Annie had finally run out of criticisms and shuffled up the stairs to her room, Kathy lay watching the moon move slowly across the window. One day without Robert seemed an eternity, and she couldn't wait to return to London.

Christmas Day was indeed a day of celebration, with the entire family attending chapel in the morning, then gathering once more at Annie's house for the best dinner the ration books could supply. Every family contributed food from their meager supply, providing a delicious feast for all. The young war workers and soldiers exchanged funny stories of their war years, laughing at the antics they had experienced and seen during the past six years. Nobody spoke of the heartache and tragedy, it was left unsaid, on Christmas Day.

The following day, as Annie and Kathy sat in the kitchen finishing their breakfast, Kathy told her mother that she was leaving soon. Mr Salt, forever Kathy's willing chauffeur, was picking her up to take her to the station for the eleven o'clock train.

"'Ow can you leave?" Annie said. "You only arrived two days ago. Are you telling me you can't stay with your mother for longer two days? You're running back to that crippled lad in London?"

"'E's not crippled," Kathy shot back. "'E was badly injured, but is recovering."

"You are such a sap," Annie shouted. "You could 'ave been a concert pianist. You could 'ave done anything you set your mind to. You could 'ave married a rich man. You could 'ave 'ad a life of luxury. You're just a nursemaid to that soldier."

Kathy jumped up from the table. She didn't have to listen to any more of her mother's tirade. Nothing ever changed. Her mother would never accept who she was or the life she had chosen.

"You can't go. I'm putting my foot down this time. Your place is 'ere with me. I can't stand by and watch you throw away your life. You were meant for great things, Kathy. I gave you everything when you were a girl. Every opportunity. Every advantage. You seem determined to throw it all away on some poor wreck of a soldier, who will never provide for you."

"Thank you for those kind words," Kathy shouted. "They will stay with me while I travel back to the man I love. You've forgotten what it's like to love somebody, Mam. I will stay with Robert until 'e's 'ealthy and strong again, and I won't even think about you. All you ever do is cause me grief."

Annie burst into tears. Heart-wrenching sobs, coming from the depths of her body. How could her daughter turn her back on her like this? She had been Annie's whole life since the day she was born. She had laid aside everything for her; her husband and Nora, her sisters, her business. Now Kathy acted as though she owed her mother nothing. After all the sacrificing, the heartache, the dedication. Annie's entire body shook with the realization that her daughter hated her.

CHAPTER 57
MARRY ME

The winter months were particularly bleak and cold that year. January, February and March saw the Londoners focused on ways to keep warm and get enough to eat.

Kathy lived in the boarding house, and trudged to and from the rehabilitation hospital on a daily basis, picking up something to eat on her way from work, and catching the last bus back to her bed.

Robert's progress was slow and tedious. He had a major setback in the middle of March when he contracted pneumonia and had to be transferred back to The Royal Herbert Hospital for treatment.

It took a further three months of intense rehab, but in June of 1946, Robert was discharged and could return to his home in Oxford.

Gloria and Donald Stevens were elated to have their son at home again. Donald hadn't seen him since Christmas Day the year before and greeted Robert with a warm hug, not wanting to ever let him go.

Kathy asked for a few days break from her job at the grocery store and joined the happy family.

The streets of Oxford were serene and quiet compared with the chaos of London, and the young couple looked forward to life outside the hospital.

The warm June day invited a trip outdoors, and Mrs Stevens packed a picnic lunch and waved Robert and Kathy off as they walked, very slowly, towards the river. With Robert relying on a walking cane for balance, it took a long time to reach the river Cherwell. They spread a woolen blanket on a grassy bank beside the rippling water, and huddled close together while they ate their picnic in the warm summer air.

The scars around Robert's eyes were less noticeable, although the left eye would always droop a little, and he would need spectacles to help him see clearly. None of it mattered to Kathy, who considered his recovery nothing short of a miracle.

"Do you remember the last time we were alone together?" whispered Robert, bending his head close to Kathy's ear. "I wish we were in that little country inn right now, cuddled up in bed, making love."

"I remember," Kathy replied. "How precious those memories are. We will be together like that again, Robert. For now, I'm content just being 'ere with you, sitting next to you and feeling your arm around me."

Robert drew her closer and kissed her lips, drinking in the taste of her and feeling the warmth spread through his body. A whistle from a passing bike-rider cautioned the lovers that they were not alone.

The decision to pick up his former life and return to veterinary college was made with input from Gloria and Donald Stevens. Robert was their only son and they had saved a generous amount of money to make sure he could attend university when the time came. They were overjoyed when he asked their advice about his future, and they reconfirmed that the education fund was still available to him.

It would take two more years of study before Robert became a vet, but now he was strong and healthy once more, he couldn't imagine doing anything else with his life. The last thing he wanted was to live in the city. The life of a country vet was his dream, and with Kathy, the Land Army girl, beside him, it could be a reality.

London was noisy, busy, dirty and full of people trying to put their lives back together. Many had lost their homes—whole neighbourhoods had been lost, leaving families with nothing. Men returning from the war found their wives and children staying with relatives or friends, at a loss to know how to find somewhere to live. The government was scrambling to build houses for the homeless, but it was no easy task when there were so many.

Kathy thought herself fortunate that she had her one room. Robert lived in residence at The Royal Veterinary College, sharing a cramped space on the fourth floor with Alwyn, a young man from Wales. Neither accommodation allowed the young couple any personal space, and they had to be satisfied with walks in the park, or by the river. When Alwyn went to visit his family in Cardiff, Robert would smuggle Kathy through a side door, and they would both scamper up the four narrow flights of stairs, before tumbling breathlessly into the dorm room, gasping for breath.

Clothing removed and scattered on the floor, they shared Robert's single bed.

Robert had made it clear that he wanted to finish his studies and be established in a practice before asking Kathy to marry him, but in the middle of his second year of studies he began to regret his stance to wait. His Welsh roommate was no substitute for Kathy. He missed her every day she wasn't with him, and hated the thought of bringing her into the building in secret, so that they could make love and spend a few hours together, in the seedy room under the eaves of the old residence.

Gloria and Donald Stevens sat quietly listening to their son as he explained his dilemma.

"I love Kathy," he began. "I made a promise to myself and to her, that we would be married after I earn my degree, and have a good position. Now, I don't know. I feel so selfish, but we want to be together, not just for a few hours here and there, but every day. I want to ask her to marry me, but how will we live? I may not find a practice as soon as I graduate later this year. I have no prospects to offer her."

"Darling," Gloria interrupted.

"No, Mother, let me finish. You have been more than generous. I can never begin to tell you how grateful I am to you for saving to pay for my education. Your generosity has enabled me to go back to college, and I don't want you to think I'm throwing that away. I don't know what to do. I only know I can't go on without Kathy. I thought I could, but I can't."

Robert put his head in his hands, not wanting to look into his parents' eyes.

His father stood up shakily, holding onto the back of his chair, and put an arm on his son's shoulder. He knew from his own experience what a difficult road his son had walked since coming home, and he loved him for the courage and persistence he had shown while recovering from his injuries.

"Thank you for coming to talk to us about this, Robert," his father began. "There's nothing you could do or say that would make us less proud of you. Whatever you decide to do will be supported by your mother and myself, but listen first to what we have to say. It may influence your decision."

"You've already come through so many challenges,"

Gloria joined in. "Your dad and I only want you to be happy, and be able to move forward with your life. You've given your heart to Kathy, and we couldn't be happier. She's a lovely girl, and has proved her love for you over and over again. You may have to struggle financially for a few years, but you'll make it."

"Your grandfather, God bless him," Donald continued. "Left you a small trust, which we intended you to have after your degree, to help you set up a practice somewhere nice. You could go ahead and get married to Kathy, and use that trust account for living expenses. Of course you would have to risk finding work in a practice with little or no financial support. In matters of the heart, money should never be the biggest issue."

Robert had listened intently to his parents, and now he choked with emotion that a solution had presented itself so easily. There was no hesitation now. He would ask Kathy to marry him when he returned to London on the afternoon train.

He hugged his father and mother. There was no need to tell them. They already knew what he would do.

"Let us know the wedding date, my dear," his mother whispered with tears in her eyes.

It was drizzling and dark when Robert arrived in London. He didn't go to his residence, but took the tube to South Kensington, and splashed through the puddles as he ran to Kathy's house. Breaking the rules, he ran upstairs and banged on her door. She came to the door dressed in a dressing gown, with a towel wrapped around her head. Her face was slick and shiny with a layer of Nivea cream, which clung in little goblets to her eyelashes.

Robert didn't seem to notice the condition of his sweetheart. He closed the door behind him and dropped to his knees.

"Marry me, Kathy," he said.

Kathy couldn't think straight. Shouldn't she be dressed in her glamorous black dress, with her hair tied up in a French bun, and her make-up perfect? Shouldn't they be sitting in a fancy restaurant sipping champagne, or walking along the Thames embankment in the moonlight?

"Please say something?" begged Robert.

Kathy blinked at him through her creamy eyelashes.

"Yes. Oh yes!" she burst out. "When? Why? 'Ow? Aren't we waiting until you're a vet?"

"We're not waiting. It's impossible. I've been to see my parents today and told them we're getting married."

Robert rose from his knees and gently removed the wet towel from Kathy's hair, watching the cascade of red curls fall in spirals around her face. He wiped away most of the cream on her face with the wet towel, so that he could kiss her properly. As he guided her towards the bed, he untied the dressing gown and ran his hands over her soft smooth body.

The house rules were already broken as soon as Robert had stepped into Kathy's room, so what did it matter if he stayed? He scattered his clothes on the floor, so that he could be next to his love. It was always like the first time, but this was special. They were to be married and Robert was overwhelmed with the love he felt for his beautiful fiancee.

Kathy couldn't wait to tell her sister, Nora, who had returned to her flat in London after the war. Norman and Nora's flat hadn't been damaged, and they gratefully opened up the dusty rooms, brushed away the cobwebs, and settled into their previous life comparatively easily.

Christopher was already seven years old and didn't remember living in London as a baby. Nora wasted no time once they were home, and gave birth to another son less than a year after the war had ended. Morgan was a delight to his parents, his brother and his Aunty Kathy, who visited regularly to play with the boys.

"Are you going 'ome to tell mother?" Nora asked her sister, trying to sound casual. "She's very anxious to see you. We took the boys up to Longton last week, and she looks old and tired."

"I 'ave no plan to visit her," Kathy answered, not meeting her sister's gaze. "We parted on bad terms, and I see no future involving 'er. She 'as always made me miserable. I do better when I don't see 'er."

Nora didn't press the issue, but worried that her sister would regret her decision.

There were good reasons for regrets.

CHAPTER 58
REGRET

The wedding day was set for March 2nd 1948, and Kathy wrote to her Aunty Rosemary to ask her to tell the rest of the family. She had seriously considered writing to her mother, but decided the news would be better accepted coming from her aunt. It was a cowardly decision. Kathy knew she should be inviting her family, particularly her mother, personally, and not in a letter. Guilt prickled at Kathy's skin.

The wedding would take place in Oxford, and family from the midlands were welcome if they chose to attend. Maybe her aunts would be there—probably not her mother.

Annie took to her bed when Rosemary read the letter to her. The familiar darkness closed in on her, but this time it didn't go away. Annie suffered a stroke two days later and the doctor told the sisters, who were gathered in Annie's bedroom, that there was little hope of recovery. He made arrangements to transfer the patient to hospital. Aunty Rosemary sent a telegram to Nora and Kathy urging them to come quickly.

Kathy left immediately, convinced that the letter she had written had made her mother ill.

Nora would join them in a day or two, after making arrangements for Norman's mother to take care of the boys.

The stroke had severely damaged Annie. She lay in the hospital bed with a blank expression on her face, eyes not focused, mouth drooping, saliva spilling. She didn't react when Kathy walked into the room and talked to her, and the nurse said she was too far gone to even know her daughter was there.

Kathy looked at the old lady in the bed, barely recognizable as her feisty mother. They had been through so much together. It had never been an easy relationship, yet Kathy wished her mother could hear her now, so that she could tell her she still loved her.

The aunties welcomed Kathy with their usual love and tenderness. No mention was made about the letter. Aunty Rosemary insisted Kathy stay with her, Nancy and Enid, but Kathy declined the invitation, preferring to stay in the old family house, where so many memories lived.

The house had deteriorated since her last visit. It smelled damp and musty, and a layer of dust and grime covered what furniture wasn't covered in sheets. A great sadness descended on Kathy as she walked through the rooms to the kitchen. This was all her fault. If she had stayed with her mother, none of this would have happened. The house would have been shiny and clean with flowers on the tables, lights everywhere. There would have been food in the pantry, probably homemade cake or scones on the kitchen table, and a kettle that wasn't rusting away on the bottom from lack of use. Everywhere she looked she saw neglect and decay, and she wept because of it.

Annie died during the night, leaving Kathy to lock herself away in the house. She wouldn't answer the door when her aunties came to call. She didn't eat, drink, or sleep. The only thing she did was blame herself for her mother's death. How could she have been so selfish? Thinking only of herself and Robert, while Annie wasted away without her.

"Walk properly. Sit properly. Eat properly."

"You should play the piano, Kathy," she heard her mother's voice behind her. "You could 'ave been a concert pianist, if only you 'ad practiced."

Echoes of the past were in all the corners of all the rooms, and Kathy couldn't bear it. She went outside to the coal shed, took the axe, marched into the living room and chopped the piano into bits.

She collapsed onto the floor in sheer exhaustion and lay there sobbing for her mother.

A loud banging on the door stirred Kathy from a stupor-like sleep.

"Kathy, open the door," Aunty May's voice filtered into the hallway through the heavy door.

"Go away," yelled Kathy. "Leave me alone."

"Let me in," Aunty May persisted. "Come on now, I need to see you."

"I want to be by myself. I won't open the door."

More knocking. More pleading. No answer.

May had no alternative but to leave. Kathy had used the dead bolt on the inside of the door, so May's spare key did nothing to gain access. She would go back to the house and try again later.

With shaky legs, Kathy wobbled to the sofa and sat staring at the large pile of debris that had once been the piano. She didn't regret chopping it up. It had been a source of mental anguish since she was a little girl. It was the one last act of defiance against her mother. She didn't know what to do with the anger she felt inside. She had secretly hoped that Annie would come to her wedding. That she would approve of Robert, and give them her blessing. Now it was too late, and Kathy felt the weight of her mother's death on her shoulders, as if she had plunged a knife into her heart.

May hurried home, not knowing what to think. She had to babysit Ann for a few hours, but she needed to see her sisters about the situation with Kathy.

"We need to visit the old aunties, Ann," explained her gran. "First Rosemary, then Lizzie, and then Daisy. You be a good girl now, and don't get in the way."

Ann didn't mind. She liked the old aunties, her Gran's sisters, and knew she would be fed milk and cookies at all three houses. She also knew, because her mum had explained it all to her, that Gran's sister, Annie, had died. Annie was the "sweet lady," who lived in the big house and always had a dish of sweets on the table in her living room. The whole family went to her house every Christmas Eve, although last Christmas was different—they had gathered at Rosemary's house instead, filling her tiny home to bursting. Ann remembered Aunty Annie being there, but she looked shriveled like a prune, and didn't even smile. Maybe she knew she would die soon.

After meeting with her sisters, May was compelled to visit Kathy again that evening. As soon as George was settled with his meal in front of him, she hurried back to Annie's house.

It was dark outside. Kathy had no idea of the time, but knew she had been sleeping on the sofa for a long time. She was stiff and cold and she wondered what had stirred her sleep.

A persistent knocking at the door, followed by Aunty May's voice begging her to let her in, forced Kathy into consciousness. She would ignore the knocking this time. She would sit in the dark and pretend she hadn't heard. May tried again and again to no avail, and finally had to admit defeat and head for home. She was freezing cold and very tired. She would try again in the morning.

The following morning, Ann ran around to Gran's house to stay with her for the morning while Dorothy worked. Her head was full of the visits of yesterday, when the old aunties were all so worried about Kathy. Surely Gran would go to see Kathy today, and would take Ann with her. The laundry tub was out when Ann walked into the kitchen. Gran must have been up very early, as the washing was already being rinsed, and Ann had missed the best part with all the bubbles. Gran always said there was nothing like hard work to take your mind off things.

Like the death of a sister?

Flowers cascaded from the white porcelain vase onto the shiny surface of the round side table beside the three-seater sofa in the living room. The aunties had wasted no time, supervised by May, whipping the old, tired house into shape. Dust cloths were removed, furniture polished, windows cleaned, and the shattered piano was hauled out of the living room by Charles. The kitchen was buzzing with activity as the younger members of the family gathered to scrub, polish and clean, before beginning the preparation of food for the expected company.

Looking clean and fresh, Kathy smiled thankfully at her family. Nora, Norman and the boys would be arriving on the afternoon train, but more importantly Robert would be there before the day was over. Her Robert.

Annie's funeral would take place the following day, and everything would be ready for the beautiful sister, whose life had been filled with mountains and valleys. She had loved one man passionately, one briefly, and one with all her heart. She had been brave and strong, and weak and sick. She had known great sorrow and great joy. She had been a successful businesswoman and an imperfect mother. Now they would all gather to honour Annie's life, and mourn her passing.

Kathy's head ached from the nightmare day she had spent locked in the house alone after Annie had died. She realized that she had been on the edge of the dark pit her mother succumbed to at difficult times of her life, and it filled her with fear. Even in death, her mother's influence reached into Kathy's mind, filling her with guilt and remorse. She found it hard to breathe. She wanted to run outside and keep running until the house was far behind her. Until the suffocating presence of Annie was lifted from her mind.

"Come and 'elp with the bedrooms, Kathy," Aunty Rosemary said, trying to distract her niece. "Your mam 'ad a lovely lot of linens stored away in the cupboard on the landing. I'm just going to make up the bed for your young man. Bring a duster and some of the pine polish, and we'll make the room comfortable for 'im."

Kathy knew what her aunty was up to, but she followed her up the stairs to prepare the bedroom at the end of the landing for Robert. It helped to be busy, particularly when she was with Aunty Rosemary.

By tea time, Nora had arrived with her family, and the house was filled with chatter and squeals as Christopher explored every room, clattering up and down the stairs, then returning to his little brother every few minutes to tickle him. It brought a smile to the drawn faces of the aunties and Kathy as they watched the antics.

Nora embraced her sister, and held her close. Tears for their mother spilled down their cheeks as they shared their memories. Memories very different from each other. Nora's of a mother who didn't pay her much attention after her sister was born. Kathy's of a mother obsessed with her, clinging and demanding. They both recognized the deep love

Annie had for each of them in her own way, and clung to that image of her.

The house was finally quiet. Nora's boys were both sleeping and the aunties had returned to their homes. Norman poured three glasses of the scotch he had brought with him from London, and handed his wife and sister-in-law a glass each.

"I think we all deserve a wee dram after such a day," Norman smiled. "I know it would be frowned upon by the pledge-signing chapel goers, but there's nothing quite like a scotch for warming a sad heart."

The two women nodded their agreement.

"Here's to Annie Gardner," Norman said, holding his glass in the air.

"Mam," said Kathy and Nora in unison, clinking their glasses with Norman's.

Kathy had looked at her watch a dozen times in five minutes. Robert was arriving at Stoke station on the late train from London. Uncle Charles had offered to pick him up.

"'E'll be here soon," Nora said. "I know you're anxious to see 'im."

Before their drinks were finished, Charles flung open the front door and announced his guest with a flourish.

"Mr Robert Stevens."

Kathy was in his arms before he could take off his coat. This was home for her—in Robert's arms, no matter the surroundings. His mouth covered hers despite the audience. Nora and Norman looked away discreetly, but Uncle Charles stood beside them with a big grin on his face. Such a demonstration of affection was never seen in his world. Holding hands was considered forward, never mind this kind of kiss.

"You taste wonderful," gasped Robert. "Where's the scotch?"

The smile left Charles' face immediately. He was one of the pledge-signing chapel-goers. He frowned at Norman, guessing he was the instigator of the whiskey drinking. Nothing good came of drinking alcohol according to Charles, but he wasn't about to speak his mind the night before Annie's funeral. He touched the front of his cap in salute to Robert, nodded to his nieces and left them to their whiskey.

"Here you go, Robert," Norman said, pouring the rich golden liquid into a glass. "Scotch it is. Nothing like it after a long train journey."

The four of them sat around the fire, sipping their drinks, content and relaxed in each other's company. Robert, who rarely shared his war experience, found it easy to talk to Norman about the horrors of battle, and being taken prisoner. He downplayed his injuries, but Norman and Nora knew what he had suffered. Likewise Norman, who had spent his war years deep underground in the middle of London, working countless hours following German troop movements and aircraft activities, told them about the responsibility he carried. The ultimate decisions of the high command were made with the information gathered by Norman and his comrades.

They talked until the early hours of the morning. Nora pretended not to notice when Robert followed Kathy into her room instead of going to the one allocated to him. Kathy would spend the night in Robert's arms and her sister thought that was perfectly fine.

The chapel on Newhall Road had seen its share of funerals, particularly for the Jenkins family. The people gathered once more as they said goodbye to Annie. Everybody dressed in black, of course. "Abide With Me" and "Bread of Heaven," the two favourite funeral hymns, were sung with gusto by the packed congregation. Scripture and prayers brought tears to all eyes. The family filed past the coffin at the front of the chapel to reach out and touch the rich oak wood and remember their mother, sister, aunty, friend. It was the way they had always said goodbye and it was right in their eyes.

Annie Gardner's house was once more filled with family, maybe for the last time. After the funeral service, and the internment at Longton Cemetery, everyone gathered for food and tea in the house that had been the centre of so many family occasions over the years.

"Hello Kathy," said a little voice beside her. "You look a lot better."

Kathy stooped down to talk to the little girl. May's granddaughter, Ann, and gazed into her eyes.

"Hello Ann," Kathy said. "I am a lot better, thanks to your gran. She's one of my guardian angels."

"Who are your others?" asked Ann

"My other aunties. Rosemary, Lizzie and Daisy. They are very precious old ladies."

Ann looked around the room and saw the four sisters, her gran and her great aunts, busy handing out cups of tea, chatting to people, smiling, and spreading their comfort.

As it turned out, Kathy had another guardian angel—her mother. When the will was read, Annie had left the house, shop and all her money to Kathy, and nothing to Nora. Strangled sobs choked Kathy as the final act of obsession filled her with more guilt and remorse. Nora ran to her side to comfort her, knowing the bequest was unwanted.

When the house was sold and the estate was free of probate, Kathy divided her generous inheritance equally between herself and her sister.

Robert had a year and a half of veterinary college left, and he returned to London after Annie's funeral to continue his studies.

The business of tying up Annie's affairs took longer than Kathy expected, and she longed to be with Robert. The contents of the house were particularly difficult to deal with. So many memories lay in those dark sombre rooms, some good, some bad.

Kathy sat at her mother's dressing table fingering the rose brooch her father had given to Annie on her fortieth birthday. The ornate jewelry box, full of rings, necklaces and her mother's beautiful jeweled watch waited for Kathy's attention.

The contents of each drawer revealed the woman who had been Kathy's mother: the soft, silky underwear in pastel shades of blue, pink and ivory, the long-sleeved lacy nightgowns with matching dressing gowns, the lambs wool cardigans, the silk blouses, the tasseled shawls and elegant wool skirts.

Hidden beneath a myriad of old greeting cards, scarves

and gloves, Kathy found a short bundle of straw stalks, tied with a blue ribbon. "Isaac September 1922" was written in tiny writing on the corner of the ribbon. The date drew a gasp of surprise from Kathy—it was the year of her birth. Whatever secret the strange memento held had gone to the grave with Annie.

"I'd like Mam's personal belongings to stay in the family," Kathy announced. She had asked Aunty Rosemary to invite the other aunties for tea so that she could share her idea with them.

"Nora would like 'er watch and two of 'er rings, and I've chosen to keep the rose brooch and a pearl necklace," Kathy continued. "Please go through the rest of 'er jewelry and keep whatever you choose. Mam also 'ad many beautiful clothes, which you are more than welcome to."

The aunties chose items from the collection and, encouraged by Kathy, took the rest to share with their children and grandchildren. Enough for every woman and girl in the family to have a small memento of Aunty Annie.

For no logical reason Kathy kept the bundle of straw. It was such an odd thing to keep among all the other memories her mother had treasured.

Robert's studies kept him busy. The courses were difficult, and he was also assigned to a clinic for his practicum. Three afternoons and every Saturday he reported to the Barnaby Veterinary Clinic for work experience. He missed Kathy desperately and wrote to her on his non-clinic days when he had a little time to himself.

As he studied and worked, he also tried to find a place for them to live. They had moved their wedding date to May 2nd, but none of the details had been worked out.

With Kathy's inheritance at their disposal, Robert finally found a lovely second-floor flat in Bayswater Road and put down a deposit to secure it. Kathy travelled to London the following weekend to give the flat her approval. It would be such fun to furnish it together. They decided to buy a few essentials before the wedding. The rest could wait until they were both living there.

"I love it," Kathy exclaimed as she whisked from room to room. "Look at the 'igh ceilings, and lovely wooden floors. We're going to be so 'appy 'ere."

"I know," Robert agreed, laughing at his exuberant fiancé. "I imagined you in every room and knew it was meant for us."

"Changing the subject," Robert said as he took Kathy's hand in his. "Will your family mind travelling to Oxford for the wedding? It will be a grand affair at Christ Church Cathedral, which is the most prestigious church in the city. Only the best for my beautiful bride."

"Oxford?" questioned Kathy. "I want to be married at Newhall Mission, my family chapel."

Robert was taken aback.

"Darling, it's a tiny insignificant little place. Don't you want an opulent, historical church with a red-carpeted centre aisle, a pipe organ, and a choir?"

"No, I don't," Kathy said quietly, looking up into Robert's questioning eyes. "I love you more than life, my darling man, but I really want to say "I do" in the chapel my grandfather built. The chapel where my mam and dad were wed and where I was baptized."

"Then that's settled," Robert said, kissing the tip of her nose. "The chapel it is."

The aunties were in a flurry of excitement as they prepared for the wedding day. May and Daisy had bedrooms for Kathy and Nora's family, and William and Florence had a spare bedroom for Robert, and borrowed a bed for Robert's parents. They set up the bed in their parlour on the main floor, so that Donald Stevens could be accommodated.

Robert's father was determined to make the journey for his son's wedding, but was now so frail that he needed a wheelchair. With Robert's help, his parents would manage the train journey and be able to stay for two nights.

The aunties were up at the crack of dawn on wedding day. Along with the other women in the family, they met at the chapel at nine sharp to transform the usually plain, dour space into a wedding chapel.

As Kathy walked into the chapel on Uncle William's arm, she was greeted with the scent of apple blossom. At the end of every pew were generous sprigs of pink, perfumed blossom tied with white ribbons. In keeping with the theme, two large branches of apple blossom, planted in large white urns, met in an arch on the small stage. Red carpets covered the aisle and the front of the chapel.

Kathy's eyes misted with tears as she fixed her eyes on Robert, waiting for her under the arch of apple blossom. He mouthed "I love you" as she walked toward him.

Mr Saunders, at the old pedal organ, played Kathy's chosen hymn as she made her way down the aisle. The aunties dabbed at their eyes and remembered their own weddings. The tiny chapel was crammed with family and friends, who sang the hymns with gusto and stood up and applauded when Rev. Jeremiah Brown (borrowed from the Methodist Church) announced the couple were now Mr and Mrs Robert Stevens. The family declared it to be the best wedding ever.

The pews were pushed aside and long tables and chairs were soon in place. A parade of neighbourhood women, who had been working behind the scenes for days, brought in plates laden with sandwiches, pork pies, sausage rolls, pickles, cheese and a cacophony of cakes, made with loving hands. The wedding cake, baked and iced by Aunty Rosemary, was the centre of attention, with three tiers of flowers made of icing, topped with a bride and groom figurine—along with a small china cow, which made Robert burst out laughing.

After a three-day honeymoon on the rugged coast of North Wales, the newlyweds made the long journey to London, and their new flat. Although Robert still had his clinic hours each week, he didn't begin his final year at the college until August, which gave him time to accompany Kathy on shopping expeditions for furnishings and household paraphernalia. It was an extension of their honeymoon, spending the long summer days together. When they weren't shopping, they were walking in the park, making love, eating lunch or dinner at ethnic restaurants, or going to a show in the West End.

All the years of heartache became part of their memories and they reveled in the joy they felt now that they were married.

Kathy wrote to her aunties regularly, telling them all about her life in London. The newlyweds travelled to Oxford frequently to visit Robert's parents and enjoy the beauty of the university city with its impressive towered college buildings and its peaceful river. Robert's father was declining in health, and without talking about it, the young couple knew his time was short. They prayed he would live to see Robert graduate as a vet, an achievement nobody had thought possible a few years ago when the war had ravaged the young soldier almost to his death.

Mr Stevens sat in his wheelchair at the front of the auditorium the following May to watch his son accept his degree. It was the proudest moment of his life.

"Time to leave London and seek a practice somewhere in the country," Robert said, holding his pregnant wife close. "Any ideas?"

"Of course," laughed Kathy. "When did you know me not to 'ave an idea. Ideas are what I do best."

"Well, spit it out."

Kathy's eyes misted over as she remembered where and when they had first met so long ago. She had loved him from that very moment.

"Cheshire, where we first met," Kathy whispered. "That's my dream, Robert. To 'ave a practice in Cheshire, where the people are friendly, the 'ills are covered in 'eather, the valleys are lush and green, they 'ave the best cheese in the world, and our children will grow up on the land."

"As always, your idea is beautiful, my Kathy," Robert said. "Cheshire is full of cattle, which is my specialty. Let's try to find something before the baby arrives. What do you think?"

Kathy nodded enthusiastically.

"Thank you, Mam," she said under her breath. The money Annie had left her would give them a good start in their new life.

They settled in a small village near Macclesfield. The local vet had retired and the practice he left suited Robert perfectly. The large cottage on the outskirts of the village was soon home for the young couple, and they couldn't have been happier.

Donald Isaac Stevens was born on September 7 1949, named after Robert's father. Kathy insisted on Isaac for a middle name. Something about the name attached to the straw bundle in her mother's dresser tugged at her heart.

ANN & MAY

1948

CHAPTER 61

THE PEAR DROP

It seemed the old aunties had talked about nothing but the Pear Drop for weeks. I listened to their discussions with great interest on my visits with my gran. It seemed the sweet shop held a very precious place in their family. The aunties talked about it like they talked about the chapel, as though it was part of them, and they all had different opinions on what should happen.

Kathy had inherited everything when her mother died. I listened to the aunties as they whispered about the large amount of money, more than anybody could imagine, accumulated over the years by Thomas' clever management of the factory. The house was put up for sale, along with most of the furnishings, and sold to the proprietors of a successful bakery nearby. However, Kathy and Nora agonized over what to do with The Pear Drop.

Gran thought Annie's daughters should sell the shop, and have done with the past. Daisy and Lizzie thought they should wait, leaving Alice in charge, for a few years before making a decision. Rosemary looked at the situation differently than her sister-in-laws, professing ties to the shop ran too deep in the family, and Kathy and Nora would never sell. I agreed with Rosemary.

The decision was finally made and the old aunties had to find another topic to talk about. I rolled my eyes as they all now seemed fixated on a certain Mr Arthur Beardmore, who had joined the Derby and Joan club. They whispered about him being a 'ladies man', who had his eye on Mrs Derbyshire. I didn't know what that meant, and wished they were still discussing sweets.

Gran had promised me a trip to The Pear Drop when the weather was nice enough, and I reminded her about it every day.

"Tomorrow," announced Gran. "We'll go tomorrow. It's supposed to be sunny and not too cold. Wait for my knock on the wall."

I was dressed for the outing before breakfast. After eating a boiled egg and toast fingers I played with my dolls at the bottom of the stairs, but couldn't get into my game. I was waiting for a knock on the wall. I knew Gran would be busy doing all her chores before going out, so I moped about the house, picking up a book to look at, then a picture to colour. Finally I stamped upstairs to plop on my bed and stare through the window, willing the sun to keep shining.

"Gran's knocking on the wall," shouted my mum. "It's time for you to go, Gran will be waiting for you."

I clattered downstairs, grabbed my coat and ran next door.

"Is it far, Gran?" I asked. "Will we be back before Grandad gets 'ome from work?"

"Longton's far enough," answered Gran, taking my hand and straightening her hat. "You're a big girl now. You can walk very far when you're four."

"Oh I don't mind the walk. I like the shops in Longton. Maybe we could go to the market to buy fruit and vegetables.

I go there sometimes with my mum to buy fish. I love seeing all the fish and watching the fish lady, in 'er rubber apron, skin and slice the fish. One day I'm going to be a fish lady in the market," I announced.

"Really," said Gran, looking down at me. "You are a funny one. You don't mind the smell?"

"No, I think fish smells wonderful."

The walk into Longton was all downhill and easy on the legs, it would be harder on the return journey, loaded with shopping. At the end of Webberly Lane we stopped outside a shop window, and Gran pointed to the display inside.

"Look, Ann," she said. "See all the bottles of sweets. This is The Pear Drop. I wanted you to see it for yourself. This is where my mam and dad met, and where Annie met 'er 'usband, and where Kathy used to work."

I stood on my tiptoes, and looked closely at the wonders in the window. It was just as I had imagined it; jars of coloured sweets, chocolate bars in a fan pattern, sticks of liquorice, barley sugar twists, and jelly babies.

A bell sounded as Gran pushed open the door.

"Well, well, Ann," a voice greeted us. "What a lovely surprise. Come on in, and look around."

Gran smiled at Aunty Alice as she came from behind the counter to stoop and talk to me.

"Look at you," Aunty Alice said. "Almost ready for school. Why don't you check out the children's corner while I talk to your Gran."

I picked up a book from the table in the corner, but my attention was on Gran and Alice as they whispered together. Why did grown- ups always think children couldn't hear them? Gran's sister Annie had been dead for months, but I could still remember the day we had visited the old aunties and the conversations that had taken place about Kathy. Since then, there had been continual discussions about Annie and Kathy, and I had listened and understood more than any of them knew.

"Alice, the shop looks lovely," Gran said, squeezing Alice's hand. "I 'ave to tell you 'ow 'appy I am that things turned out the way they did. You and our Charlie deserve it. You stepped in and 'elped Annie when she needed it most, and this is your just reward."

"I needed to 'ear you say that, May," Alice said. "Me and Charlie often wonder 'ow the family feels about Kathy's decision. She could 'ave sold The Pear Drop along with the 'ouse."

"Kathy and Nora made the right choice, Alice," Gran said. "We were all in agreement that to 'and over the title of the shop to you and Charlie was the very best decision. This old place 'as been part of our family for decades. I can still see my mam, in 'er starched white apron, behind that counter, smiling 'er wonderful smile. Now you're going to be 'ere taking care of the shop until the next generation takes over— one of your own girls maybe. It will stay in the family, and that's the main thing."

Alice hugged her sister-in-law with tears in her eyes.

"I won't let the family down," she said. "The Pear Drop will be kept in good order, just as Annie would have wished."

I put down the book I'd been looking at and went to stand beside my gran, while Alice busied herself on the other side of the counter. She smiled at me as she came to say goodbye to us.

"Ann, 'ere are some sweets for you to take 'ome," Alice said, handing me a small white bag tied with blue ribbon. "They are pear drops, your great-grandad's favourites."

"Thank you, Aunty Alice," I said politely.

Gran and I were quiet as we walked to the market to shop for fruit and vegetables.

"Gran," I said, "I don't think I want to be a fish lady anymore. I would rather work at The Pear Drop."

It was a joy to write this book. As with my previous novels it is based on a true story and spans three generations of my paternal grandmother's family.

I remember hearing my gran talk about her parents and her nine siblings, many of whom I visited frequently when I was very young. My gran died when I was sixteen years of age, back in 1960. Asthmatic Aunty Lizzie lived until she was almost 100 years old. Newhall Mission Chapel was the centre of our lives, and I have many fond memories of the wonderful leaders and congregation who unknowingly influenced my life.

Gran's beautiful sister, Annie, had an interesting life, which captured my imagination when I was thinking about writing another novel. I remember her vaguely, mainly because she always had sweets in a dish on the table in her living room.

As the story unfolded, I drew on family experience with depression, and explored how it was managed in families when there were no drugs or therapists to give relief from the worst symptoms. Without her sisters' help, Annie would surely not have recovered from some of her darkest episodes. She loved three men, two of them passionately, and lived much of her life as a leader in her extended family as well as her businesses.

The novel covers the years from the 1880's to 1949, a fascinating time in history, when many people lived through two world wars, and the hardship of poverty. It's a time when people showed great strength and fortitude despite their circumstances. The Jenkins' family lived through these times, sending husbands, sons and sweethearts to fight, not once, but twice in their lifetimes.

As we live through the COVID-19 virus crises of 2020, we are reminded that no generation since the last world war has faced a world crises like this one. This time we cannot see our enemy, and are united, as every country works together to combat this killer virus. Not since 1918, when the Spanish Flu killed more than ten million people worldwide, have we seen every country in lockdown as the whole world grinds to a halt. We have no idea what our world will look like on the other side of this crisis, only that we will survive, and hopefully become better people because of it.

Based on a true story, spanning half a century, follow the lives of two very different people from opposite backgrounds. What happens when a middle-aged, wealthy aristocrat meets a young impoverished girl? In an era of strict class and social boundaries, when the rich and the poor of England each had their own firm, clearly defined limits, scandal could ruin the lives of not only the people involved, but reach into families and communities.

When Edward meets Gertrude, his hope for the future is suddenly transformed. But there's a big problem—he's already married. Will they risk the scandal? Will they both find what they are looking for?

Young Dorothy is trapped in a life of poverty and heartache. Abandoned by a mother who never loved her, she is forced to live with grandparents who care even less for her than they do for their own bratty children. Dorothy must persevere and hold on to the distant memory of her loving father with only a tin of letters and a small toy soldier to remind her of her former life of wealth and privilege.

With war breaking out across Europe, and Dorothy moving into adulthood, she wonders whether her father's wealth and influence will be enough to rescue her from the life she has been living. Or will a chance encounter with a handsome soldier on a train be her ticket to freedom?

ACKNOWLEDGMENTS

Once again my sister, Christine Podmore, was my right-hand researcher and constant support. She charted our family tree five generations back, with dates of births, marriages, and deaths, all of which were invaluable to me as I put the story of Annie together. Christine, I am forever grateful for your meticulous work and your sound advise on all aspects of life in the Potteries during the early part of the 20th century.

Thank you to my faithful proofreaders, Christine, my daughter, Tracey, and my husband, David. Each of you pointed out different issues for me to take a second look at and corrected a myriad of errors. The time-line issues were difficult to deal with, but with Christine's charts, and Tracey's math skills, everything was worked out in the end.

Thank you Lauren Craft for editing the book. Thank you for your words of encouragement, your sound advice, and your great insight. The changes you suggested worked so well - you always challenge me to do better.

Thank you Roseanna White for your work on the cover. It looks amazing—just how I imagined the Pear Drop would be. You are always so enthusiastic, and work with us to get it just right.

A huge thank you so my son, Matthew Brough of Thicket Books, who walked the journey of writing this novel with me from beginning to end. Your expertise amazes me, and I am so grateful to you and Cheryl for the hard work you put in behind the scenes, publishing and promoting my novels. The writing is fun, but you do all the work.

David, I couldn't do this without you. Thank you for your support and every day encouragement. Thank you for every time you made food and cups of tea for me, so that I could keep writing. You happily read each chapter as soon as it was written, and urged me on. I love you.

ABOUT THE AUTHOR

Ann Brough is in her mid-seventies and lives with her husband, David, on the shores of beautiful Lake Winnipeg in the province of Manitoba, Canada. She has been a keen storyteller for her whole life, and ventured into writing novels at the tender age of seventy three. This is Ann's third book and, like the first two, it is based on true facts remembered and recorded by her mother and grandmother. It is Ann's belief that all families have stories to tell—some fascinating and exciting. She is inspired by the hardships and heartaches her ancestors experienced, and was excited to write what she knows about their lives. All three novels are based in Staffordshire, England, where Ann grew up.

Ann and David have a growing extended family. With three married children and five grandchildren (now six, as their eldest grand daughter married in 2018). Everybody loves the lake and summers are filled with family, food, sand, campfires, swimming and wonderful memories.

This latest book attempts to emphasize the difference between Ann's mother's experience, growing up in an abusive household where alcohol was prevalent and children were only tolerated, and her father's family, who lived in the same area but attended a temperance chapel, and whose children were cherished and loved.

The influence of Ann's paternal grandmother, May Podmore, has been apparent throughout her life.

For more about Ann and her other books visit www.annbrough.com

www.ingramcontent.com/pod-product-compliance
Lightning Source LLC
Chambersburg PA
CBHW020920110726
47900CB00001B/229